Forbidden magic

Forbidden magic

A. C. Smith

First published in 2024 by Provincial Publishing, Sydney

A catalogue record for this book is available from the National Library of Australia

ISBN: 978-0-6454900-2-2

Cover design and illustration by: Bridget Acreman

For those who live with hope,

and those whose dreams came true.

Book two of the Iwizadi Trilogy

Prologue

A very long time ago, there was a powerful magician named Iwizadi. All the children of the world grew up hearing his name. As time went on and the stories about him were told and retold, there became so many different versions that a child growing up in a small town belonging to the Capital Country would hear a completely different tale to a child in the eastern nation of Naha. It is amazing how dramatically the simple passing of time can change a story; how much a story can change with just one retelling.

Different as they were, most of the stories had common elements. For example, everyone knew that Iwizadi was from an ancient city named Libalele, and he had a brother named Umwahu, with whom he was locked in a lifelong feud. But that's where the similarities stopped.

The Iwizadi of the Capital was an outlaw, whereas the Iwizadi of Arazi in the north was a fierce warrior. The Umwahu of Nelasive was a tyrant, who took the throne of Libalele by force, whereas the Umwahu of Nyika was a humble and unlikely regent, forced to govern until Iwizadi was ready to take control.

Like all children around the world, Zaria loved the story. She pestered her parents and house servants to tell it to her every night at bedtime, and she knew it back to front — the

Naha version, that is. She knew every detail of it by the time she was five years old, and could tell it better than anybody not long after that.

She loved how Iwizadi was only trying to do what he thought was right. She loved that he was misunderstood, and that people never saw the good he was trying to do. But most of all, she loved the magic.

It was magic that captivated all the children; the reason they begged their parents to tell the story over and over again. Their big imaginations could barely fit in their small heads.

So, when children begged to hear more about magic, their parents added little flourishes and embellishments to the story. They teased just a little more each time, feeding their children's insatiable appetites for the wonderful, the extraordinary, the magical things that make a story special and transport them to another world.

Is it any wonder then, that between the time that Iwizadi lived, and the time Zaria learned about him, that the stories barely resembled reality?

Most children in Naha didn't move far from their place of birth when they grew up. As a result, most children – and adults – never learned that there were a thousand variations on the story of Iwizadi.

Zaria, like everyone else, knew the very real, physical limitations of her repressive city. But she did not know the boundaries of her imagination. She often struggled to contain her imagination within the expectations imposed on her since birth, and she had spent her childhood frustrated by the lack of imagination shown around her. The only time she felt at home was when she heard – and later told – the stories. She was as guilty of embellishments as anyone else.

Her mind had conjured vivid imaginings of Iwizadi,

Umwahu, Libalele, and above all, magic. She could escape into the stories at any time, and she could take people with her when she told them. They were worlds of her creation, free from the problems of her everyday surroundings.

The children of Naha all knew another story, too: that they were at war with their neighbours in Nyika to the south. They all knew that the Nyikan people must never be allowed to cross the river Pechen that separated their nations. If that ever happened, they were told Naha would be lost forever. The only time the adults' imagination matched that of the children was when they invented fear. They told stories to give voice to their fear of what the Nyikan people would do if they ever crossed the river into Naha. And little children have a way of believing things their parents tell them.

All the children of Naha grew up fearful of Nyika and wondrous of Iwizadi, their fear eventually eclipsing their wonder as they grew up. All the children except Zaria. As a young woman, she always preferred to invent stories of magic and faraway lands than to invent fears of the various ways a Nyikan could torture a Nahan child. Her father could not understand why she clung onto childish fantasies and did not devote her life to running the country.

Unlike her peers, she didn't lose her childlike imagination as she got older. As young people her age began to join the military and talk endlessly about Nyika, she felt conflicted. She felt in her heart that either something was wrong with her, or something was wrong with everyone else, and it made her feel lonely, even with others around. It was hard to grow up and see her peers lose their imaginations, and sometimes she wished she could be the same as them.

Iwizadi was different to the people around him too. Zaria knew this from the stories and she liked to emphasise that about him whenever she told them. He was the one who thought differently, who acted differently, and whose legend lived on forever. She knew it got him in trouble, too. The people turned on him, and this part of the story was scarier than any rumours about what the Nyikans would do to a naughty child. Zaria was terrified that one day, her childhood friends would turn on her for being different, just like the people of Libalele had done to Iwizadi.

So, she pretended to be like everyone else. She stopped talking about Iwizadi when it became clear that kids her age shouldn't talk about fairy tales as if they were real. She tried to silence her imagination when it distracted her from fitting in with others. But as a tiny act of defiance, and as a way of retaining her sense of integrity, she never helped to spread rumours about Nyika. She vowed that if she used her imagination for anything, it would be for spreading wonder and hope, and not fear.

Iwizadi was forced to leave Libalele when the people grew wary of him. He was different, and his dedication to magic made the superstitious people anxious. They didn't understand the things he could do, or the progress he envisioned for the city. His brother Umwahu saw things going badly, and stepped in to help. Iwizadi was heir to the throne, but as the old king's health declined, the people became more and more restless. They started to fear what Iwizadi would do to them as their leader. They feared the unknown more than anything, just like Zaria's neighbours and friends and family.

Zaria sometimes felt misunderstood like Iwizadi.

When eventually the old king died, the people refused to allow Iwizadi to lead them, and drove him out of the city. Umwahu was put in charge instead, and this seemed to please the people, who saw him as a safe choice; someone who thought like they did and would keep things the same.

But it did not please Umwahu, who simply did not want to be a leader. And nor did it please Iwizadi, who promised to take revenge on Umwahu and the Libaleleans, and disappeared, never to be heard from again.

At this point in the story, it was up to the storyteller to moralise, and make up some lesson for the children listening. Parents used to make up all kinds of things to make their children better members of society. They would say it is important to listen to your elders, or you should always try to fit in with others.

Zaria sometimes felt like Umwahu: in the wrong place at the wrong time.

Above all, she felt frustrated at where she was in her life. And it was her frustration, and refusal to give up her naïve sense of wonder that led her to accidentally discover magic one day when she was still a child. She instinctively knew that she had to keep it a secret, or else she would end up like Iwizadi: exiled and outcast. She knew people would fear her, and she wanted to be loved. Loved for who she was, not for who she felt like she had to pretend to be.

Magic was for Zaria not only a source of great joy, hope, and wonder. It was equally a source of fear and frustration. She loved that she felt an extra layer of connection to the hero of her stories, but when she looked around and saw the ignorant and suspicious people of Naha, she felt frustrated at her impotence to share magic with them.

Iwizadi never came back to challenge Umwahu. Zaria used to think this was the scariest part of the story. It wasn't just a sad ending, but to her it meant that fear had won over hope. It meant that he had spent the rest of his life suffering, after leaving his city. And she was frightened that it might happen to her too.

After years of practicing magic in secret, she had become

quite skilful at it. She could do all kinds of things that would make her younger self green with envy. But it was only when she was twenty-one, that her reality was turned upside-down. There came a moment that would change her life, and the future of the world.

She had a dream.

It was a dream unlike any other. It was a dream of great clarity. She found herself in a round room. There was a large oak desk in front of her, and several smaller desks arranged around the room to face the large one. There was a beautiful rug covering most of the stone floor, patterned with planets and stars. A window to her left looked out over a sweeping valley. There was a bright blue river cutting across the landscape, and a shining city had been built along its banks. Distantly, the shape of an enormous eagle caught her attention.

While she was looking out the window, Zaria felt safe. She knew it was a dream, and she knew it was not hers, but she felt like she belonged there. After feeling her whole life that she didn't belong in her own city, it was a powerful and strange feeling.

She heard a door behind her swing open, and turned to see what happened. A man was there. He glided through the doorway towards her and stopped in front of the big desk. She tried to look at him, but his face was blurry no matter how hard she tried to focus. From every angle he was like a ghost.

"It's you," she said, trying and failing to see him clearly. "I know it's you."

"It is me," he answered. "I'm going to tell you about Libalele. There's something I want you to do."

Chapter 1

"Tell me, Haforn: how is my father?" A short, young man stood on a rocky outcrop of the mountains that circled around the valley, and addressed the sea eagle that had come to perch on his arm. He reserved a small level of formality for the sea eagle, as they were not particularly close.

"The gulls have received little information from Chuluun so far. We know he has made it across the great wide sea and he has begun to sail around the coast of the western continent." Distantly on the far side of the mountains away from the city, the man and the eagle could see the coast. A great grey storm cloud floated over the sea without threatening to come to land. If it ever did reach the shore, the mountains would swallow it up before it reached the valley in which the city was built.

"I guess that is better than no news, even if there is little to say." He sat down on the rocky slope, and watched the storm harmlessly gather.

"I wish I could tell you more, Khuch Chaddhal, but it is hard to get information across the sea."

"I know. There is not a lot we can do."

"Do not despair. We are watching him always. If anything goes wrong, we will know with only the smallest delay." He was talking about the network of birds that old Tesver had managed to establish all over the Western continent before achieving mastery over Bird magic and transforming into a tree.

"Thank you. It's just so unfair." He picked up a pebble and flicked it aimlessly away, where it came to an abrupt halt after stirring up a tiny dust cloud.

"What is?"

"That after waiting a lifetime to come back home, he has to leave right away again. And for what? So that others can take our home away from us!" Several weeks after Chuluun had left, Khuch still simmered with rage when he thought about it.

"The birds are on your side."

"I know you are, Haforn."

"I do not want Chuluun to fail either. If he comes back alone, who knows what will happen?"

"It's a terrible thought that things could somehow get worse than they already are." Chuluun's task was to convince a nation of foreigners to come home with him to inhabit the island and displace his own people.

"I suspect Iwizadi has already conceived of ways to make your life worse."

"I suspect you are right. No matter what, I just want him to return in one piece. And quickly. Things are not looking good for us, with Aisling taking instructions from Iwizadi, and Ychir stirring up trouble."

"We will just have to wait and hope that he succeeds."

"The Khun are good at waiting." His face was plastered with a broad, grim smile.

"So are the eagles."

"I suppose no news is good news. Thank you for meeting me out here. Not everyone in Khot trusts Bird magic anymore."

"I understand your words," the sea eagle said carefully. "But I have never understood humans. Maybe I never will."

"You'd better go now, before someone sees us."

Haforn launched from Khuch's arm into the sky, and within seconds had become just a small dot in the distant sky, and then was swallowed up by the storm, leaving Khuch alone with his thoughts. He began the long hike back to the city, taking the small, winding trail through the mountains surrounding the valley. It was overgrown from being largely unused during the long war, except by some stubborn farmers and their children. Khuch didn't know any of that, however. He never saw Gazar during the occupation. He had only recently found the trail as he explored his new island home.

He could see the brilliant river Gol majestically making its way from the peak in the centre of the valley southward towards the gap in the mountains and out to sea. Curious how the central peak had never been named. Perhaps it had a name in the ancient language of the people who had once occupied the valley before the Khun; the same people who had returned and now were causing all the Khun's problems. Maybe it didn't need a name.

Chuluun had been gone only a week, but things were happening so quickly in Khot that it might be unrecognisable by the time he returned.

If he returned.

When he left, the city was divided, and it had only gotten worse. There were those who had high hopes for the city's future and prayed for Chuluun's safe passage, and there were those who openly expressed desire for him and the new leaders to fail and never return. Compromises had to be made, and everyone was forced to decide how much they were willing to give up.

But Chuluun was forced into an impossible situation. How could they blame him for something that wasn't his fault? Khuch thought it was completely unfair. Only Iwizadi knew about the place he was ordered to go – Halasat – and only Iwizadi knew what kind of people lived there. The Khun, including Chuluun, were left with only questions, and now only the vague rumours from foreign birds could give Khuch any hope that his father was alive.

How did it fall apart so quickly? It was only a little over a month earlier that the Khun had returned to Gazar – Blue Island as it was known to the rest of the world – and resettled in their ancient city, Khot. In that short time, they had been able to restore their homes to a basic condition, begin growing food again like in the old days, and forge conspiracies against Iwizadi and Aisling.

Khuch tripped over a gnarled root and nearly fell off the side of the mountain. For all its beauty, the land itself was far more dangerous than the forest he had grown up in with Aisling, across the sea to the west.

Like Aisling, he grinned: dangerous despite her beauty. Khuch rarely joked, but when he did, his jokes were full of sarcasm and twisted layers of meaning. The Khun were not exactly famous for their sense of humour. They were more known for their struggle, and the endless wars fought over their homeland.

Gazar was caught between warring states. It occupied a strategic position in the war between Naha and Nyika. It was also unlucky to have enormous quantities of raw Noi that the rest of the world scrabbled to control.

Too much was happening too quickly, and he needed time to digest it all. He and many other Khun had spent years waiting to take action, and when it had finally come, they were overwhelmed by it. They were not ready. They assumed wrongly that when the time came, all their struggles would be over and they could go back to life as they used to know it. But it was not the case.

After returning to their beloved homeland, things quickly went wrong, and new struggles began. New threats emerged.

First, there was the question of who was in charge. The Khun had always insisted that they were autonomous – that only Khun could lead Khun. Even during the occupation of the most recent and most savage war, they had maintained their independence to some small degree, even if it was under tight controls. But their expectation was dashed when Iwizadi had suddenly shown up and claimed ownership over Gazar. It was a great insult, and many Khun seethed with rage about the situation. They had returned home with a fair leader among them already – Khuch's father Chuluun – but Iwizadi made it clear that he didn't want Chuluun around. Chuluun was coerced into running a personal errand for the wizard. He sent Chuluun to the unknown western nation of Halasat to convince its people to come live on Gazar. To prevent the Khun being killed in front of him, Chuluun agreed reluctantly.

Then Iwizadi had placed Aisling in charge, shocking everyone, and again threatened to murder all the Khun when they protested. Iwizadi's magic was unmatched and they had no choice but to agree to their new leader. He said that she was his direct descendant and the legitimate heir to the city. He would not take no for an answer and again through threatening people he got his way.

Aisling was opposed to accepting the responsibility because she was young and inexperienced, and thought a Khun would be better suited, but Chuluun helped convince her it was the right thing to do. Iwizadi was not a man to cross, even if they could not see the wisdom in his decisions. She relied on Iwizadi heavily and like many others did not see why he couldn't just govern the city himself.

Khuch, and many others, felt like prisoners in their own land. And even though he outwardly supported his wife Aisling, he surprised himself when a seed of resentment found its way into the love that he felt for her. He was not the only one who resented her and Iwizadi, and there was a growing organisation amongst the Khun who most strongly wanted independence, led by Ychir.

Then there was also the threat of Substance M. The government in charge of the Capital had somehow learned of the Khun's secret: magic. The Khun assumed it had been revealed by one of the many refugees who had moved to the Capital during the war. Over many years, the Capital had experimented with ways of extracting and refining magic, until eventually they had managed to weaponize it.

The Khun who were there on that day will never forget the battle they fought over Khot. They will never forget the terror they felt, seeing soldiers artificially impregnating themselves with false magic.

They will also never forget that it was Aisling who eventually stopped them. Even if she had to use their own weapon against them. As grateful as they were to be back in their home country, they felt that their situation was fragile; that at any moment, the soldiers could return to wage war again, fiercer than ever. Many were too proud to admit that Aisling's actions had been what eventually saved them.

Immediately after Iwizadi placed Aisling in charge of the city and retreated to his study, some of the Khun held a meeting to discuss their future.

"On the plus side, she did stop the soldiers and she saved our lives," said Sanakh. She was one of Chuluun's closest allies and supporters, who had known Aisling since she was five years old.

"But we cannot forget the simple fact that she is not Khun and Gazar can never be in the hands of a foreigner again." Ychir's opinions were very popular. He too had been in the small group of thirty who had lived in the forest for eleven years with Aisling, but he was combative by nature. He believed in the purity of the Khun and in tradition. He had been arguing with Chuluun for years, and now that Chuluun was out of the picture, he saw an opportunity to seize leadership through a hard-line nationalistic ideology. It was quickly spreading and taking hold.

"Chuluun has accepted Aisling as one of our own, Ychir," Sanakh protested.

"Oh, shut up about Chuluun!" Ychir argued. "He lied about Iwizadi. And we would have been home years ago if he hadn't held us back for so long. You don't know him like I do. He's not some saint like you make him out to be."

"Held us back?" another Khun protested. "Have you forgotten that the war was still going until recently?"

"It doesn't change the fact that Aisling is not Khun."

"Not Khun?" Sanakh shrieked, her voice getting away from her. "You helped raise her! She is the same as any of us!"

Khuch had watched during the meeting. Needless to say, no agreement was reached, and tensions continued to simmer. He was unique in his position, as the only Khun present to be married to a foreigner. He remained silent and contemplative, trying to think how Chuluun would settle the debate. Ychir of course saw his unwillingness to fight as weakness.

It was peculiar, Khuch reflected, how Iwizadi seemed to invite chaos. He had admitted to having meddled in the affairs of many important people around the world. He had personally created a leadership crisis among the Khun and almost encouraged Ychir's rebelliousness. Khuch had a feeling as he stopped at the river Gol for a drink, that Iwizadi was only warming up to bring more and more problems to their lives. He sighed as he thought that things were only going to get worse before getting better.

The magic water made him feel rested and energised, and he continued walking home towards Khot. The sun began to set, and the glowflowers that grew in the valley began their nightly moon worship. A few minutes later, some of them had begun to open their petals and drink in the moonlight, giving back a warm, welcoming blue light in return. In the springtime, they released thousands of glowing spores into the air that hung about, illuminating the air, dancing a peculiar, beautiful waltz.

As he walked through Khot towards his home near the base of the mountain, he was proud of how much life there was in the city. Until a month ago, he had only ever met a few dozen Khun. Now, he was surrounded by them. There were thousands that had been hiding around the world and returned to Gazar when they heard the good news, as well as many that had remained there during the war. Both categories were reserved and said little about their experiences.

The city was built on a network of tiny streets at random angles and it was easy to get lost. The streets in the centre were cobblestone, but further out they were less ornately paved. Khun architecture was simple, and most buildings were painted a bright white, or off-white colour on the outside and had brown tiled roofs. Residences were mostly one-storey with a large front garden.

And they had rebuilt the city so quickly. When they

arrived, it had been heavily damaged from fighting and neglect. A few foreigners had chosen to settle after the occupying forces mysteriously retreated, and they were happy to welcome home the estranged population. Already, the city was thriving and businesses were springing up like weeds. There was no shortage of pride among the Khun for their city and their land.

Khuch passed a tavern and heard a familiar voice. Without wanting to invite danger, he slowed down just enough to hear what Ychir was saying and kept moving.

"…has no right to be here…"

This was followed by a loud cheer from what must have been fifty or a hundred voices.

It was a delicate situation. The people were not happy, and Ychir was leading a fast-growing faction. It would have been wise for Khuch to keep going, but he wanted to know who Ychir was talking about. If it was Iwizadi, he agreed. If it was Aisling, he did not. Or at least, he wanted to think that he did not. A small part of him thought they both belonged back in the west where they grew up.

But before he could turn around and eavesdrop anymore, two large men burst from the tavern, singing badly, swaying and stumbling. Khuch quickly turned a corner and continued on his way home. The singing was interrupted by a violent fit of coughing that echoed through the empty, darkening streets.

Before opening the door, he sighed and hesitated. Things between him and Aisling had started to fall apart almost as soon as the trouble with Iwizadi had begun. He put his hand on the brass handle and waited there, listening and thinking. It was the stress of it all, he decided. She was stressed trying to lead well, and he was stressed being caught between two cultures. It was hard to communicate with her. He opened the door and went inside.

The home was like an oasis of calm in the tense environment of the city. Khuch and Aisling lived with Aisling's mother, Maria. Orn the eagle was there too. He often visited, but he lived on his own schedule and was untameable. Sky King, the other birds all called him, even Haforn the sea eagle. Khuch met Aisling with a small kiss and greeted the others politely. They resumed their conversation and he went into the kitchen to prepare some food for them all.

"You shouldn't be so open about it, mum," Aisling warned her mother about Orn's visits. Khuch emerged from the kitchen with a few plates. "You know how they feel about Bird magic."

"Oh, I don't care about them," Maria dismissed the warning as she brushed Orn's feathers. He leaned into her touch, as if in love with her. "Orn is an eagle. He is royalty. They'll come to their senses soon." She had shoulder-length dark hair, cut in the style of the Khun, and she was very clearly related to Aisling. She had the same face shape, and small nose. They had the same posture and mannerisms, despite Aisling growing up without her.

"Aisling is right," Khuch joined in, sitting down and starting to eat. The others didn't know that he had been meeting with Haforn on his exploratory walks in the mountains.

"Oh, you two are so… perfect for each other!" Maria deflected the conversation. Aisling beamed at Khuch.

"I agree with them too," Orn said. "It's not safe for us if I visit as often as I do. Maybe we can continue our conversation in private later, Maria. I will do what I can here."

She nodded in reluctant agreement as if she just wanted

them to stop talking about it, and Orn bid farewell to the others.

"What's he talking about, mum?" Aisling asked when she was sure that Orn had flown away and couldn't hear them.

"It's nothing," Maria started, trying to think of a plausible lie. But her mind was no help. She was still getting used to hearing Aisling call her 'mum', after being separated for so many years.

"It's about *him*, isn't it?" Khuch drilled. Aisling could see that he was right. "Again."

"Mum! You promised you'd drop it!" She was angry. She had started feeling recently as if Maria was trying to undermine her leadership. "You said you'd start to trust us."

"I trust you," Maria said. "But not *him*. I don't trust that he has done anything good for you or our friends out there."

"For the last time-" Aisling began, but silenced herself. It was an argument they'd had many times before, and it led nowhere. Every time, Maria promised to abandon her suspicions, and Aisling defended Iwizadi. Khuch refused to join in; it was not his argument. He didn't want to upset his wife, but if he had been forced to choose a side, he would have sided with Maria in a heartbeat. He could not trust Iwizadi like Aisling could, and found it strange that she could.

There was a rumour circulating that she was under a spell, just a mouthpiece for him leading from the shadows. If Ychir didn't start the rumour, he encouraged it.

There was no spell, though. For all her good intentions, Aisling was naïve. She trusted Iwizadi after he had helped her escape from the Capital's human experiments. She wanted people to see that he was helping, like he had helped her. She wanted to believe that whatever he was planning was going to benefit everybody, even if they couldn't see the whole picture. Even if some of his actions resulted in temporary setbacks. Like sending Chuluun away for a while.

"Orn still has suspicions," Maria continued, speaking to her food. "We only want to know that he won't hurt us."

"So, it's Orn now? Not you?" Aisling dropped a spoon loudly into the bowl in front of her.

"It's everyone!" Maria returned with her voice louder than she would have liked.

"Khuch!" Aisling turned to him for support. "What do you think? Do you trust Iwizadi?"

He was silent, but that was the wrong answer.

"Not you too…" She took his hand. "I need someone on my side."

Khuch looked her in the eyes, revealing very little. He had inherited his father's face of stone. Her face on the other hand, was expressive enough for both of them. Even so, she knew him well enough to read his impassive gaze. She threw down his hand.

"I am sorry, *Tsenkher*," Khuch said, using a Khun term of endearment. "I do not think he is helping us. He will throw us out whenever he decides."

"Great. Thanks for nothing." She left the table and collected a few items from near the door. She put on her coat and boots. "I thought you, of all people, would support me."

"I do support you," he tried.

"Yeah, right." She opened the front door to go, letting in a gust of cool wind.

"Not him." He went towards her. "Remember how he betrayed your uncle. Don't go."

She paused, remembering how Iwizadi had played on her uncle Jack's prideful nature, tricking him into a fatal showdown. Jack had not been very kind to anybody, but seeing him die the way he did, writhing in pain and desperation, even Aisling admitted to herself that Iwizadi could have handled the situation better.

"I have work to do. The city doesn't run itself."

She threw the door shut after her and stomped towards the palace that was carved into the face of the central peak. It was used as both the government offices and Iwizadi's private residence. Entry was restricted to only a few people. Originally, Maria was authorised, but Iwizadi took away her privileges when she began trying to find out more about him. It should have served as a warning to Aisling that maybe there was more to him than she trusted, but she defended him, saying that he had a right to privacy like anyone else.

"She won't listen," Khuch lamented.

"She will," Maria said. "But it will be too late. She will learn the hard way. She's so much like her father."

Aisling needed to speak with Iwizadi. She needed advice. What was she going to do about the growing unhappiness in the city? Or the growing unhappiness in her heart?

"Most complicated problems have simple solutions." Chuluun's voice echoed through her mind. What would he have done in her situation, if he was still the leader in Khot? He made everything look so simple.

"Maybe I am looking for complicated solutions," she said to herself.

Her anger was subsiding, and she had stopped stomping. Now she strolled towards the entry to the palace, admiring its ornate stonework. It was ancient. The Khun said it was already built when they first arrived on Gazar, but there was no sign of other people living there. The city had a much longer history than anyone could remember.

She stopped outside the entryway and instead of

Chuluun, she thought of her own father, Peter. It was still a fresh wound, and no matter how she tried to get on with life, with the complexities of leading Khot, with the tricky diplomacy involved in keeping the Khun happy, his face still surfaced in her mind's eye too often.

Since losing him only five weeks earlier, she had barely used Fire magic at all. The few times she did, it felt different. It felt like she could lose control of her anger at any moment. She could feel the Fire magic tugging at her, pulling her towards its burning centre, begging her to let her anger take over, desperate for her to fuel its core. But she knew that if she gave in to the temptation, she would be consumed, and not in the way Peter had been. The first time Fire magic turned on her like that, she cried. She finally understood how Peter felt every time he used it. How he could have learned to control such an angry spirit was beyond her.

But Peter hadn't been destroyed by the Fire. No, he had allowed himself to become one with it. He was there in every spark. Whenever someone used Fire magic, he was there, lending his strength. The Khun, especially Chuluun, were impressed with Peter. He was the only foreigner they knew to have achieved mastery of any type of magic.

Aisling stared at the Gol and remembered the service they held for Peter. The masters were revered in Khun culture. They were the people who had cheated death and given themselves to magic. She was proud to know how they felt about him, but it didn't take away from the hurt.

She entered the palace and was greeted by the landing at the base of the waterfall, the scene of terrible memories. Where the water fell from was a mystery. It flowed endlessly from the peak, no matter the season. It came crashing down into a natural harbour, around which the palace was built, with a private dock enclosed in a cave before the Gol spurted out from a huge opening. This was where Iwizadi had first addressed the Khun after the battle for Khot. It was where he showed that he could not be stopped by force.

A beautiful set of stairs was carved into the rock. It climbed upward, past several chambers used by various officials, and each landing showed signs of wear from centuries of use. As the leader of Khot, Aisling knew the rooms well. She worked in the mountain with a team of Khun. She suspected Iwizadi had threatened them in some way, because they showed the same resistance to her as everyone else. It was like they were working because they were forced.

Iwizadi had revealed to her privately that she was the heir to Gazar, that she was descended from the same ancient race that had built the palace; that she was descended from him. She never told anyone, not even Khuch. It was the first secret she had kept from him since they were children and she had denied she had a crush on him. It was for the best, she thought. She didn't want people to know and thought no good could come from knowing.

She continued climbing the stairs, admiring the ornately carved banister. Nothing about the grand hallways suggested that she was inside a mountain. The halls and rooms were lit with the glow spheres that the Khun could produce with Light magic.

Light magic was the first magic she ever saw, when she was five years old and Chuluun made his hand glow in front of her and Peter. If there was any magic that she could choose to master, it would be Light magic. As far as she knew, there had never been a Light master. In fact, mastery was exceptionally rare and masters were revered almost as gods. She pictured her dad's face again.

"Come in," came a voice from the top room as Aisling approached the door. It swung open before her, revealing Iwizadi's study.

It was a room that many people had seen, but few had visited. Aisling herself had seen it many times in her dreams before she first visited in waking. She remembered that everything about it was exactly as she had seen – or rather, been shown: every stone, the view from the window, the door handle, the desk, the feeling of safety. She looked at a spot in the middle of the floor out of habit, remembering where her uncle had been murdered.

"I know why you are here," he spoke. His voice was like honey, and it instantly cleared Aisling's mind of any doubts she had about him. "But I cannot help you this time."

"What do you mean? Why not?" she was dismayed. "You always help."

"Not this time." He shrugged. "I am busy."

"With what?"

"I do not have to explain everything I do to you, Aisling." He closed the book he was writing in and stood up to stretch. He coughed a few times like there was hair in his throat. "We are alone in this place. There is only you and me here to represent our ancient people. I often think about this, and I expect that we might receive unwelcome guests."

"What guests?" Whenever Iwizadi spoke, Aisling felt like she had no control over her body. She felt that he commanded her to stand still and listen. She felt that the words she spoke were not her own, rather they were his, and he was engaged in a conversation with himself.

"Umwahu." The name shocked her. "He is coming for me. I don't know when, but I feel like time is running out."

"What? How? Isn't he dead?"

"He is like me," Iwizadi laughed. "Do you expect

something as banal as time to kill him?"

"I guess not." She looked at the floor, suddenly regretting coming. She tried to count to stones, but there was no pattern to their placement and she gave up. "Why would he come for you?"

"It is an old story between us. I am certain that he will come for me before this year is over. Libalele will be caught in the middle." Iwizadi always referred to Khot by its original name, refusing to speak Khun unless it was necessary. But Aisling was appalled by his disrespectful attitude and flippant disregard for the Khun, after all their recent hard work rebuilding the city that he claimed to love.

"Caught in the middle?" she spoke up, this time with her own words. "Can't he visit you somewhere else?"

"No," he said forcefully. "This is where I belong. Everything I am doing is for the good of Libalele. When Chuluun returns with the descendants from Halasat, we can make this city the seat of the world's power as it was destined. I only hope he returns before Umwahu."

"What about the Khun?"

"I am sick of hearing about them."

"So, when Umwahu comes, the Khun will suffer because you're too selfish to go somewhere else." Aisling instantly regretted letting her anger speak. Iwizadi's eyes flashed gold and he rounded on her. She was lifted a foot off the ground by some invisible force and held pinned against the wall.

"Selfish? You think I'm being selfish?" He seemed to grow to fill the room, and the lights dimmed, casting demonic shadows on his face. "After I have given you a city? I am returning our lost people to their homes. I have graciously given the Khun a place to live, even if they think they are entitled to something more. I have single-handedly ended the war here. I am working towards creating a brighter future for everyone, while you complain about a handful of unhappy thugs. What do you want me to do? What else do you want from me?"

Aisling fell to the floor as the spell was released, landing awkwardly. She rubbed her knee where it banged on the stone. The questions were rhetorical, and Iwizadi continued his monologue. She found herself agreeing with some, but not all of his points.

"Look out there, Aisling." Iwizadi's voice was melodic again, and the lights had returned to normal. He gestured out the window. "What do you see?"

"I see Khot," she answered obtusely. She had inherited her dad's defiance and it often chose dangerous moments to surface.

"Libalele," he corrected her arrogantly. He coughed deeply once. "One month ago, this city was in ruins. Now look. See how it shines. See how beautiful it is. This is because of me."

"It's because the Khun are proud of their home. They worked to rebuild it." She didn't like that Iwizadi was taking credit for the Khun's hard work.

"They worked," he agreed. "And they are proud. But Libalele is not theirs. They have built it for our people when they return."

"Our people?" Aisling tried to hide the disgust in her voice. "Maybe they are your people, but mine are already here, and I want to do what's right for them. You told me to lead them, and I will."

"Aisling, your people are on their way. Try to get this idea about being a Khun out of your head. You hear the way they talk about you. You know they don't accept you. Why would you insist that you are one of them when they so clearly do not want you? When our true people return, they will embrace you."

"You are a liar," she said in Khun. "I know what they say about me, but it's just Ychir. He's been like that my whole life. You should hear what they say about you. Nobody wants you here. They don't trust you, and it makes my job harder when they think you are the one who is really in charge."

"It sounds like you have a lot to learn about leadership," he answered in his own language. "When Umwahu comes, they will be glad to have me."

"What's that supposed to mean?"

"It means you have to look at the bigger picture, Aisling." He sat down again. "Heavens, maybe you are more like them than I thought. Please just try to look past the small details."

"What is he going to do?"

"He has already begun." Iwizadi was referring to his persistent cough. Many Khun had recently picked up a similar sickness. "He will start by unleashing the horrors he has created, then he will come and destroy everything."

"What horrors? Why don't you ever just say what you mean? How can we stop him? How can I help?" Iwizadi sat down and opened his book again and flicked through the pages, looking for something. He stopped finally, and turned it around and slid it across the desk so Aisling could see. She sat down opposite him and read.

"This is where the spell starts," he explained.

"What spell?" Aisling was intrigued, but it was so convoluted and detailed and long that she couldn't understand it at all. Her thirst for magic always triumphed over any other emotion she was feeling. Khuch had used this fact several times to deflect arguments over the years.

"The spell to destroy Umwahu," Iwizadi said with

venom.

"Why?" Aisling tried to remember the version of the Iwizadi story she grew up hearing and what it said about Umwahu. She had recently learned that there was more than one way to tell it.

"I don't have to explain everything to you," Iwizadi snapped.

"I have a right to know if my people are in danger!" she continued using Khun.

"No matter what I do, they will always be in danger," he answered cryptically, with remarkable control over his voice and again stifling a cough. There was no sense of anger in the room anymore, just calm discussion. "Danger from you, from me, from the wars, from Umwahu… from each other."

Aisling stared at him defiantly, and it seemed to please him. He laughed.

"Good, Aisling. They will need a strong leader. You are learning. Prove that I was right about you." He took the book back and closed it in front of him.

"How can I lead them if I don't know where we are or where we are going? If Umwahu is coming and he is a danger to the Khun, I have to be able to help them, to protect them."

"Look around. You know what they say about us. Your people need unity. They might be united in hatred against me, but when Umwahu is here, they will forget me and unite against him. They will always fight against something, and they will get used to me when there is a bigger threat knocking down their doors."

"I don't want to wait for Umwahu to arrive before uniting them. And so far, the only thing uniting them is that they want us gone. Why don't we let Ychir take charge? I could step aside and let him lead. They would be much happier that way."

"If you give an inch, they will take a mile," he cautioned her, seeing through her personal desire to step down. "Giving Ychir that one concession will lead to him uniting all the Khun against us. It will be dangerous for you and your family. They will turn on you, and I will have no choice but to subdue them by force. I would prefer not to do that."

"I get what you mean," she slumped into a chair and let her long skinny arms fall by her sides. "I was just thinking of how to get him on our side. If he doesn't hate us, he could be useful for uniting the Khun with us."

"It is a good idea, but forget Ychir. You will not be able to win his support."

"Then what? I have no ways left to unite them."

"Yes, you do." She perked up hearing him say that and sat forward on her chair. "You've been only thinking about how to unite them with you. But I will tell you one thing about leadership: it doesn't matter if your people like you or not. You can unite them against you, and you will achieve your goal."

"It makes sense, but-"

"And Ychir has already begun the hard work for you. All you have to do is make one very unpopular decision and he will do the rest of turning them against you."

"And if they are united – even against me – I will be able to keep them safe from Umwahu when he comes." She gulped.

"Yes. If you simply tell them to support you in case of invasion, they will resist."

"So, what would be the most unpopular thing I can do?"

"Take away their magic."

"What? Magic is the way we live. It's what makes us

different to the rest of the world. Magic is what keeps us safe. You want me to take it away from them? I couldn't! But… you're right. It would instantly turn everyone against me and help Ychir." She fidgeted in her chair. Another trait inherited from Peter; she could never sit still for too long.

"The greatest threat to you is an unhappy people willing to use magic against you. You know how strong they can be when they have to be." Iwizadi began trying to convince Aisling to really believe in her decision.

"I know…" she thought back to the battle they fought to defend Khot. "But none of the spells they used were lethal. I'm not so sure about this plan."

"Were they necessary? Were those spells essential for their day-to-day living?" Iwizadi still pushed on with his reasoning.

Aisling remembered the various spells used on that day. She remembered seeing how the Khun could cast spells together as a group to be stronger; how together they had made the entire city invisible. She remembered the spells they used to paralyse the soldiers. Maybe Iwizadi had a point. Their unity was what kept them safe from external threats, and she needed them to be safe from Umwahu. And when they were faced with a bigger threat, they bonded and forgot their other disagreements.

"What if we could only use essential spells for our daily lives," she thought out loud. "Then Ychir would have to think that I'm doing something that benefits no one, and he will tell all his supporters. They will all hate me."

"It is certainly an option." Iwizadi thought back to his own past.

"That way, we can still use magic, but only the ones that are not dangerous."

"If you think it is a good idea…"

"I do," she stated, now convinced that she was on the right track.

"There will be resistance. You should expect Ychir to lead an uprising."

"I understand." She nodded. "But I want to unite the people, no matter what. It will be good for them but bad for us. I think I am starting to understand now that leadership means making unpopular decisions."

"They could object to you controlling their lives too tightly. Ychir could become violent. I am prepared to use force to help you. After all, I would also like them to unite against Umwahu. But are you prepared to use force to defend yourself against them?"

"It's in the name of their safety, even if they don't know it," Aisling reasoned, uncomfortably. "Chuluun always said 'complicated problems usually have simple solutions.' But I'm starting to doubt if that's true."

"You are sure you want to go through with this?"

"Yes. I don't see any other way."

"How will you decide which magics are essential?"

"Anything that can cause harm will be banned."

"Even Fire? How will they heat their homes?"

"Okay then, not Fire." She thought of her dad again.

"How about Light? It can be used to blind someone."

"Umm-"

"And Water? You remember how it can be used to drown a man." She looked at the spot on the floor where her uncle had drowned, pictured his dying movements, struggling against Iwizadi's own spell.

"Maybe it's not as easy as I thought."

"And Bird magic? You should know how dangerous spies can be to a leader."

"Bird magic isn't dangerous," she tried to convince

herself. She thought of her mother's relationship with Orn, and how they were plotting something; how Maria was banned from the mountain after trying to uncover information about Iwizadi.

"No? How then did your uncle know the right time to invade last month?"

"I don't-"

"You think it had nothing to do with the traitorous crow living outside his window? You think information isn't dangerous?"

It dawned on Aisling that out of all the magics that she knew, Bird magic was the least useful to everyone. Firstly, not everyone could use it properly. And secondly, it was not essential to their living in the same way as Light and Fire and Water. Even Time and Matter spells were useful for food production. If she was to ban any magic, it would have to be Bird magic.

"If I ban non-essential magic, how would I enforce it? Wouldn't everyone just keep doing things the same?"

"A good leader must be firm," Iwizadi said dreamily, as if losing interest in the topic.

"Yeah, you're right."

"The law enforcement in this city is weak as it is."

"Well, we haven't had much need for it," Aisling said. "There isn't much crime."

"And would you rather wait until you have a crime epidemic to establish good procedures? Ychir's gang is getting more restless every day."

"No, you're right again," she thought about it. "We need stronger police so that when there is crime, we can fight it."

"And I expect that when you make your announcement there will be an increase in crime."

"Then should I not ban any magic?" Aisling doubted

herself. "I thought if they were united as a people they would not resort to crime."

"Aisling, there is going to be crime no matter what. We know that they are unhappy with you as leader. So, show them that they have a good leader. Be strong, and make the choices that will help them. Even if they can't see it. It is better to be feared than liked."

"Okay," she got up and moved to leave the room. "But I'm going to say goodbye to Orn now. At least until things change again in the future. When they are happy again, I can remove the ban. When they are united and safe, and Ychir has backed down, I mean."

Iwizadi watched her leave, and resumed his studies, shaking his head. He had bigger things to worry about than whether or not the Khun were satisfied with their leader. She had a lot to learn.

He opened his book to continue writing, paused, and flipped back to the page where the spell started, several pages earlier.

"Dammit!" he exclaimed, and rested his head in his hands. "I've made the damn thing too complicated. It's not going to work! I'll have to start again now, try something else."

He was struck with a fit of coughing, doubled over in pain, leaning on his desk for support. Little flecks of blood covered his wrinkled, brown hand. When he recovered, he examined the blood as if he had never seen it before. He brought his hand to his face and sniffed it, licked it. Satisfied but worried, he cleaned up and sat down again, with a troubled look on his face.

"How are you doing this, Umwahu?" he asked no one in particular. "How did you escape?"

Suddenly, Iwizadi sat upright and his long limbs stiffened.

A glazed expression came over him and he began to write in the book while staring straight ahead, his thin mouth whispering chants the whole time. He scribbled in his trance for a couple of minutes, then just as suddenly as it began, he regained control.

He looked down at the page in front of him and felt sickened by the words he saw:

You are going back, and I will put you there myself. I am coming for you. Soon. I will make sure you never take another waking step. You will never dream again. And neither will Libalele.

There was no question in his mind as to whether the threat was genuine or not. One thousand years earlier, Umwahu's promise to destroy him had been brushed off by a younger, more arrogant Iwizadi. Now, it took on a new and frightening reality. Iwizadi went over to the window and shouted at the top of his voice.

"You'll never catch me! I'm never going back! This city is mine!"

Aisling heard the shouts as she exited the palace. She tried to pick out the words. *Never.* That was all she could hear clearly. But there was something different in his voice, and she hesitated, wondering if she should go back up to check on him.

A thought flitted through her mind: maybe she should just let Umwahu take Iwizadi. Would that make the Khun happy? They want to be free. But no, he said Khot would be caught in the middle of their fight. She had to try to avoid that.

As for Aisling herself, more than anything, she just wanted to belong. She had been raised among Khun, and felt like one of them. But because she was born a foreigner, there were some who would never accept her. She spoke Khun, she used magic just like them, she fought on their side in battle, but none of that mattered because she looked different to them. It felt very unfair. The one person who welcomed her identity was Iwizadi, and she felt nothing in common with him and his mysterious origins. Worse, if she accepted his culture as her own, the Khun would rebel against her and she would lose her real sense of self.

She decided to stop by the Gol on her way back home. It was easy to find thanks to the proliferation of glowflowers that grew on its banks. She found a path through the waist-high flowers and came to face the river. It started quite narrow near the base of the peak, and widened as it got closer to the sea. Where Aisling now stood it was only about fifteen metres across, but moving swiftly.

The blue light from the flowers on both banks lit the scene and she could see her reflection clearly. She was looking tired and thin from working hard and stressing about the city. Her blonde hair had grown long and was tied messily to keep out of her face. She picked up a rock and threw it at her reflection.

"I don't want to lead them." Her voice came out softly and sadly, and it sounded like someone else was saying the words.

Her reflection pieced itself back together after the rock tore it apart. It was funny how even through the water she could see her tears reflected. She half expected the magic river to absorb them.

"Why did he put me in charge?" But it was a foolish question. Iwizadi did whatever he wanted through threats and violence. If he wanted her to do something, she did it. Before leaving, Chuluun helped her accept the situation, saying that it wasn't forever, that things would get better.

"It's easy for you to say," she had said.

"How do you mean?" His deep voice felt like a handful of jagged rocks.

"You always say things will get better. That's why we all came here with you," she paused to breathe. "It should be you."

"But it is not," he answered calmly. "We have overcome one trial, and now we are faced with another. It is life."

"Please don't go." She hugged him. In a way that many Khun would be uncomfortable doing, he hugged back.

"I must," he released her. "You know what he will do if I refuse."

"I know."

"And you know what he will do if you refuse."

"Yeah."

"We all have parts to play."

Aisling looked downriver to where the Gol widened suddenly and its current slowed to a trickle. At its widest, it would have been nearly one hundred metres across. There were magical things under its surface, breathing in its power. She started to wander down the banks until she reached a point where the water was at its calmest. It was the place where the ceremony to honour her dad's transformation was held.

She held a hand out in front of her, keeping her elbow bent at her side, and a ball of fire grew in her palm. It was a fire that changed colours repeatedly, randomly, rapidly, from orange to blue to green to red.

"I know you are here, but I miss you." The fireball grew a tendril, that wrapped around her wrist. When it touched her, she felt encased in a warm, comforting hug.

She crouched down and gently placed the fireball on the surface of the river, where unaffected by the water it started to float away, never losing intensity. The feeling of its warmth quickly faded however, and when eventually the fireball had floated into the distance, she was left standing there staring at the place it used to be, feeling the cold around her.

When she arrived home, Khuch and Maria were playing cards together. They stopped to look at her.

"I'm sorry," she said. They assumed she was apologising for their argument earlier, but she felt sorrier that she would be making Bird magic a crime. It was not the right moment to tell them.

"It's alright," Maria said, and got up to hug her. Khuch was silent, staring at his cards.

"I think I'll go to bed now." She looked at Khuch, then went into the bedroom. Through the wall, she heard Maria hissing at Khuch:

"Go after her, you idiot." He did as he was told.

Maria went outside for some air, and enjoyed being alone with her thoughts. She tried to put out of her mind any ways that Khuch and Aisling might be arguing or apologising.

It was rare that she had a moment to breathe. Most of her days were occupied with helping rebuild the city, or learning everything she could about its history. She was learning to speak passable Khun from Sanakh, who often visited and had become a good friend.

She had learned that Khot, or Libalele, had a history as mysterious as it was complicated. The Khun seemed to have kept mostly oral histories, that while mostly consistent, still carried a risk of inaccuracy. In addition to that, their stories were heavily ritualised and focused on specific events, leading to a very incomplete picture.

Nobody for example, could explain where the Khun were living before arriving on Gazar. In their creation myth, the

Khun simply *were*. They said they had always been there. But they also said that the palace had existed before they arrived. It was impossible to reconcile the two stories.

The Khun also had no idea who had built the palace or how old it was. They said it was empty when they found it.

Their creation myth was called the *Buteelin Domog*. It told the story of how in the beginning, the Khun were surrounded by blackness. They wandered in the darkness for eternity until they fell. They fell for years and years without end until eventually, they splashed into the Gol. Half of the Khun drowned instantly, but the other half survived and were imbued with the river's magic. Glowflowers sprung up from the dirt at every place one of the dead washed ashore. The Gol was from that moment on the sacred source of life, and the glowflowers its guardians.

The central peak was for the most orthodox Khun a place of death. It was the bridge to the void from which they came, and they all avoided going there. All of this story was recorded in the Book of Boloi, which Iwizadi had confiscated when he appeared, sparking outrage in the population. Chuluun was particularly offended, after having guarded the holy book for all the years he had been in exile.

Maria was not only interested in the history of the Khun. The reason behind many of her arguments with Aisling was a strong distrust of Iwizadi. Everything they knew about him was shrouded in mystery and secrets. She wanted to know where he was born. She wanted to know what really happened when he was last living in the city, one thousand years earlier. She wanted to know more about the people who built the palace.

But whenever she tried to find out more, she met dead ends. The Khun had no idea about him, other than their version of the same fairy tale told all over the world. It seemed like everywhere she looked were dead ends.

She still had a few tricks up her sleeve though. Even before coming to Khot, Maria had been adept at Mind magic. She had a stronger power than most at reading and manipulating the thoughts of others. It was a power that could be used for great harm, and indeed when she worked for the Capital's Department of Magical Research, she had used her powers more for harm than for good.

Orn shared her suspicions, and wanted answers as much as she did. He flew to meet her now, as she stood outside her home. She wasn't wearing her leather glove, so he politely landed next to her.

"Can we continue our discussion?" he asked.

"I was thinking about it, but I didn't expect you to come so soon." Maria sat on a large rock near the door. Like most homes in Khot, theirs was a small building with an emphasis on outdoor spaces and a large garden. Most Khun grew some foods for themselves in the fertile soil, with a strong helping of magic.

"I would like to help," Orn said, hopping over to be closer to Maria. "I think I can find out more if I go abroad."

"I think so too." She stroked his feathers. "I've already learned everything I can from the Khun here. I think maybe I know more about their history now than they do."

"You haven't tried the thing we talked about yet."

"No," she looked into his eyes. "It's too dangerous and I'm scared."

"I think it is the only way we can get the answers we seek."

"Maybe," she held her hands together on her lap, her back hunched forwards a little. She shared the same crippling indecisiveness as Aisling, and wished she could be more like Peter, who had always acted first and thought about consequences later. "But he will know immediately."

"If you don't try it, you will never stop thinking about it." He hopped onto her lap. His talons cut into her thigh but she didn't mind. "I know you, Maria. I know you cannot fight this obsession. You need to try."

"I know you're right, Orn-"

"-But it doesn't make it any easier." He finished her sentences often. "You've practiced on me many times, remember? I never notice when you are in my mind."

"Yes, but-"

"-But it's different because I am an eagle. Well so what? My mind is just like any other. *His* will be the same, too."

"How can you be so sure?"

"Eagles are born to be sure of everything."

"And," Maria thought about Orn's decision. "You are sure you will be leaving."

"Yes. I will learn more about him through travelling the world. I want to see the places he has been, speak with those who have seen him. I will learn the truth about his past."

"And I will learn the truth about his future." Maria transferred Orn to her arm, got up and stretched, feeling more assured about her direction.

"Do you want to practice one more time before I go?" Orn suggested.

"That would be nice."

"Then tell me," he spoke slowly. "Which direction am I planning to fly first?"

Maria held her body as still as she could, emptying her thoughts so that her mind could be filled with Orn's. She imagined a plume of smoke drifting from her forehead outwards towards Orn. It danced through the air between them, seeking him out, and when it found him, it latched onto his forehead, connecting them.

She was used to it now, but when she first started using Mind magic, the initial jolt of connection was like being beaten with a stick. She prepared to feel Orn's mind enter hers and fill the space she had emptied for it, and when it came, it was no more shocking than a mosquito bite.

He was right: an eagle's mind was no different to a human's. They had the same hopes and fears. She allowed a moment for his thoughts to settle into place. From experience she knew that if she rushed before things found their places, she could be horribly disoriented and uncomfortable, and as a result more easily detected.

Orn was making it easy for her, though. In the centre of his thoughts was him flying north-east to the icy kingdom of Arazi…with Haforn the sea eagle. She saw them cruising over the sea and into the colder clime. She saw the setting sun cast long shadows ahead of them and felt a strong sense of dread. Orn was afraid.

She snapped back to reality, sending Orn's thoughts back where they belonged, and replacing them with her own.

"You're taking Haforn with you?" she exclaimed.

"Yes. I have some concerns about the journey."

"I saw."

"I can trust him."

"So can I." They remained silent for a moment. Maria no longer needed the same time to recover after performing a Mind spell as she used to. "Did you feel anything at all when I was looking around?"

"Nothing."

"Do you think I can do this?"

"I am certain."

"Please keep me updated when you find something."

"It might not be a good idea," Orn warned. Maria's confused expression urged him to explain. "There is something brewing here against the birds. But if you can find me with Mind magic, it should be safe to communicate that way."

"I've never cast over such a long distance. Is it even possible?"

"I know you will try. Now I am going. I trust that you will find what you are looking for." He hopped onto her arm, preparing to go.

"Goodbye for now. Please be safe."

"You too." And Orn launched from her arm into the sky. She wished she had been wearing her glove as she looked at the gashes that he had left on her.

Orn helped give Maria more confidence in her ability, but he had made it easy for her. Whenever they trained, he had his thoughts front and centre. With Iwizadi, she would have to poke around, investigate for much longer, and expose herself to being found out.

Every type of magic had a risk of harming the user. Fire magic used the power of a person's anger, but it could easily get out of control. Water magic could come gushing from a person if they concentrated too hard on stemming its flow. Even Bird magic, one of the oldest magics known, could turn on the user. Aisling and Khuch often talked about their old friend Tesver, who had followed the path to Bird magic mastery and slowly transformed into a tree. Mind magic was relatively unknown, as it was not so frequently used. What dangers did it pose to users?

While Maria was contemplating the dangers to herself from Mind magic, a few metres away and separated by two walls, Aisling was thinking about a different type of magic.

Back when they fought the battle to save Khot from the Capital, she had given a name to the magic Khuch had always done for her: Love magic. When she needed strength, he was there to cast some unknown spell to help. He could combine it with Light magic, as he had done with the stone she kept by her bed – the stone that always glowed with the colour she wanted to see. She had been thinking a lot about Love magic, hoping to surprise Khuch with it one day. But unlike the other, more mundane types of magic, she couldn't see the results of her practice. Fire magic could produce fire or heat, Water magic made water, but how could she see the love she created? How, when fear and hatred were taking place in the hearts of the Khun around her, even Khuch?

When Khuch cast it, it was easy to see. It filled her with warmth and confidence. She had tried to cast it on her reflection, but the best she could do was make herself shiver. Stubborn as always, she promised herself never to give up trying until she could do it better than him.

He had fallen asleep quickly, as he always did, while she tossed and turned, unable to get comfortable.

Chuluun had to return before anything else went wrong on Gazar; before anyone else came to invade. It was all she could think about as she lay there awake, waiting for the fatigue of the endless night to take over.

Eventually, as she let her tiredness win over her restless mind and drifted off to a restless sleep, far away in the east, a woman was waking up from a fitful dream.

Chapter 2

She saw him again. He was always the same, always faceless, with words as vague as his appearance. In the past she had always felt as though the meaning of the dreams was impossible to decipher, but this time, she knew that it was time to act. She had heard him talk many times of his city, a faraway place with a name she found hard to pronounce – Libalele – and felt the vague pull of his words reeling her in. Last night however, she somehow knew that the time had come, and everything he had ever told her was coming together.

He knew about the disease. He knew that all over Naha, people were falling ill and dying from an invisible predator. It started with a tickle, and that then became a cough. The cough grew worse until people started losing blood from their noses and coughing up other pieces of bodily tissue. There seemed to be nothing for it once it had taken hold. Parents were terrified that their children would fall ill. The castle staff were not immune either, which caused the king great concern.

Naturally, everyone had an opinion about the disease and their own home remedies. Some people swore by a foul concoction made mostly from raw ginger root. Others believed prayer the only solution that worked to heal the sick.

A dishevelled man was taken away from the castle gates in hysterics, screaming his raspy voice between coughs: "This is what you deserve for what you did on the island!"

Zaria saw them lead him away through a window in the castle. There were rumours spreading about the brutality of their soldiers during the excursion into Blue Island – *occupation* the critics called it. The king and the other people in charge of Naha hated those critics and there were severe penalties for anyone caught openly criticising the recent events of the war.

"Those poor souls!" the man yelled as he was led into the castle dungeon. "It's your fault we're sick! It is God's way of punishing us!"

Officially however, the cause of the illness was a new type of mosquito. The King's counsellors had invented a story that couldn't be easily disproven and seemed to quash any criticisms, at least for a while. They made sure to spread the story aggressively so that people couldn't escape it. The whole city was built around a swampy inlet on the east coast, and it was true that there were constant mosquitoes. The people of Naha were used to mild illnesses spreading from time to time, so many of them believed the official story.

When Zaria awoke from her most recent dream, it was barely sunrise. She felt ill-rested and determined to find a way to see him as soon as possible.

He had said something about the disease, too. He asked her if it had affected Naha and she said yes, it was the mosquitoes. He said that was a lie, and she said she knew.

He said he had a cure, if she could come get it.

But that was easier said than done. Naha had been a city state at war with Nyika since long before Zaria was born. There were controls on movement, curfews, and rations. It wasn't that easy to leave. She needed a plan and a lucky opportunity.

Fortunately – or unfortunately depending who was asked – the soldiers had recently returned from Blue Island. Some of them were glad to be home, while others were annoyed, feeling that they had been recalled unexpectedly early when things were going well. Ultimately though, a soldier's opinions counted for very little, and they had no say in where and when they were deployed. The same conflicts existed amongst the decision-makers too.

Not long after the withdrawal, King Timofea himself got involved, deciding to hold an inquiry. He thought the sudden decision to withdraw from Blue Island was highly suspicious, and undermined his government's attempts to gain a strategic hold in the war with Nyika. Zaria was present as she was one of the King's daughters and had been repeatedly urged to show more interest in state affairs, and less interest in fruitless stories about magicians. She was only mildly excited to hear what had happened, but Timofea was like a child at the circus. He had questions and he was determined to get answers. Someone was responsible. Someone would be punished.

Together they made their way into the conference room, where a group of about twenty people were waiting. They all stood up to attention as Timofea entered and found his place. He pompously sat down, lowering his thin frame into the chair at the head of the table. He brushed a hand back through his unkempt, black hair and then rubbed the bridge of his nose with tiredness. The thick bags under his eyes made him look much older than he really was.

"We are here today to discuss the withdrawal of troops from Blue Island," he began, looking at each of the officials present in turn. He raised his thick eyebrows, which combined with his droopy dark eye bags made him look like a caricature of himself. "I expect an explanation as to why the decision was made, considering we had established victory already. Why did you abandon our hard-won asset? Who is responsible?"

"Sir," began a man in military outfit seated partway down the long table, on the King's left. "Some of our officers received advance warning of a surprise offensive unit. It was considered prudent not to risk high casualties from this unknown enemy."

"Yes, this is the official story I have seen in the reports," Timofea replied. He took a sip of water and stared at the man who spoke, deeply unsatisfied. "General Andrei, I would like to dig deeper into the meaning of the report, not parrot the words that have already raised so many questions. I would have expected our army to defend its position rather than flee at the first rumour of trouble."

"Of course, sir." General Andrei lowered his gaze to the papers in front of him. Included was a topographical map of Blue Island, showing its most advantageous positions. The Noi lights that powered the room flickered slightly.

"Can someone, anyone, fill me in on the situation exactly as it had occurred leading up to the retreat?" the King demanded.

"Sir," a woman in a grey suit answered. "As this military's official historian and veteran from the island, I can provide some details." She was sitting perfectly upright and rigid, and had an expression of self-importance on her face. Her large brown eyes were slightly too big for her face and made her look like a doll.

"Go on then, Athena." He looked bored at her, having hoped to receive a short, snappy military reply, rather than a propaganda-laced essay. He realised the inquiry might take longer than expected. He sighed. Whatever, he was King of a nation fighting an endless and unwinnable war; there wasn't much else excitement. He might as well allow this circus to continue and have fun with it.

"You recall the operation to establish a stronghold on Blue Island was conceived by your predecessor, the late Queen Danika the Bright, named for the huge amounts of Noi powered technology installed in Naha during her reign. It was determined that Blue Island offered the most strategic position against Nyika's sparsely populated west coast, while also providing a foothold to the Capital in the western continent, if your eminence should ever decide to expand our ambitions."

"Yes, I remember that, Athena." He affected impatience, as a way of showing his power, but really did find her narrative engaging. Some of the military men present wriggled uncomfortably. She coughed lightly and continued.

"Movements began twenty-one years ago. The journey to the island was difficult – still is difficult – and initially took two months. That time is now one month due to advances in Noi technology. Our early exploration was met with some token resistance by the locals. We pacified them, and began the process of civilising them.

"After one year, we started receiving reports that the locals were guarding an enormous quantity of Noi, which they had not yet exploited. Their society is one without Noi, relying on primitive technologies.

"The discovery of the Noi deposits changed the thinking at the time. We saw Blue Island then as more than just a well-positioned military base. It was determined that a colony should be established on the island, and the Noi exported back here to the major cities."

Athena felt her voice cracking and stopped to take a sip

of water. She coughed into her glass while doing so, accidentally splashing the man next to her. He wiped his face with the back of his sleeve, and tried not to look offended. She stifled another cough before continuing.

"Our first colony was successful for approximately six months, before spies from Nyika and Arazi had learned of our movements. Nyika sent soldiers of their own, deciding that they wanted to occupy the island instead of us. Of course, we could not let them gain control of it, so we sent three more units."

"And in the process, weakened our defences here in the city," added General Andrei disapprovingly.

"Indeed. Go on Athena," said Timofea. Despite his impatience, he was enjoying the story. She had a way of summarising everything that pleased him more than he had expected.

"Yes. The decision to send more troops was almost unanimous." She cast a sidelong glance at General Andrei. "By that time, most people agreed that Blue Island's importance in both the war and in Noi production was beyond expectations. It would have been a disaster had we lost control over it. The decision reached at the time was to defend it against the Nyikans at all costs, and fighting began. Many soldiers on both sides were lost, and the locals fled."

"Did those orders ever change?" the King asked.

"No, sir," Athena said humbly. "The situation did change however, when Arazi tried to use the fighting between us and Nyika as a distraction and sneak in to steal the Noi production."

"Cozbi…" the King spat the name. Most of the military men present had personal grievances against the Arazi tyrant and his ruthless bandits.

"Yes. It was Cozbi who ordered the Arazi fleets to

intercept our transportation routes. His pirates infiltrated our production lines and claimed the largest of our mines.

"Up until that point we assume, the Nyikans were unaware of the vast Noi deposits on Blue Island. A temporary alliance was struck up between us to oust the Arazi thieves. We promised a share of the Noi in return. Eventually they demanded seventy percent in return for fighting off the Arazi, and leaving us alone on the island."

"Ransom money," General Andrei whispered under his breath. Everyone heard, but since they all agreed they said nothing, even King Timofea.

"The deal was expensive, yes. But we were still left with vastly more Noi than we would otherwise have had from our small scattered deposits in the foothills of the Kuravi Plani."

"Please stick to the facts, Athena. I am not here to debate the wisdom of the ill-advised alliance," the King reprimanded her.

"Yes, sir. The Nyikans held up their end of the bargain and fought with us against the Arazi for several years. It was during the alliance, some fourteen years ago, that you succeeded Danika the Bright as King of Naha."

It had begun raining. From the conference room, they had a spectacular view of the blue light given off by Noi in the city below. It rained often on their swampy land, and a heavy mist hung in the air.

"Does it rain often on Blue Island?" Timofea asked. Of all the people in the room, only he and Zaria had not visited the colony.

"Not often, sir," General Andrei answered. "It is more often than not a cloudless sunshine. And the soil is rich for crops."

"If it weren't for those damned foreign bastards, we

might be able to enjoy it there!" he erupted. Athena burst into a fit of coughing and guzzled the rest of her water. "Bring her another," the King said to a servant without bothering to turn and look at him. "Are we getting to the point yet, Athena? Why did we retreat?"

"It gets complicated here sir. We have only scattered intelligence coming from the western continent, but it seems that about that same time, they somehow learned about the Noi deposits too, and got worryingly ambitious."

"Greedy pigs," General Andrei muttered.

"Indeed," the King conceded. Despite General Andrei's involvement in the withdrawal, Timofea had a soft spot for him and his bold attitude. "Is their land not exceedingly rich in Noi as it is?"

"It is, sir. But they are, as the General rightly states, greedy pigs."

"Please stick to the history, and leave out your editorials."

"Yes, sir. Thanks to the agreement with Nyika we had been able to drive out the Arazi after some years of fighting. It was then agreed that the alliance would continue in the colony, so long as the threat remained from the Capital in the west. We negotiated a better deal regarding the Noi extraction at that point and split the production fifty-fifty with Nyika.

"Then seven years ago, the Nyikans betrayed us and took control of the mine with the help of some mercenaries from Arazi. At the same time, they began small skirmishes closer to home, even daring to cross the border a few times.

"We had to decide if we should pour more troops into the Island to reclaim the valuable Noi mine, or to strengthen our defences at home. Knowing that a round trip to the Island could take up to four months, we thought it would be wiser to defend ourselves here.

"So, for the last six and a half years, our soldiers on Blue Island have been waiting, hoping that the Nyikan-Arazi alliance will fail, and trying to stay alive."

"We were stuck, sir," General Andrei spoke up and shrugged his shoulders with an exaggerated slowness.

"Then our intelligence at last came through from the west, that the Capital was advancing its interests with a new weapon. They already had far more advanced technology than any of us or the Nyikans or Arazi-"

"What weapon?" the King interrupted.

"We don't know, sir," General Andrei answered. The King grunted and nodded at Athena to continue. She choked back another cough and continued. She seemed to be annoyed at how the cough was interfering with her polished appearance.

"Whatever new weapon they had, it spooked a lot of the soldiers and officers in the colony. A lot of the Nyikans and Arazi were worried too, and some of them started to leave."

"Would that not have been the moment to regain control? Why the hell did we decide to leave too?" the King asked angrily. The officers in the room all looked uncomfortable and did not want to answer.

"It was decided that whatever weapon they had, if it could frighten away the Nyikan and Arazi armies, it would be too dangerous for us to remain too," General Andrei summarised. The King looked unimpressed.

"And now we reach the official reason stated in the report. We have gone in a circle, people. Can't somebody tell me anything new? Did any of you have proof of the new weapon? What was the intelligence you received?"

"Sir," a wiry man furthest from the King spoke up. "There was no direct proof."

"What was the intelligence, General Rainer?" he asked

again. There was a silence in the room. "Why won't anyone answer me? Give me a straight answer."

The generals exchanged nervous glances, daring each other to remain silent. But General Rainer was the first to break.

"We had dreams, sir." He tried to maintain his dignity, but admitting it out loud was almost too shameful.

"Dreams!" The King was furious, but suddenly Zaria was more interested in what was happening. "You abandoned our most strategic asset, that we fought to control for twenty-one years…because you had dreams? It was *my* dream, it was Danika the Bright's dream to establish a colony. We had it!"

"Yes, sir."

"And you're telling me now, all of you, that you gave up and walked away because of dreams?"

"Yes, sir."

"If you would be so kind as to tell me what was the content of these dreams?"

"Sir, every single Nahan on the island reported the same dream independently," General Rainer said quietly. Zaria was straining to hear him from her place across the table.

"Speak up! And Athena, do not record any of this in the official history."

"Every one of us had the same dream independently." General Rainer answered reluctantly.

"What dream?"

"There was a man-"

"A man!" the King ridiculed. "You retreated because you all dreamed of a man!" But Zaria was leaning further and further forward.

"Yes, sir. A man. And a room. A round room."

"What did this man look like?"

"None of us know, sir."

"How do you mean?"

"None of us could remember his face. It was like he was underwater."

Zaria had to choke back a gasp. Her father rudely pushed her glass of water closer to her and grunted.

"Well, what happened in this dream that was so frightening? What did he say? What did he do? Did he show you the weapon?"

"In a way, sir."

"What the hell does that mean, 'in a way'? Either he showed you or not!"

"Sir, the Nyikans and Arazi all saw it too."

"So what? What did you see?"

"The island was on fire. The mine, the town, our bases, and all of us. He was standing there, watching it, making it happen." Hearing this shocked Zaria, whose experiences with Iwizadi had always been instructive and enlightening. She didn't want to think the same man was capable of such destruction and terror.

"And?"

"There were others on the island."

"What others?"

"Soldiers, wearing Capital uniform."

"Just ordinary soldiers?"

"No, sir. They could make things happen with their hands."

"Things? What things?"

"They could make the natives gasp for air. They could topple buildings from a distance."

"And then what?" The King was unimpressed, but Zaria was desperate for more.

"There was a girl, sir. A child."

"A girl?"

"She could do things with her hands too, but even more powerfully. We saw death sir."

There was a heavy silence in the room as the King decided what to say next. Nobody dared move, fearing that the stiff fabric of their uniform would make too much noise. Timofea pinched the bridge of his nose and rubbed his eyes with one hand, and used the other hand to hold the weight of his head, propped up on the table on one elbow.

"A dream is not intelligence enough to base these types of decisions upon. You have made me look like a fool. How do you know it was not a trick to make us leave, so that Nyika could gain control unopposed?"

"I-"

"The war is not over, and Blue Island is crucially important to our victory. We will be returning there as soon as preparations are made. You two: General Andrei, General Rainer, you will each receive the Medal of Cowardice, which you will wear at all times. You will be cashiered: demoted to rank of private, and you will be the first to set foot on the island and last to leave. Am I clear?"

"Yes sir," they both chanted, somewhat relieved that their punishment was not worse. Zaria could not believe her luck. The same day she decided to go see Iwizadi in person, her father had ordered the army to go back there. That had to be a sign from the universe pushing her towards her destiny. It was now or never; this was the only official way to leave the city. She wouldn't have to sneak out if she was going on official business. All she had to do was convince the army to take her with them, and the easiest way to do that was to enlist. She decided to speak to the disgraced generals in private when the meeting was over, because she wanted to know more about the dreams without getting her father involved.

"Captain Vasiliy," the King directed his attention to the man two places to his right, next to Zaria. "Congratulations, you are now General Vasiliy. You will be leading the way."

"Thank you, sir," Vasiliy replied automatically. He looked nervously at his two former superiors down the table. They did not meet his eye. "We will begin preparation immediately."

"Athena," the King addressed the historian. "I need to talk to you in private. Think of a way we can turn this cowardice in our favour. The people will demand to know why all our soldiers are back. The soldiers will need an official reason to tell their families when they inevitably ask about it."

"Yes sir," she looked thoughtful. "Perhaps some sort of evacuation drill?" The King grunted, which Athena took to mean "try again".

"We can only hope now," the King began slowly summarising. "That our enemies have not taken advantage of our absence on Blue Island. A lot can have happened in the time since you deserted your posts, and a lot can happen in the time it takes you to resume them. If we are lucky, you will find everything just as you left it. If, by some miracle, your dreams turned out to be true visions of a weapon from the west, I swear to formally apologise for my actions taken here today and restore things to order. I refer to you two privates, specifically."

"Yes sir."

"Send word back immediately upon arrival. I wish to know the situation without delay." This was a good opportunity for Zaria. She decided to chime in, still promising to talk to Andrei and Rainer in private afterwards.

"Let me go," she said. "I would like to see for myself."

Everyone was taken aback, for they had not expected her to say anything during the meeting, let alone volunteer to be involved in official business.

"Zaria, are you sure?" Her father was most stunned out of everyone. "You have never shown an interest in this before."

"Yes, I am sure." She felt the inquisitive stares from everyone there and made up an explanation. "I would like to be more involved in politics and I see this as a good opportunity to begin. After all, you just need me to report what I see."

"General Vasiliy?" the King addressed the newest General, implicitly asking what he thought.

"I welcome Miss Zaria, sir."

"Fine then. Athena, after our meeting, I want you to explain everything we know about Blue Island to Zaria. She needs to be able to understand the things that she reports on."

"Yes sir."

"And I believe that brings our meeting to a close. I have answers now, unsatisfactory as they are. We have a way forward now. I want all members of the military to understand perfectly well that dreams are not actionable intelligence. Regardless if they all share the same hallucination."

Everyone stood up as the King made his way out first. Athena followed him, and Zaria stayed behind to talk to the privates about their dreams.

Unfortunately, she could not get them alone, as the rest of the people there all left together as a group, and the privates were swept up in the middle of the exodus.

"Everything alright? First time can be nerve-wracking." A younger officer stopped to ask her. His name was Iskander and he was a Major. She had known him for several years, ever since he first enlisted and went on basic training camp. A year earlier, he was stationed in the castle in an administrative role and Zaria had more opportunity to interact with him. During that year they developed a type of romance that never blossomed. She waited for him to make a move, but he never did, knowing that it would be highly improper. She understood, but wished he would do something anyway, even though he was too serious of a soldier to ever break the rules.

She thought he had a kind face; too kind to be in the army. But at the same time, he was too energetic for a desk job, and she was happy for him when he was transferred to active duty again, even though she wouldn't be seeing him around the castle anymore. She decided then that she would never again waste her heart waiting for a man.

"I was just wondering how long the journey to Blue Island will take exactly." Zaria knew it was about a month, but had to make something up so she didn't look suspicious. She decided then that she would ask Iskander about the dreams too. He might be more approachable than Andrei or Rainer, in fact, seeing as his pride was still intact and they already knew each other.

"If there are no delays, it will take twenty-five nights." While saying this, his smile told Zaria that he was looking forward to the journey. Perhaps it wouldn't be so bad if she managed to get stuck with him for a month. "But if there are any delays it could take much longer."

"What delays could there be?"

"Serious storms, mechanical problems." He brushed a loose strand of hair out of his eyes. He had a blonde wave longer than most other men in the army, but still tidy. Zaria thought it suited him. "Raids, if we're unlucky."

"Raids?" She was a little surprised. "Is the route not through Naha entirely?"

"It is," he said measuredly, as if not wanting to be overheard. "You must surely be aware that in the provinces Naha is not as united as the city might want to believe."

"You mean our own countrymen attack our army?"

"Stranger things have happened."

Zaria was beginning to regret volunteering, but she forced herself to reason that it was the safest way to leave the city.

"I hope I have not made you change your mind, Zaria. Your presence would be welcomed among the troops. Word is you are a gifted storyteller. You could help with raising morale." This made her blush, the way he was flattering her. Was he flirting, she wondered? She remembered the dreams.

"Speaking of stories, I am intrigued by the dreams that General Rainer spoke of." She could not immediately tell if Iskander had also dreamed of Iwizadi or not. Apparently, every soldier on the island had.

"Private Rainer," he corrected. Even with his handsome face and broad jaw, he managed to look very serious, revealing to Zaria his devotion to the army.

"Sorry, yes."

"Can I tell you something?" He stepped closer towards her and she could see that the lines under his eyes were not unattractive like they could be for some men. She could smell the soap from his stiff, fresh uniform. He lowered his voice to a whisper. "I have had the same dream. It was not a lie. And it was not exaggerated. Private Rainer did not do justice to the horrors we all saw. It is worse than you can imagine. We were all being watched by someone."

"I believe you."

"To tell you the truth, I am worried that we will be

marching to our deaths."

"Then why are you going?" She took his hands. He had calluses and scratches all over. She ran her thumbs over them gently, feeling the rough bumps and scar tissue.

"We are soldiers. This is what we do." She nodded, understanding. He took a step back, as if realising he was too close all of a sudden, regaining his military composure. "You are brave for wanting to come with us."

"I don't want to spend my life locked up in this city," she confessed.

"I am the same," he nodded. "You remember how restless I was back when I was working here. When you get a taste for adventure, it is hard to eat anything else." She thought about Iwizadi, and the stories, and adventure, and she was excited. More excited than she could remember ever being.

"How soon do you think we will be leaving?"

"Probably the day after tomorrow. We need time to pack supplies for the trip, but there is no time to lose. You will also need to get travel permits and have your briefing with Athena."

"I am looking forward to it."

"I hope you enjoy the journey, because you will be making it twice. At least the soldiers will have the luxury of setting up a base." She liked the way he looked when he made a joke, how the corner of his mouth twisted up and a little dimple sunk into his cheek.

They left the meeting room and Iskander farewelled her. He had a lot of work to do to ensure the army would be ready to go. As he walked away, she felt her old feelings for him resurfacing, in spite of her decision not to wait for him.

It was still early in the day, and after packing some of her belongings, she spent most of the rest of the day with

Athena learning everything there was to know about Blue Island. She was fascinated by its indigenous people, who lived without Noi. It was almost impossible to imagine life without Noi, and she hoped to see them first hand. But Athena warned her that most of them had fled or been victims of the war. It bothered her the way Athena talked about them, as if they were less than human, just objects in the way, but she held her tongue.

"You know they are a primitive people," Athena told her. "They have some superstitions about the mountain and the land. They seem to think that the river gives them special powers."

Zaria hung on to every word about the natives. The Khun, she learned they called themselves. In their language it meant 'people' apparently. Few of the soldiers had learned to speak it to any degree, but there were supposedly many Khun who had learned to speak Nahan. Zaria hoped that she would have a chance to meet one of them and ask about what powers they believed the river gave them. Maybe when she arrived, she could send a messenger back in her place. After all, her plan was to find Iwizadi and the cure to the disease, and she was not happy about simply turning around as soon as she arrived. There had to be another solution. She did not want to return without the cure.

She thought that if the Khun were a society who did not use Noi, they might have another form of energy. Maybe something magical. The more Athena talked about them and the island, the less far-fetched it sounded. It sounded magical to her.

"There are some remarkably beautiful flowers there," Athena mentioned. "They grow in the soil there by the river. As far as we know, it is the only place in the world where they have been seen. The natives call them glowflowers, because they glow. Sometimes you have to admire their simplistic thinking, don't you? Our scientists have not worked out how exactly the flowers emit light, but it probably has something to do with them absorbing Noi from the ground through their roots."

It must be magic, Zaria thought. She was determined to stay on the island and learn more. Maybe the cure could wait.

Iskander was right about the departure. The day after the meeting there was a great deal of noise and movement in the barracks as soldiers prepared for another long tour. Most of them hadn't even unpacked after their journey home. Normally, they spent six months at a time on tour, and they were busy packing trucks with everything they could possibly need to survive. An entire truck was filled with tools to repair any kind of mechanical failure or damage to the structures they would build. Others were stuffed full with foods and gardening supplies.

Iskander's previous position had involved overseeing the supplies and ensuring the right things were packed for excursions, so he was very interested in the process and chatted with the woman who had taken over his old position while they watched the soldiers hard at work.

The Nahan army was proud of its inclusive attitude. Women had always been involved, unlike the Nyikan and Arazi armies. Some women had risen to the rank of general, with many soldiers saying that they were the most conniving leaders with the best strategies.

Zaria received her official documents and could hardly sleep that night. When she did, she dreamed of Iwizadi again. Through his blurry face, she thought maybe she saw him smile and heard him whisper the words 'good, good'.

Early in the morning she saw the full scale of the

expedition. There were at least one hundred trucks waiting to go. Some of them were laden with equipment, while about half would carry soldiers. It was an impressive sight. They were due to depart at nine, driving west through the city, then out past the hazy Noi mining sites in the Kuravi Plani, then out into the distant provinces. As a civilian, Zaria was treated with more leniency than the other soldiers, but she was still expected to follow any orders from General Vasiliy in emergency situations. She had a place in his truck. Iskander had pulled some strings and made certain that he would be riding in the same truck with her.

King Timofea addressed the soldiers before they departed, reminding them that they were not to abandon their posts again should they be presented with nightmares. The job of a soldier is to follow orders, not to run away in the face of fear. He gave Zaria and Athena a separate farewell, warning them of the dangers they faced. Athena thanked him and joined the soldiers to leave. Zaria hugged him around the waist, astonished to feel how bony he was. She remembered a time where he was portly and fun. That was before her mother had died. He hugged her back and she said goodbye and went to where Iskander and Vasiliy were waiting for her.

When they started driving, she realised that military trucks did not have the modern suspension that was in other Noicars, and it was going to be a bumpy month.

While there was a general uneasiness amongst the troops about going back to Blue Island, General Vasiliy appeared more concerned by the sickness that affected people with no apparent pattern. At any time, there could be five or ten soldiers stricken with the disease. They had not yet worked out how it spread.

"We don't know the cause," he told Zaria and Iskander

as they chugged through the narrow city streets from the barracks. When they reached the main street, they would be able to drive a little faster. Many people in the city stopped to stare at the enormous convoy. Some waved half-heartedly, but most wore blank expressions, fatigued by the unending war. Vasiliy spoke Nahan with a slight provincial accent. He was born somewhere near the west coast, and migrated to the city with his parents when he was young. Most of the time, his speech was textbook proper, but sometimes a trace of his native tongue came through.

"Is it not mosquitoes?" Zaria asked them. They snorted.

"When you see Blue Island, you will understand," Vasiliy told her. "They have no swamp and no mosquitoes, and that is where the disease began."

"You brought it back to the city?" She was shocked. Iskander remained silent in the presence of his commanding officer. "And through all the provinces?"

"It was not us. It was the Nyikan dogs and Arazi pirates. There were attempted raids on our coastal base several times. From there it spread."

"Couldn't it be contained?"

"Impossible. We had supply lines in many directions. If we cut off supply, there would have been disaster. Besides, we didn't know what was going on until it had started to spread. We don't even know how it spreads, but it seems to follow us wherever we go."

The truck reached the main street, and the sharp turn pushed Zaria into close contact with Iskander. She made no effort to resist the motion of the truck, and he made no sign of discomfort. She let her thigh remain pressed against his for a minute before shuffling back into position.

"There is something I read once," she said, trying to remember it. "It said that raw Noi can cause sickness."

"That's our best theory at the moment," Vasiliy agreed. "But we cannot prove it. And even if it's true, look around you. Everything we do is thanks to Noi."

"Maybe if the people knew that Noi was making them sick-" she began, but both Vasiliy and Iskander started shaking their heads.

"They won't give it up," Vasiliy said simply. "You are talking about changing the way that people live completely. It is not possible." Zaria thought about the magic she knew how to perform, and knew that he was wrong. There was a better way, she thought. But she was yet to learn that magic had its own dangers.

The rest of the day passed without event. They chatted sometimes, and watched the scenery. Zaria was enthralled watching the landscape change as they made their way west. Only a few times in her life had she been outside the city gates, and never beyond the Kuravi Plani. In fact, other than Vasiliy, she didn't know anybody from the provinces, though she knew that the city had a large number of immigrants.

At the city gates they had to stop and chat to some soldiers who controlled the road in and out. They asked to see her documents, even though she was riding with the general.

The landscape was extremely different to the city, and she wondered if the city had any room to expand, crowded as it was. It was built on what seemed to be the only solid ground as far as the horizon. All around them was murky swamp, and the road was a dangerous sort of semi-submerged bridge. It was extremely difficult to see where it was built and where its edges fell away into the grey sludge, and she was impressed with their driver's ability. A constant haze hung in the air, making the light from the sun dimmer than its full brightness, but that was what she was used to having grown up in the city.

By the end of the first day of travel, they could see the first peaks of the Kuravi Plani rising on the horizon, silhouetted by the setting sun. If it weren't for the haze, they would have had a very hard time driving directly west into the sun.

They set up camp and rested for the night. The soldiers were extraordinarily efficient, having done this countless times before, and Zaria was impressed by their precise movements. Everyone knew their roles and what everyone else was doing. Soon, there was a basic meal prepared, then soon after that it was time for sleep. Her mind felt dizzy as she lay down, after being jostled and jolted all day on the road. She was too tired to want to stay up and talk to anyone, but lots of the soldiers played cards until it was late.

The following day was much the same as the first. As the peaks drew closer, the ground became firmer and the haze thinner. Around midday, the first Noi excavation came into view on their left. It was nowhere near the size of those in the western continent, but Zaria did not know that and she thought it was enormous; it must have been as wide as the city she was from. The blue glow of the raw Noi shone brightly. It was the furthest she had been from her birthplace.

In the afternoon of the second day, the road began to wind steeply upwards through the hills. She understood now how difficult the journey would have been before the invention of the latest Noi conversion engine. No wonder it had taken two months at first. It was also good that the road was not going straight west anymore, since the swampy haze was no longer present to protect their eyes from the sunset.

The climate in the Kuravi Plani was completely different to the city. Zaria thought the air smelt better, without the stench of mud and rotting wood. The sun felt hotter, more direct, but the air lacked the humidity she knew and she shivered. There were no mosquitoes, and the trees were different. There were birds and other creatures everywhere. Iskander saw her awestruck expression when they first entered the hills and laughed.

"This is nothing. Wait until you see the island."

"I know it is still weeks away but I am feeling impatient. How can I maintain this excitement the whole way there?"

"I'm sure there will be things along the way to distract you." He was thinking about potential dangers and difficulties, but she was thinking about him.

"I'm sure you're right."

"We are making good time," Vasiliy commented, a subtle compliment to their driver. "Sometimes the road through the swamp takes two, maybe three days. We were lucky with the weather. Any rain and you would not be feeling so optimistic."

"He's right," Iskander said to Zaria. "There is not much that is more demoralising than a night in the swamp in a storm."

"I can imagine," she said gloomily.

"When it rains," Vasiliy continued, "You cannot see the road. It is a nightmare driving through the swamp, trying to guess where the road is. We have lost many vehicles this way."

"Well, I am glad to have avoided that experience," Zaria laughed.

"Don't be so happy," Vasiliy replied grimly. "You still have to come back through it."

"That's your life motto, isn't it? 'Don't be so happy'," she teased him. Iskander and the driver held back laughs. Vasiliy scowled and grunted, not wanting to admit that she was probably right.

"When is there ever time to be happy?" he tried to defend himself. "There is too much work to do to be happy."

The second night, they made camp in an elevated valley. Zaria hadn't noticed during the day, but they had steadily driven quite high up into the hills. The road had been relatively smooth and free of obstacles, and she wondered if Vasiliy felt something like happiness about it.

From their camp, Zaria walked a little bit away to where she could get a good view of the area around the hills. She saw the swamp, but could not make out the wet road they had travelled on. She could see a few smaller Noi mines glowing powerfully. Though it was now too far away to see, there was a faint hazy glow to the east that she recognised as coming from the city. She looked back at the campsite and saw the blue light of Noi on everything: the vehicles, the lights, even their weapons. It was impossible to imagine life without it. How did the Khun live? She needed to know. Maybe Vasiliy was right, and it would be impossible to convince people to change their reliance on it. But if only they knew about magic! Surely they would want it!

The thing that most impressed her about the night was the clear view of stars. There was nothing like it in the city due to the combination of Noi and the smog coming off the swamp, and she stared upwards for a long time at constellations she did not recognise. The wind started to pick up and she got cold, so she went back to join the others for a hot drink and a meal.

She sat near Iskander, and after everyone had eaten, he tried to get her involved in the conversation.

"Zaria, why don't you tell us one of your famous stories?

You know, we find it tiresome to talk about the war all the time." She felt put on the spot and awkwardly looked at the expectant faces around her.

"I guess it would be tiresome," she agreed, to some laughs that gave her confidence. "But what would I know about tiresome, living locked up in the castle and all…"

More laughter. That was a good sign. She relaxed a little and tried to think of something to entertain them. They were all relaxed around the table, about ten people. They were soldiers in high spirits, not yet worn out by the war. Any story would do.

"How about one of the classics?" somebody suggested.

"A fairy tale? Like a children's story?" she was surprised to hear, but also relieved as these were the ones she knew best.

"Iwizadi," someone else said. "Tell us Iwizadi." There was all-round agreement.

"Okay, okay. Listen," she started, thinking of all the times she'd told the story to little kids at home.

"I will tell you the *tragedy* of Iwizadi, BUT-" she paused to make sure she had their attention. Small children, soldiers, they act exactly the same. She had barely said one sentence and they were already leaning forward to listen.

"But it isn't the story as you know it. This is the *true* story." There were murmurs of approval. "A long, long time ago, in a country not far from here, there was a shining city. It was called Libalele, after its valley and its river, and the people who lived there were said to live to twice the age of anyone else in the world.

"The people were so proud of their city, and they worked hard to make it the best city in the world. Many people visited Libalele from around the world to see for themselves. The visitors were always impressed, and envious of the city.

"But the people had a secret, one that they guarded closely. The reason the city was so brilliant and clean and modern lay with the people. You see, of all the people in the world, the people of Libalele were alone in their ability to use magic."

Zaria stopped to sip at her tea, and her audience waited eagerly for her to continue. The night was getting colder and the tea felt good. The scene was set. Time to add some drama.

"But not everyone could use magic the same way. Some people were weak, and others were strong. One man was stronger than all the others. His name was Iwizadi. He had powers that made even the strongest magic users envious.

"They used to say to each other, 'how does he do it?', and 'I could never do a spell like that', when they saw him do things so easily and so powerfully.

"Over time, their jealousy slowly changed to worry, and they feared that he might use his supreme power for harm. The people went to see his brother Umwahu, who was just like you and me. He was an ordinary man, with an ordinary job and a family. The people thought that he knew Iwizadi best of all, so they asked him for advice. 'What should we do about Iwizadi?' they asked. 'We are scared that he is becoming too powerful'.

"'Why should you fear that?' Umwahu asked plainly. He knew Iwizadi was a simple man, who enjoyed learning for the sake of learning, and inventing new spells for the sake of inventing new spells. He knew Iwizadi had no motives bigger than that. 'Because,' said the people, 'what if he turns his magic against us all?'

"Umwahu laughed at the idea, but saw that the people were serious. He wanted to tell them everything would be alright, but they would not listen. He tried to tell them that Iwizadi was not a threat to them, but they would not listen. Eventually he told them that he would speak to Iwizadi on their behalf, and make him see their concerns. They were pleased with Umwahu, and went away.

"Umwahu told Iwizadi about the people, and Iwizadi laughed. He said they had nothing to worry about, he was not interested in power, only magic. Umwahu went back to the people.

"'It is not good enough,' they said. 'We don't believe him.' Umwahu asked what would make them believe, but they scratched their heads because they didn't know. 'What do you want him to do?' Umwahu asked the people. 'We want him to stop showing off his powers, and promise not to learn any more magic.' Umwahu said he would bring the message to Iwizadi, but he knew his brother would not like it. He would not understand, and he would refuse. The people went away, satisfied that Umwahu was helping them."

Zaria needed to pause to catch her breath. Her throat felt a little dry, but she put it down to the cold mountain air.

"Iwizadi refused, because he could not understand why the people were worried. Umwahu went to tell the people. This time, they did not ask him to deliver any messages. This time, they decided enough was enough, and they went to Iwizadi themselves. If he refused to give up his tremendous power, they would make him leave. It was not alright for one person in their city to be so different, and so difficult.

"They went to where he lived, and saw him happily studying some books. He greeted them cheerfully, oblivious to their intentions. They ordered him to leave the city. They told him he was too dangerous. 'Me? Dangerous?' he did not understand. They gave him until sunset to leave.

"Iwizadi went to Umwahu and asked what the people were doing. 'I warned you,'' Umwahu replied. 'But you did not listen.' The two brothers knew that Iwizadi would never stop learning and practicing magic. He would only ever get stronger.

"Umwahu said that there would always be a place for Iwizadi, if only he chose to fit in it. Iwizadi said he could not imagine how. Umwahu said that for such a smart person, he completely lacked wisdom."

Zaria paused for a while as if realising something about herself. She reflected on the story as she always did, empathising with the foolish wizard.

"Then what? Is that the end?" one of the soldiers asked.

"You know it's not, you idiot," one of the others answered. People made hushing sounds and looked at Zaria to continue.

"Life in the city continued, but it wasn't long before the people started to notice Iwizadi's absence. They noticed how things didn't seem to work as well as they had before. They noticed that there were more arguments and that public works took longer. They noticed that the sun beat down harder, and the rains came in heavier, and the winds blew through the streets with violence.

"They went to visit Umwahu again, and asked if Iwizadi was responsible for keeping things working well. Umwahu said that he was. 'Please bring him back!' they begged him. 'Find him and tell him to come back!' Umwahu said he would try, but he did not know where Iwizadi was. By that stage, he was long gone.

"They wanted him to go, because he was not like them. Then they wanted him back, but it was their own fault he was gone. They never knew all the good he did for them, until he was no longer around to do it."

Everyone around the table was silent for a moment longer while thinking about Zaria's little summary at the end. Then they burst into applause, laughing and smiling. Many of them had not heard the story since they were children, and thoroughly enjoyed hearing it again. Zaria enjoyed their approval, having spent her life among people who thought she was strange. For once, her unconventional attitude and passion had brought happiness to others. She enjoyed the feeling and wondered if it was what normal people felt all the time.

It was getting late, and despite the good mood in the campsite, they all went to bed ahead of another long day of driving. Zaria crawled into her tent and snuggled into her sleeping bag. The soldiers all treated her very well and she was happy to be there.

The night was still and the air hung heavy around the camp. It was the deadest part of the night, and a slight frost was settling into the grass, and it would crackle into a million pieces in the morning when everyone woke up and broke it with their steps. From inside her tent, Zaria heard a faint crunch of frost. It must have been someone visiting the latrine during the night, she reasoned, and closed her eyes again.

A moment later, there was a yell, followed by more loud voices, and lights came on in every tent. Terrified of what she might see, she unzipped her tent and poked out her head.

There was a lot of commotion near the vehicles, and soldiers running all over the place. Iskander rushed to her tent and roughly pulled her to her feet.

"Nyikans. Come with me now." There was no time to explain anything else. He ran fast, pulling her with him in one hand, with his weapon gripped tightly in the other. She stumbled awkwardly trying to match his pace, groggy with the mixture of adrenaline and deep sleep. There were more screams, and chaos all around them. In the darkness, she saw the lights coming from the soldiers' weapons floating in mid-air, ghostly and beautiful, but tactically foolish. They painted streams and patterns in the night.

Iskander was leading her towards one of the trucks, and they did not stop running until they reached it. The campsite was a mess of confusion and blood. He opened the door and pushed her into the cab of the truck and told her to remain hidden in the footwell.

"What is happening?" she shouted between gasps for air.

"Nyikan raid," Iskander handed her a small weapon. "This is the way they do battle. Surprise attacks in the night. I have to fight, because it is my job. You should be safe in here. I will be back for you."

For her whole life, the war had not been real for her. It had been just another story that people told to death. But in that moment, the entirety of what she knew about Nyika had come true, and she would not be able to digest the horrors of what she saw for some time. Iskander was about to turn back to the battle when she grabbed him by the shirt front and kissed him. She was almost as surprised as he was. He pulled away and was about to turn back to the skirmish, when her eyes were drawn to something over his shoulder. He saw the direction of her gaze change and in an instant knew that he was in mortal danger.

A Nyikan soldier had followed them to the truck and snuck up behind Iskander, waiting for the right moment to emerge from the shadows and strike. They were no ordinary bandits. They were trained soldiers, relying on the darkness of night to make them invisible. They dressed in black, painted themselves dark colours, and even abandoned their

Noi-powered weapons so that the blue glow would not betray them like those belonging to the Nahan soldiers did. They were like shadows. Demonic shadows.

Iskander groaned and spat some blood, and tried to overcome the agonising pain in his side where the knife entered him. In a heroic effort and with a pained roar, he pushed back hard on the Nyikan soldier and threw him to the ground, landing on top of him. He tried to aim his own weapon and shoot him dead, but his grip loosened and it fell from his hand as the Nyikan took a second knife and shoved it through Iskander's forearm. He howled in pain, and headbutted the soldier. They scrambled for dominance on the ground, the Nyikan dizzy from being flung around, Iskander twice his size but badly wounded. With his good arm he managed to land a blow with the base of his fist on the man's neck, crippling him.

Zaria watched horrified from the cab, and held her own weapon out in front of her. It was nearly impossible to see the Nyikan man, and she was terrified of misfiring and hurting Iskander even further. The Nyikan could see her though, as the light from her weapon gave her away. They grappled on the ground in front of her, barely three metres away, the Nyikan man trying to make Iskander roll onto the handle of the knife that was still stuck in his side.

"Shoot him, Zaria!" he called out through a mouthful of blood.

She wanted to. But it was too risky. She had another plan, but it would mean revealing her deepest secret. In the moment, she decided that there was no other choice.

Iskander was relieved to feel the struggle weakening despite not hearing a shot from Zaria's weapon, and managed to crawl to one side of the man. He went to reclaim his weapon and finish the fight, but then he saw that the man seemed to be having a seizure of some kind. The man was clawing at his throat and having trouble breathing. He began writhing in horrific ways as if he were drowning. His eyes were fixed on Zaria in the cab, who was staring back at him with inhuman focus, unblinking, her mouth partially open and her lips moving silently.

"What are you doing to him?" Iskander yelled, not understanding what he was seeing. His focus on the battle was disturbed by his blood loss and confusion. She did not stop, not until the man's eyes rolled back and his arms fell limp by his sides, and his ghastly choking and spluttering had ceased. Iskander, through his own pain, imagined that he must be having some kind of near-death hallucination. He looked up to see Zaria jump out of the cab and run towards him. She pulled him towards her, crying. He smiled and closed his eyes, weakly falling into her embrace.

"Iskander!" she yelled, shaking him. He made no sign that he had heard her. An immense dark stain had spread across his uniform.

The screaming from the camp was getting less and less chaotic. The frantic movement of the Noi weapons in the blackness of night had ceased, as the surviving soldiers surveyed the damage. Zaria had to act fast before any of the Nahan soldiers found them and saw what she about to do. She gently laid Iskander down, and stabbed the already-dead Nyikan in the neck with his own knife. Just in case anyone wanted to question how he had died. He made no indication that he felt it, and she was relieved that he was not alive to experience even more pain.

She breathed deeply to regain her composure and wiped away her tears. She made sure Iskander was still breathing, laboured though it was, then she began to visualise a healthy, beating heart. She stared hard at his fading body and visualised the heart pumping blood through every part of him, from the top of his head to the ends of his limbs. The stream of blood from his mouth slowed and then stopped, and she could see his chest rising and falling more steadily than it had been. She knelt down and wiped the corner of his mouth on her sleeve, and felt his breath on her hand. His eyes began to flutter open.

She focused on the gash that had been torn in his arm. It was a dirty cut, one that would not ordinarily heal, and likely would become infected. Slowly, the edges of the wound began to close together and soon it was not visible, except for the blood that had dried on his skin already.

"Zaria," he said with more strength than before. She silenced him and looked closely at the knife protruding from his left side. She slowly gripped the handle, silencing his weak protests and ignoring the groans of pain he made. Her other hand she used to stroke his face, and in her mind, she visualised him intact. She imagined his body fit and healthy, strong and handsome. She imagined his skin unbroken and firm. She stared into his eyes, sending these visions to him, calming him, wordlessly saying 'trust me'.

With a sickening gasp from Iskander's mouth and a slimy sucking from his body, the knife was out of the wound, and Iskander crunched upwards expecting tremendous pain and blood.

But there was nothing. He put his hand on where the wound should have been and felt just his skin as he had always known it. He looked at the place he had been stabbed and saw that his uniform had been pierced. But he was alive and well, and he could not understand it.

Zaria saw that he was alright and let the knife fall from her hand into the dirt. He sat up and hugged her tightly and she hugged him just as hard, relieved that he was alright. She kissed him again, but he quickly pulled back.

"What did you do?" he whispered, slightly horrified. A minute ago, he had been on the brink of death. "How am I alive?"

Zaria had dreaded a moment like this for years, and no matter how she imagined it happening, she was not ready for it. She didn't know what to say.

"How did you kill him? What happened to my wound?" She tried pulling him close again, but he resisted.

"I had to save you," she said.

"What did you do?" He moved to get up, surprised to find that he felt completely healthy and rested. He grabbed her and pushed her into the cab again, this time following her in and shutting the door. "You did something back there. Tell me. No one can hear us in here."

"I can make things happen if I think about them." She looked forwards out the windscreen, not daring to imagine the look on his face. He smelt of sweat and blood from the fight. She saw her own clothes had blood from the Nyikan on them and shivered.

"I would not normally believe such a thing," he said quietly. "But I saw him die. I died too."

"It was too hard to shoot him in the dark with you moving. I had to do something."

"He looked like he was drowning."

"He did."

"And me?"

"I can heal people."

"Zaria, do you know what the army would do if they knew about this?"

"I had no choice. He was going to kill you."

"He did kill me. He should have killed you too."

"But I saved you."

"It isn't natural."

"It is to me."

"I am going to return to the general for head count. It sounds like the fighting is over for now. But you should wait in here until we know for sure."

"Are you going to tell him about it?"

"I haven't decided."

"I didn't want to lose you." She began to cry.

"You might be the key to winning this war. The army would love to know your…magic…and how it could learn from you." He saw that this was upsetting her greatly. "On the other hand, it could work out for the best if we keep this secret to ourselves."

"Please." She nodded vigorously.

"I am going back to report now. Maybe we should talk this through ourselves before making any decisions."

"Thank you."

"I should thank you too." He bowed his head. "As much as I believe in fate taking its course, I really didn't want to die."

"I hope not."

Iskander left to survey the aftermath of the fight and assess what damage had been done. Zaria watched him go and was alone with her thoughts, standing next to the truck. After the horrific yelling and chaos of the fight, the silence surrounding her felt in sharp contrast. It was mildly uncomfortable. She wondered what Iskander would do, and hoped that he would not tell a soul.

A hand reached out from behind her and covered her mouth, while another held a knife against her throat. She had not heard the Nyikan approach and now she was completely vulnerable. She could not perform magic under that sort of pressure.

"I saw what you did." His voice was gritty and he spoke her language with a strong accent. Even though the Nyikans had a language similar to hers, it was still obvious where he was from. His breath on her neck made her cringe. "If you struggle, you will be killed. They'll pay big money for you alive." She nodded and made no sound, though her breathing was fast and heavy.

Another man emerged from the shadows and tied her hands tightly behind her back. Then he took a bag made of a thick black fabric and covered her with it, from head down to her knees, so she could walk clumsily, but she was made blind and rendered invisible in the night.

"Not a sound," the first man warned, poking her sharply with a knife through the bag. They led her away from the camp and through some difficult paths. She was impressed with how easily they moved. She felt them going downhill for some time, then up again and down again for what must have been an hour at least.

Eventually, when she was almost too tired to go any further, they came to a stop and she heard some voices talking in Nyikan. She could see her ankles illuminated by the blue of Noi and deduced that she was in their camp.

Her command of the Nyikan language was rudimentary at best, relying mostly on what their two languages had in common. Other than some basic words, she was not able to decipher their conversation and regretted not having paid more attention during her classes when she was younger. She saw that somebody stood between her and the source of the light, and a gruff voice addressed her in fairly broken Nahan.

"He says you drowned my man. How?"

Iskander's words came to her then, what an army would do if they knew about her ability. She felt a knife poke into her back.

"How?" She wanted to see his face.

"I don't know."

The knife broke her skin just enough to make her bleed and gasp in pain. It was especially terrifying not being able to see.

"How?" He was unrelenting and she knew he would not give up unless she answered.

"I don't know," she said weakly. She sobbed as she felt the point of the knife return, threatening to poke her again. Would it be worse to be stabbed in an open wound or to have a new one made?

"How?" No emotion.

"Do you want me to show you?" Zaria surprised herself at her burst of courage. She said the words in Nyikan, their strange vowels feeling wrong in her mouth. The knife retreated and the bag was torn away from her. She stood blinking in the light, taking in the scene around her, and the great ugly man in front. He glared at her for a moment, then burst out laughing. The other men nearby laughed too, stopping just after he did.

"Bring out the other prisoner," he barked at some men nearby. Two of them disappeared into a tent, then reappeared seconds later with another person covered in a black bag like she had been. The person had no shoes she could see, like somebody who had been taken in the night while sleeping. She gulped, knowing that it was one of hers, but hoping she was wrong.

The Nyikans removed the bag and Zaria was horrified to recognise the man in front of her. He saw that she still had her hands tied behind her back, but showed no signs of fear. There was a reason Rainer was a general before her father had mocked him.

He wore the medal of cowardice proudly, almost defiantly. His skin was heavily darkened from working out in the sun, and it was hard to tell his original colour. His hair was close-cropped in a very traditional military style. He looked quickly from left to right with the dark eyes that hid behind a heavy brow, examining the scene around him, surprised to recognise Zaria but making a deliberate effort not to show any recognition on his face.

"Show me," the Nyikan in charge ordered her, pointing at Rainer. "Drown him."

Zaria stared at Rainer, shaking her head, wishing she was anywhere else. It started to rain, but the soldiers were unperturbed by it. A soldier cut loose her hands and stood by her side with the tip of his knife poking into the side of her neck.

"Now."

Rainer didn't know what was going to happen, but he began to look more worried when he saw that Zaria was repeatedly whispering 'I'm sorry'.

"If you do not drown him, we kill you both. It is very simple." The leader sat down casually and picked at his nails.

Rainer understood the threat of killing well enough, but he did not know what was meant by drowning. He had lived his adult life under the threat of death in battle and survived longer than many men were expected to survive. He had come to terms with knowing that he could be shot, or stabbed, or even starved to death in war. But drowning was different to him. There had never been reports of Nyikans drowning prisoners. Some forms of torture were below even their low standards.

"You have to do it, Zaria," Rainer said steadily.

"Shut up." A soldier kicked him behind his knees savagely and he fell forwards, getting a mouthful of mud.

"Do it," the man in charge ordered.

Zaria tried to imagine a way out, but her mind was too frantic. She found resistance in her mind when she began to cast a spell, but fought through it.

Rainer felt the binding around his wrists loosen, but made no movement other than a tiny smirk at Zaria to let her know he was free. He still had no idea what the soldiers wanted her to do, or how his bindings had come loose, but he wanted her to know that he was ready to fight his way out.

Zaria wanted the soldiers to let their guard down for just a second, and she knew the only way out would be sharing her magic with Rainer. It was very risky, but it should work.

She concentrated on him where he stood pretending to be bound. The soldiers noticed her posture and expression change, and they watched her closely, trying to see how it worked. She imagined a tendril of smoke reaching dancing outward from her head and seeking out Rainer. When she felt that it reached him, she focused on sending him the following message:

"Pretend to drown. Then when I say go, I attack them and you fall to the ground playing dead."

Rainer twitched a bit, and she knew that he had heard her. He didn't understand how he heard her voice in his head, or how she intended to attack ten men unarmed, but he figured it was their best, if not only chance at escape. She had, after all, freed his hands without touching anything.

The soldiers' attention was focused on Rainer when he started straining to breathe. He jerked his body this way and that, and made the veins in his neck stick out as far as they would go. He held his breath and constricted his blood flow until his face turned red, then purple. It was an exceptional performance. The soldiers were amazed, and Zaria saw that not one of them was watching her anymore. The soldier who had seen her drown the other Nyikan watched especially closely.

"Now," she sent the word into his mind and he dropped. The soldiers and the leader stepped closer to him to examine him. They were afraid to touch him, but they had to make sure he was dead. The leader knelt down to check if he was breathing, and just as he was about to discover the lie, Zaria called out. "Hey! Shitheads!"

It was too late for them to defend themselves, and after a bright flash of light, they felt their skin prickling. They burst into sheets of sweat and collapsed, vomiting. Rainer picked himself up and stole a knife from the nearest body, systematically slashing the throats of all the soldiers, who were writhing in agony. When the last soldier was dead, he looked around at the carnage.

"What has happened here?" He turned to Zaria, the long knife still gripped tightly in his hand, its blade dripping blood onto the dark, muddy ground. He stepped towards her. "Explain."

"I saved your life," she explained. "Are you not pleased?"

"I heard your voice in my head, and I played your game, and now these men are dead against all odds. I am grateful for my life, but I am wary of the one who wields such power." He took another step closer, menacingly.

"We should find our way back to the convoy."

"Impossible. They will have counted us as casualties by now and moved on. There is no way we can catch them." He wiped the knife clean on one of the dead soldier's shirts.

"Then I will make it to Blue Island without them," Zaria decided. Despite his apprehension and distrust, Rainer laughed.

"You really think you can just find your own way across

the provinces on your own? You have no idea of the danger or even the route."

"Then you will come with me," she said.

"No," he refused. "My duty is to find the nearest station and report my status. And yours too I suppose."

"And my duty is to go to Blue Island, and return word of the situation there. With or without you, I am going." She started towards one of the Nyikan tents, praying that an appeal to duty would convince him to come. "For now though, I will try to get some sleep before setting out in the morning."

"You are insane. I will figure out our location and take us to the nearest base in the morning."

"You've seen what I'm capable of," came her voice from inside a tent. "You know that I will be fine on my own. It would simply be much easier for me to complete my mission if I had you working with me, rather than against me."

"And what exactly was that, earlier?" He admitted to himself that a woman capable of putting ideas in his mind and of murdering ten men without taking a step probably would manage quite well on her own.

"Magic," her voice answered. Rainer stood a little dumbfounded under the hastily constructed shelter that the Nyikan men had set up. Their bodies lay nearby in the mud, rain washing their blood into fetid pools at their sides. In the absence of any logical answer, magic seemed about as good a guess as any. Rainer quickly decided that maybe he could use her protection rather than the other way around. He did not enjoy the prospect of facing the unknown wilderness of the provinces on his own, desperately looking for a waystation.

"I will sleep now too," he called out to her. "And in the

morning, I will decide what to do."

Inside Zaria's tent, she sat shivering. It was the most horrible night of her life, and no number of war stories could have prepared her for the sort of violence she witnessed – and participated in – that night. She cried for the soldiers who had died, both Nahan and Nyikan, and worried what Iskander and Rainer would do with her secret. Would they tell others? Or would they let her remain hidden? Who would believe them if they told?

She slept fitfully, feeling guilty about the dead soldiers lying nearby, and the one she had drowned and stabbed in the neck to save Iskander. At daybreak she crawled from the tent and raided the Nyikan soldiers' supplies. They packed light, but she found everything she needed to survive and recover her strength. Rainer had already taken his fill of their things by the looks of it, and she saw him approaching from further off. He was wearing a pair of boots that he had stolen from one of the dead soldiers.

"I have decided to come with you," he announced without any other pleasantries.

"How reasonable of you."

"I have looked around a bit this morning, but I see no recognisable landmarks. I have no idea where we are, but I suggest we head northwest until we find the road again."

"That sounds fair."

They ate some of the Nyikans' food, and packed a bag with supplies to last several days.

"They did not pack much," Rainer commented. "This is bad news for us."

"Why?" Zaria was dismantling her tent.

"Because if they packed this light, there is likely a larger group not far from here."

They hurried to pack the rest of their supplies, then

quickly set off. Zaria followed Rainer's advice and took a pair of boots before they began trekking through the wild landscape. The best-fitting pair was still a little too big for her.

"With any luck, we will see something useful within an hour or two," he said, pushing back branches. "Normally I would be cutting these branches down, but if there are more of them behind us, I don't want them to see where we go."

It was indisputable logic, but it made progress very slow. Zaria wondered if perhaps it would have been worth getting away faster and cutting a path, but Rainer was firm that slow and safe was the best method. He said he had faced this enemy before and knew how they operated.

At midday, they had barely covered any distance. They had made it only a few hills away from the starting point, and stopped in a dense area of bushes to eat and drink. It was a very wild country. The sounds of the birds were different to what Zaria knew, and there were ants and other crawling things everywhere.

But she was free. She was outside the city, with no one to tell her what to do or where to go. Except Rainer, but she had her own type of influence over him. Forgetting the danger of being pursued, she enjoyed the first moment of freedom she could remember, smiling to herself. She caught Rainer looking at her and quickly wiped the smile off her face, embarrassed, but he smiled a little too. At what, she didn't know.

Rainer didn't talk much, except when he explained obstacles or was deciding on which route to take. That suited Zaria fine, who felt no particular affection for him, and wanted to reach the island as soon as possible. Though she admitted it would have been a more pleasant journey if they could chat at least a little.

That night, they found a hidden place to rest amongst some boulders. Rainer insisted that they abstain from making a fire and would have covered any Noi equipment, had they still had any.

They sat, eating a cold meal of packaged rations, when Rainer stopped and listened. He put his food down silently and went to look around. He pointed back in the direction they had come from.

"Look: smoke." So, he was right. "If we are lucky, there will be nothing to give away our path."

"And if we are not?"

"You have seen how easily they move in the night." Rainer went back to pick up the remnants of his meal. "I will watch them while you sleep. Then it will be your turn."

"Okay." And she lay down to rest, knowing that the threat had not yet passed.

Chapter 3

"Look what I can do," the young boy named Iwizadi called out to his brother Umwahu.

"No, I don't care," came the response.

"This one's really cool! I promise!" Iwizadi ran along the bank of the river to where Umwahu was sitting under a tree, lazily holding a fishing rod. The heat of the sun pounded down and he was glad for the shade.

"I told you I'm not interested." He pulled his hat forwards to cover his eyes and lay back to rest.

"Fine, next time." Iwizadi sat down where he was in the sun and played around with the shapes he was making in the air.

"Dad said you shouldn't do that. Why do I always have to babysit you?" Umwahu said without taking the hat off his eyes.

The various colourful blobs he was creating all shattered and disappeared.

"Why?" Little Iwizadi instead picked up a shell from next to him, wedged in the muddy bank, and examined the shape. His mind instantly turned to wondering how he could create that same shape out of Light. Umwahu took his hat off and rolled onto his side. He jammed the fishing rod into the earth.

"You know why. Remember what he said?"

"Yeah, I remember." Iwizadi sighed. He jumped up and ran out to where Umwahu would have to roll over to see him. "You're just jealous because you can't do any magic."

"Shut up! Yes, I can."

"Then why don't you prove it?"

"I don't feel like it. Now hurry up and catch a fish so we can go home. It's too hot out here and I'm tired."

Umwahu was the older brother, and always called the shots. He liked bossing Iwizadi around, making him do his chores for him. Iwizadi didn't usually mind too much. Even with Umwahu around, he was in a world of his own thoughts, constantly dreaming of new ways to play with magic.

Catching a fish was an easy one, but he didn't want to let Umwahu know his secret. Umwahu might have thought his younger brother was a pushover, but Iwizadi was very good at keeping secrets. He went to take over the fishing rod and reeled in the line so as to cast it out further into the river.

He waded into the water, which felt cool on his skin. The rod was far too big for him, since it was their dad's and Iwizadi was only very small for his age. He cast strongly out into the river, which impressed Umwahu, even though he tried to not notice and instead scoffed and rolled his eyes. Iwizadi turned back to make sure Umwahu had gone back to sleep before playing with some magic on the bait. It only took a minute before a fish had been attracted to the magic bait and started tugging on the line. He struggled to pull it out, his tiny arms pulling with all their strength against the energy of the flailing fish. With a huge effort, he managed to drag it through the surface of the water and onto the shore.

"I got one!" he called out, and Umwahu sat up.

"Already?" he replied jealously. "I was sitting here nearly an hour and got nothing."

Iwizadi reeled in a large river trout, big enough for two meals for their family. Umwahu packed it away into a special bag they used for carrying fish.

"Tell dad I caught it."

"Why?"

"Because if you don't, I'll tell him about you doing magic you're not supposed to again."

"That's not fair."

"Yes, it is. You broke the rules."

"Why is all the magic I like against the rules?"

Umwahu shrugged and started walking home. Iwizadi trotted to catch up, his little legs having a hard time matching his brother's pace.

"Why does dad say only some magic is allowed?"

"It's not dad's rules."

"Then who makes the rules?"

"Shut up."

"I hate this place. Why can't I do the magic I like?"

They were often seen walking from the river to their home through the city. It was a funny sight, Umwahu carrying the huge heavy fish bag over his shoulder while Iwizadi struggled to keep up. They took the same route as always that day, past the familiar shops and over the roads they knew well.

"Caught another big one today, lads?" Miss Indali sang out as they passed her fruit stall. They beamed up at her.

"Big enough to feed the whole city!" Mister Inyama called to them and waved. It was a very friendly place to grow up. Despite its large population, most people in the city knew the boys. Umwahu was very popular and people enjoyed talking with him. He was known for his exceptional ability to kick a ball. Iwizadi was considered cute, and was known for doing well at school. He enjoyed reading and people thought he was shy.

They made it home and saw that it was late in the afternoon. Their dad was out at his job, but should be home soon. Umwahu dumped the fish on the table to prepare it.

Magic was permitted at home, but only certain kinds; the kinds of magic that made their daily lives easy, for tasks like washing and making light. Anything else was viewed with suspicion, including the artistic magic that Iwizadi most loved.

Umwahu grabbed a knife and began de-scaling the fish. He made a huge mess, and told Iwizadi to clean up as the scales went flying across the room in all directions.

Iwizadi had his preferred method of cleaning, but knew that Umwahu wouldn't like it. So, he took out the broom and swept up all the scales he could see.

"Stop doing it so messily," he told Umwahu.

"Or what? It's nearly finished anyway."

"It's annoying."

"You're annoying."

Iwizadi pouted and finished sweeping up the scales, while Umwahu focused on gutting and filleting the fish. No matter how many times he did it, the smell of fish gizzards always made him screw up his face and hold his breath. He flung some sloppy organ at his brother, who objected loudly.

Iwizadi put the broom away and Umwahu finished his task. Iwizadi saw that Umwahu had made more mess and left disgusting inedible pieces of the fish everywhere on and near the table. It was one of the accepted uses of magic to clean things, so Iwizadi quietly and efficiently blasted away the offal with some jets of water that he conjured up from nothing. Soon, the table and floor were clean, and the mess swept outside in the spell.

"You should do that outside; it stinks of fish in here." Their dad came in and admired the size of the fillets. "This is a big one. Good job boys."

Iwizadi swallowed his tongue, not wanting to say anything about the injustice from earlier that day. Umwahu hadn't done anything, he wanted to say, but nor did he want Umwahu to talk about his using magic for fun.

"I caught it myself!" Umwahu boasted. Iwizadi stood nearby and watched as his dad praised his brother. Umwahu had always tried to make his life miserable, for as long as he could remember. He was a bully, and he seemed to wish Iwizadi had never been born.

In their city, magic wasn't for fun. It was a tool for work, and nothing else. Long before Iwizadi was born, the people in charge made a law that any magic not used for work, where other tools were inefficient or dangerous, was a crime. They reasoned that it would protect the people from any accidental or malicious damage caused by magic, and they knew that magic often had unexpected, negative effects on a user. It was for everyone's safety.

Punishments for accidental magic injuries were small, but crimes where magic enabled, or worsened the damage carried severe penalties. The most severe was a type of magical prison called the Nightmare. Nobody returned from it once they were sentenced.

Their dad, Bulumko, had explained the situation many times, but Iwizadi could not accept it. Why were the artworks he created in mid-air with combinations of Light and Water magic considered dangerous? To whom? He saw no possible harm in them, and decided that the law must be mistaken. After all, how could art be a crime?

But it didn't matter to Bulumko whether his son saw reason in the law or not. Their society was built on laws, and he believed in justice, no matter what.

"We will have this tonight when your mother returns from her trip," Bulumko said, and set about magically making some ice to keep the fish fresh. "Umwahu, have you got homework to do?"

"Yes." He went out of the kitchen.

"Iwizadi, I guess you have done yours already?"

"Yes." Bulumko chuckled.

"Come with me, then. I will teach you how to make the hot coals for the barbecue."

"Why can't we use Fire magic to cook? It's so fast. The fish could be ready in seconds," he asked for the thousandth time.

"I have told you before, it is a crime." Bulumko originally thought that Iwizadi was oppositional and defiant, but his son's naïve persistence had led him to change his opinion. He now thought Iwizadi must be some sort of idiot. He just couldn't understand why his son didn't accept it. "And cooking is a fun time anyway. Come on now, let's go outside and get started."

Bulumko lit a fire in the coal pit they had outside.

"Why is Umwahu so mean all the time?" Iwizadi poked the coals and helped the fire take hold.

"Why? What has he done now?" Bulumko sighed.

"He's always mean to me." His childish innocence was plastered on his pouty face.

"He will grow out of it one day. It's just a little jealousy."

"Jealousy? Why?"

"Elder siblings are often like that. They think that having a younger sibling will take something away from him. It's nothing to worry about. One day he will realise that having a brother is a good thing."

"What if he never does?"

Bulumko chuckled and rubbed Iwizadi's hair.

"It might feel like that, but one day he will grow up. Trust me. You are both still very young."

Later, when the barbecue was ready, Bulumko wrapped the fish in foil and placed the pieces on a rack above the flame. Their mother Uzima came home just at that moment, exactly at the time they expected her. Bulumko went to help her with her baggage, leaving Umwahu and Iwizadi in charge of the cooking.

"Hey Iwizadi, wouldn't it be funny if the fire went out." He tipped some water onto the coals and they sizzled and released a lot of smoke.

"No! Stop that! Dad put us in charge."

"I'm just having a bit of fun." Umwahu tipped out another splash of water. The fire was still strong enough to cook dinner, but it was starting to show signs of weakness.

"It's not fun, it's just mean." Iwizadi got closer to the flame and blew on it and prodded it with a stick to keep it burning strong. He was determined to cook dinner without magic, since Bulumko had said cooking was fun. He wasn't expecting to feel water on the back of his head, but Umwahu tipped out all of his glass without warning. More of the water spilt onto the coals, and it looked like it was struggling to stay lit. Umwahu hooted with laughter, and Iwizadi panicked. He wanted to show his dad that he was responsible and surprise his mum with a nice dinner, but Umwahu was making everything in his life so much harder. Water dripped down his face and neck and he flicked it out of his eyes.

Iwizadi decided the right thing to do would be to help the coals along with magic, just a little bit, not enough for anyone to complain about or even enough to know. He was angry with his brother, and his Fire magic was cast very strongly; much stronger than normal. Very quickly, he had the coals burning like they had been before Umwahu's prank, and wondered why such a useful magic was illegal. The law must have made a mistake. Umwahu wasn't laughing anymore when he saw the result of Iwizadi's spell. But the spell had enhanced his anger with his brother. He felt like he was on fire when Umwahu next spoke.

"I'm telling," he said. The magic in Iwizadi flared up, like he hadn't quite put out his internal fire and it had caught alight again.

"But I didn't do anything wrong. You did! You always do."

"You did a crime in our house. Dad will be mad." It was getting worse and he was scared, even though he wouldn't admit it. There was a feeling in his soul that was unfamiliar, like he was not in control of his magic. He wished Umwahu would just go away, but thinking about him again made his internal fire burn even stronger and more out of control.

"I'm helping. You're making trouble." Iwizadi stood firm by his choice to use magic, but felt like something was wrong with him. He had never felt so volatile after casting a spell. He was scared because he did not understand it. But Umwahu bore down on him without giving up. "Now leave me alone."

"If I don't tell, what can you do for me in return? I'm open to making a deal."

"Just go away."

"What if I don't?" Umwahu felt hot and started sweating. He wiped his face aimlessly and stumbled towards his brother. He saw Iwizadi standing steadily with the coals burning ferociously behind him. Umwahu was then scared, he had never seen Iwizadi do anything to stand up for himself. "What is- are you doing this?"

"I told you to leave me alone." Iwizadi's voice felt like it was not his own, but he couldn't control it. The voice of the Fire had taken over his mouth. The anger towards Umwahu he had spent years not showing was all coming out at once. He remembered every argument, every time Umwahu stole his food, every time Umwahu bullied him without reason, and with every memory, the flames grew hotter inside him. He felt like he might burn, but he didn't care. He didn't want to put it out now.

Umwahu fell to the ground, his clothes soaked with sweat and urine. The coals from the barbecue had been so hot and motile that a few of them had popped out of their bed. Some wood nearby was showing signs of burning. The fish was beyond saving.

"Stop it! Iwizadi, stop!"

The boys' parents came outside and rushed to Umwahu, trying to revive him. Iwizadi continued standing in the middle of the scene, unable to release his spell. Even if he wanted to, he could not overcome the hold that the Fire magic had on him. The parents were yelling at him, but he couldn't hear their words above the roaring of the flames of his spirit. He did not want to let the spell go. He wanted to make Umwahu hurt.

Bulumko struck Iwizadi hard across the face, knocking him to the ground. The Fire released Iwizadi, who rolled on the ground in a daze. Umwahu was unconscious and was carried away by his mother. The wooden objects in the garden were now aflame, and the fire was spreading to their home and the neighbouring buildings.

A sinister thought flitted through Bulumko's mind that he could leave Iwizadi there. The penalty for this type of magic accident would be severe, depending on the extent of the damage. If he was unlucky, Iwizadi could end up in the Nightmare, and surely that was worse than death. It could be blamed on him.

He shook away the thought, picked up Iwizadi and ran from the burning building.

It took hours to get the blaze under control, even with people casting Water magic. When eventually it came time to answer questions, Bulumko ordered Iwizadi not to say anything. Umwahu was taken to the healer, and not expected to come home for a few days.

Justice was swift and straightforward. The city council determined that magic was the cause of the fire, due to the difficulty in both extinguishing it and in treating Umwahu's injuries. A natural fire would not have contained the same level of malice.

Bulumko's house was damaged beyond repair, and would have to be torn down and rebuilt. Thirty-five other buildings were damaged to a lesser extent. Eight people had been trapped inside their homes and died, and many others suffered from burns and other injuries.

There was definitely intention to harm in the spell, the council concluded. Initially they were divided as to who cast the spell, and it nearly came to the point where Bulumko was charged, despite the evidence that he was with his wife in another part of the house when the fire started. They said he should have been supervising Iwizadi.

Umwahu eventually woke up and wasted no time in blaming Iwizadi. He wanted to continue showing Iwizadi that he was the dominant brother. He wanted to get rid of Iwizadi, like how he never wanted him there in the first place. The council trusted Umwahu's accusation but they still did not want to believe that a child had wielded such destructive force. There had to be another explanation. What had provoked him to do such a terrible thing?

But no one could find any evidence of Umwahu's wrongdoings. He had never hurt Iwizadi physically, and no one was ever a witness to his bullying. Despite the initial objections, the council eventually came to an agreement and the investigation was closed. Iwizadi was named as the instigator of the blaze, and labelled a threat to peaceful living. Umwahu's record was clean, and he would get what he wanted.

But the matter of sentencing was a new argument. Some council members thought that the law should be followed to the letter, and that a person harbouring such murderous and violent intent must be removed from society. Others argued that he was too young and could be educated.

Those who believed in rehabilitation and education were slowly won over by the sight of Umwahu, covered in untreatable burns. For burns caused by natural fire, the healers could do wonderful things, but for those caused by Fire magic, they were not so effective. All they could do was reduce his pain.

After months of argument, the council members agreed that the law should be followed, regardless of Iwizadi's young age. He was to be sent to the Nightmare. Umwahu was pleased, but their parents were shocked. No amount of begging or bargaining could change the council's hard-reached decision, and they took a long time to grieve.

The day came for Iwizadi to say goodbye to his family. His parents watched sadly as he was led away by the police. Umwahu glared and silently cheered. Justice, he thought, had finally been served.

The Nightmare was considered the most perfect punishment for those who committed magical crimes. It was built as a way to contain all the people who had shown themselves to be incapable of abiding by Libalele's strict laws of magic use. The laws were designed to protect everyone, but some people just did not agree with them, whether through malice or ignorance.

It was a rare occurrence for someone to be sentenced to the Nightmare. The last time was before Iwizadi was born. A councilwoman thought that she could gain more power if there were fewer other councillors, and managed to murder three before being found out. She too used Fire magic, and lost control of her anger. Some people said that the Nightmare was a place of pure fire. Most did not want to know.

The entrance to the Nightmare was at the top of the central peak, at the place where the water erupted. Only the councillors knew the spell to open the door, and were always reluctant to perform it. In theory, the door was one way only, but magic was only limited to the imagination, and they feared that eventually an inmate would discover how to come back through.

Perhaps the most horrifying thing about the Nightmare was that it was a place without time and without space. Inmates entered for eternity, and were forced to exist without purpose. Without time, they could not age. Without space, there was no magic to cast, and nothing to do. They simply entered and were lost to the world and to themselves.

But staring at the gaping void that opened before him that day, Iwizadi had no idea of what awaited him. He stepped forward bravely, but not before offering one final gesture to the city. As he walked into the void and let it close behind him, he left colourful bubbles of Light floating in his wake. As if to say he was right and they were wrong about magic. One of the councillors there to witness it later said it was the most beautiful thing he'd ever seen. He'd gone his whole life without knowing that magic could be beautiful, and tore himself up with guilt for having sent a small child into the Nightmare.

Nothing could have prepared Iwizadi for the sheer emptiness he would face in the Nightmare. He stepped inside it and felt dizzy from the lack of any visual reference. Everything was black, just pure darkness. He wheeled about on the spot and saw the split in the fabric of space through which he had come, leading back to the world he knew. He saw his trail of bubbles, and the awestruck looks on the faces of those present, and then the door was gone.

He was nowhere.

Umwahu was once again an only child, just as he had planned. But his hopes of reliving the experience he remembered were ruined by the sadness from his parents. They didn't share his excitement at being their only son again. He didn't understand why not. He assumed they would be as happy as he was to be free from his freak of a brother, who was a criminal, and whose constant magic was a worry to the family. Umwahu was glad to be rid of Iwizadi, whose proclivity for magic made his own power look infantile. Umwahu hated being upstaged by his younger brother.

Over several years, Umwahu used his popularity and his disfigurement to rise in power in the government. He discovered very early on that he could manipulate people's feelings by drawing attention to his burns. The day he became a councillor, he felt intense pride and loved the attention he got from everyone. He had made a career on the philosophy that all magic was dangerous if used by the wrong person, citing himself as an example of a victim. He fought for stronger laws restricting its use, and frequently showed off his scars. He never fully healed, and proudly wore his burns as a reminder that magic should never be allowed in the public's hands again, except for strictly controlled, official reasons. One such exemption was when the Nightmare had to be opened for a new inmate.

He was tremendously eloquent, and even the other councillors rarely disagreed with him. He could convince anyone of anything, and one slow change at a time, he stole all the magic away from the city and its people.

"How did it happen without anyone noticing?" they used to ask each other. Nobody foresaw it getting to the extent that it did, but they kept agreeing, one change at a time, that everything Umwahu proposed was for the best.

The final ban to be imposed was on the healers. It took a lot of convincing, but Umwahu by that stage was already very good at convincing people to do things they didn't want to do. He argued that the healers were a danger to others, because they could choose who to save and who to leave. They could be targeted by factions he argued. The people filled in the gaps with their own fears: if foreigners came to invade, and the healers sided with the foreigners, they would be overrun.

His mission complete, Umwahu's next goal was to change the laws restricting his own power in government. As it was, he would have to retire from the council after ten years, ready or not. And then he didn't know what he would do with his life. He wanted to ensure that never happened.

But he was for once in his life stuck for ideas. The laws in that area were much less vague than those dictating the correct and safe uses of magic that he had worked hard to change. It was a much more challenging goal.

A memory sometimes surfaced that bothered Umwahu. Iwizadi came into his mind whenever he saw his burns. The memory of him standing there in front of the fire, watching as he suffered haunted him. He could picture Iwizadi's tiny skinny body wearing his second-hand clothes that were too big for him, his big ears sticking out too far. He would be like that forever. A memory. A ghost. Their parents had managed to move on, but sometimes they talked about him wistfully as if he were missing, or long-dead.

The people were quick to adapt to their new living situation. Without magic to do the things they used to do thoughtlessly, they looked for other ways. When Light magic was banned, they first used oil lamps instead. They worked just fine, but ensuring a constant supply of oil was tiresome, as was lighting them safely. It wasn't long before some clever people discovered that the glowing blue substance that they found underground could generate massive amounts of energy. It was not long before it became widespread and Umwahu was praised for showing them the way forward to a new stage of their social evolution.

But Iwizadi was there in every decision he made. When Umwahu looked in the mirror and saw a middle-aged man staring back, he knew that locked in the Nightmare, out of time and space, his brother was still a six-year-old boy, slowly going insane. It was the cruel irony of the Nightmare that only the most creative people went in, and there was nothing in there to use creatively.

In order to change the laws surrounding leadership, Umwahu needed a unanimous vote from the councillors and majority support from the citizens. It was a large task. He knew he could rely on some councillors, but others would oppose his attempt to gain more power. There was no way to hide his intention behind words or a tragic backstory this time.

Nevertheless, after a few months of lobbying, he had

gained support from the majority of the people. Since his magic reforms, accidental deaths and injuries had plummeted, and in general crimes were down. They loved him for those results. Some people did not support him and missed the freedom to use magic, but their voices were small by comparison. Initially when the bans were implemented, some councillors held reservations that people would denounce their neighbours to settle personal disputes, but fortunately that never happened. They all simply got on with living in the best way they could. And they were happy to support Umwahu, who had made their lives measurably safer.

The councillors took note, and a few of Umwahu's opponents were won over to his side. One by one, they were convinced that he was a man worthy of changing the laws. A man deserving of more time in leadership.

When finally the decision was unanimous and Umwahu succeeded in changing the laws, he decided it was time to gloat. He had everything he ever wanted, and Iwizadi had nothing. He had power, fame, respect, and fear. He climbed the stairway to the top of the mountain and went to the source of the water. The source was in a small cave, and gurgled upwards from within the mountain. It shuffled outwards to where it suddenly dropped hundreds of metres. The violence of the drop was so sudden compared to the calm interior of the cave, and a small barrier was put up to prevent anyone curious enough to look over the drop from accidentally falling.

Umwahu performed one of the only legal spells left, the one that opened the portal to the Nightmare. It was also the only spell he could ever do without any difficulty, which pleased him greatly, knowing that Iwizadi couldn't do it. The portal opened in the rock wall of the cave and Umwahu involuntarily shivered when he looked inside. It was true emptiness. It was darker than dark, and just looking at it made him feel hollow.

But it was not exactly as he remembered. Admittedly, it had been many years since he last looked inside, but he remembered it being somehow emptier. He remembered the nothingness was stronger. Was it possible that the Nightmare could weaken over time? It was created so long ago, and no living person knew how exactly it was done.

"Iwizadi!" he called into the empty space, not really sure if Iwizadi would even hear him through the void. "Iwizadi! Come here, it's Umwahu!" He almost expected nothing to happen. Why would Iwizadi come to see him? After all, he had made sure he was sent inside in the first place.

A young man peered around the edge of the portal. He would have been about fifteen years old. He was very thin and tall, but Umwahu instantly recognised him. He had the same soft, white hair as he remembered his younger brother having, and the same shaped face. But he had grown up and his ears no longer stuck out too far.

"Impossible," Umwahu said. There was no time in the Nightmare. His brother was supposed to be a child. "How have you aged?"

"Good to see you too, brother," Iwizadi creaked. "It has been a while. Or at least, I assume it has. It is very hard to keep track of time in here." He was more confident than Umwahu remembered him being. Umwahu was thoroughly unnerved by Iwizadi having aged. It was not supposed to happen. He thought about closing the portal immediately and going back to the councillors. But he had come to rub his success in his brother's face, and he was really very curious to find out how Iwizadi had done it. He needed to know if it was a trick or if Iwizadi really had managed to upstage him from inside the prison.

"You were supposed to be a child for eternity. There is no time in the Nightmare."

"Ah, I suppose it has been exceedingly difficult to keep track of things in here. How long has it really been? You are looking very old." Was that a hint of arrogance? Umwahu was feeling like he was not in control of the situation. He remembered the feelings of jealousy and hatred he had felt when his mother first brought home a baby brother.

"Nearly thirty years."

"Thirty years!" Iwizadi grinned. "Hard to believe. It feels like much less." He really was gloating proudly.

"It should have felt like forever to you."

"Well, I admit that when I first came in, it was a challenge. I don't know if you've ever been in here, it's really very disorienting when you find yourself outside of the world."

"I'm sure it is. That's the point. You were supposed to suffer in there."

"I did. To a point. Now, I think I quite like it. I've made it a bit more homely."

"Homely? There's nothing in there. How could you make it homely?"

"Don't worry too hard about it. Anyway, I'm sure you have come to visit for a reason? It must be important, seeing as it's your first time visiting in thirty years." Umwahu could sense the anger in Iwizadi's voice that had caused the accident all those years earlier. He had his own anger to match it.

"Yes, I came to tell you about my great success. I have campaigned to extend my term as councillor and now I am proud to say I am going to be in power until I die."

"Happy for you." Iwizadi looked at his nails. "But just letting you know, I'm going to live longer, and I will always be more powerful. You realise that without time, I will live forever."

It was a troubling thing for Umwahu to hear. He was angry at his brother for not suffering the way he was supposed to.

"Why are you so happy?"

"You don't understand, do you? This place, if you could even call it a place when I arrived, has been a blessing."

"A blessing? You're in prison." Umwahu couldn't believe what he was hearing.

"It is complete freedom. I can spend my entire life in here thinking about magic and learning about magic, and my life is as long as I want it to be. It's amazing. And the best part is, I am finally away from you."

Umwahu felt all the old things he used to feel when they were kids. He wanted to tease Iwizadi, and show him he was bigger, stronger, more important, more popular. But Iwizadi so calmly told him life was better without Umwahu in it. He was seething. And the longer Iwizadi stood there calmly, the angrier he became.

"You haven't explained yet, how you have aged without time. And how are you learning without space? There is not supposed to be anything in there for you to learn."

"Ah well. One thing I have learned is that magic is only as powerful as the minds that imagine it. I'll admit that it is a very powerful mind that created the Nightmare, and it did take a lot of effort for me to figure it out."

"What do you mean, 'figure it out?' You can't just figure out the Nightmare."

"You've spent so much of your life fearing magic and banning it, that you never bothered to learn how it works."

"I didn't tell you about banning-"

"You didn't. Councillor Nekinso did. Or to be more

precise, I saw it in his mind."

"You still haven't explained." Umwahu made a mental note to talk to Nekinso later.

"Talking to Nekinso won't do you any good. He doesn't know that I've been in his mind."

"How-"

"I have to thank you, Umwahu. This is the most fun I've had in- how long did you say? Thirty years?"

"I think I'd better explain to the councillors that something has gone wrong with the Nightmare." Umwahu made a move to back away and close the portal.

"But we haven't finished talking, brother." Iwizadi grinned again. Umwahu noticed that Iwizadi had not blinked throughout their conversation and he shivered.

Umwahu went to turn away and close the portal, but found that he was paralysed. His legs didn't respond when he wanted to step away. He couldn't turn his body.

"Why don't you stay awhile? I'm sure you'd be interested to see what I've done with the place. Won't you come in?"

Umwahu struggled to move, and fought to close the portal. But he couldn't control his thoughts enough to do it, and the gaping hole in the universe remained barely a metre ahead of him.

"I really admire the architecture of this place," Iwizadi said. "It took me a lot of time to reverse engineer it, but I think now I quite like it in here. It will be a shame to leave. At the start, I had nothing but darkness. But I knew that you had put others in here before me. So, I went looking for them. And instead of fierce magic criminals, I found babbling shells of humans.

"Do you understand now? There was other matter. And where there is matter, there is magic. Even when I was a little boy, I understood that. Nobody will miss those people.

We don't even know how many years they had been in here. I took the cells that made up their bodies, and the atoms that made up those cells, and I used them to create space. And when I had space, I had a place to practice magic.

"The best part, the part that you and the councillors failed to understand, is that by removing time, you made it so that I had an eternity to gain power. You thought it was a punishment, but I feel as though I have been handed the keys to the universe. There is no magic on this earth that is beyond me. There is nothing I cannot do."

Umwahu felt himself rise into the air, still unable to move independently.

"Put me down!" he shouted.

"You love to give orders, don't you? You always did. Why did you hate me so much, Umwahu? Why did you try to get rid of me? Why did you hurt our little family?"

"Stop this at once."

"Or what? Another magical prison? It would only be a matter of time before I learn its rules too and break them. Now answer me? Why do you hate me?"

"Because you were an accident!" Umwahu spat the words out that he had held onto for far too long. "Mum and dad wanted to have me, but you were different. You weren't there when mum came home from a trip in tears and had to explain to dad that she was attacked by another man. Even though I was too young to know what it meant, I knew that someone had ruined our family. And that someone was you. We didn't want you, but there you were anyway. And even though you hurt mum, she still loved you. And dad raised you just like me."

"So, I should be sorry for being born? Somehow you think that I caused mum to suffer?"

"You did."

"How can you remain blind to the facts, Umwahu? Mum and dad stayed strong together and raised two children, until one of those children was vengeful enough to tear them apart. It was you, Umwahu, who destroyed the family, while it was me who brought them closer."

"You liar. At least they wanted me."

"Do they still want you? Not even thirty years has made you see the flaws in your thinking?" They paused for some breaths and let their emotions drift away, recognising the futility of their argument. Umwahu broke the silence. When they resumed talking, it was calm and detached, separate from the emotionally charged argument they were having before.

"Time. How are you not a child anymore?"

"You know, space and time are quite similar. Once you know how to create one, it's not hard to create the other."

"You created time?"

"To some extent." Iwizadi looked at his brother's lined face and his own teenage body. "It seems I was a little off in some respects. Not a bad effort though, if I'm honest."

"Put me down," he repeated.

"Or what? You'll tell?" The emotions came back from where they were hiding just below the surface.

"Let me go."

"I still have questions for the great lifelong leader of Libalele."

"They'll come looking for me."

"I'll welcome them all into my new home."

"What do you want?"

"You've made a bit of a mess of the city."

"A mess? I made this place great."

"No. You've taken from it. Nothing you ever did was for the city; it was all for you. Like how you sent me away for your own selfish plans. You somehow thought I ruined our family, but really you ruined it yourself when you sent me here. You banned magic for yourself, so your own pathetic skills could be forgotten. You changed the rules so that you can win the game. Thirty years, and you haven't changed at all. The city is worse without magic. You should have done the opposite, and given them more. Now they are living in fear of being taken to the Nightmare, and they are tearing up the earth itself to replace the magic they lost."

"You're just a sore loser. I am a winner."

"You know, your new laws have sent quite a few people my way. You should have seen the looks on their faces when I explained that the Nightmare means freedom to do anything."

"So, what do you want?"

"I am going to make Libalele great again. I am going to remove all the things that are wrong with it, and start again. You, the old-fashioned council, and the ignorant people who are digging up the earth's blood. And I have my army ready in here to fight with me and start again."

"How do you plan to do that?" Umwahu was still struggling against the spell that held him captive mid-air.

"It's quite simple, really. I just have to get out of here."

"Impossible. No one has ever left the Nightmare."

Iwizadi laughed. It was a high-pitched, piercing laugh and it chilled Umwahu to the bone.

"Magic," Iwizadi began, and traced the outline of the portal with a bony finger, "is only as strong as the imagination."

There was a spark as he touched the portal.

"Whoever created the magic of this portal was quite imaginative." He took a step back. "But then again, they didn't have infinite time to dream."

Iwizadi stood facing his brother and pushed his thoughts out of his mind. He often used Mind magic to read the thoughts of the councillors and learn what was happening in the city. It wasn't usually as easy as it was now, with Umwahu frozen and dangling before the open portal. When Iwizadi felt his mind clear and receptive, he set about sending his searching thoughts out. The people who designed the Nightmare, he had worked out, did not consider the possibility of Mind magic being used across its boundaries. He sent a tentacle of thoughts out to grab Umwahu, and when he found his target, he grabbed on tightly. He felt the slight bump as Umwahu's thoughts filled the space in his mind, and immediately began his next spell.

It was easier said than done, but Iwizadi knew that if he could imagine something, he could create a spell to do it. He sent his own thoughts out of the Nightmare and into Umwahu's vacant mind. Umwahu groaned in discomfort, and Iwizadi had to push to squash his mind into the smaller space.

Umwahu felt his awareness changing. His perception of the portal shifted. He didn't feel himself passing through it, but he knew that something had changed. He was still paralysed, held in the air by Iwizadi's spell, but the air felt different. It felt emptier. It took a moment to realise with dread that he was on the wrong side of the portal, staring out at Iwizadi.

The spell worked. Iwizadi finished it off by releasing his mental grip on Umwahu, who fell in an unceremonious heap.

"What have you done?" Umwahu screamed and tried moving through the portal. The sparks prevented him from passing through.

"I have escaped," Iwizadi said matter-of-factly. "I have to

admit, I'm not used to the feeling of this air. Or this passing of time. Maybe I will have to do something about the time out here too. I really did like it in the Nightmare. I hope you like it too. My servants will give you a nice welcome party."

"You'll be sorry! I should have killed you when I had the chance!"

"No, brother. I won't be sorry. I will be busy. You've made a terrible mess of this city. There will be a lot for me and my friends to clean up." He looked at the wall opposite the portal, and effortlessly opened a new one. "You can all come out now."

Slowly, cautiously, a middle-aged lady reached through the new portal from the Nightmare into the cave, peering furtively as she came into a world of fixed space and time.

"It worked," she addressed him with admiration. "You did it." She was dressed in a simple jumpsuit that meant she was held in prison before entering the Nightmare. She walked over to Iwizadi and kissed his hand.

A man climbed through the portal and had the same dazed expression. Then another. And another one after that. In a short time, the cave was filled with the people Umwahu had deemed the most dangerous magic users in the city; people the council had decided were a threat to society. Eleven plus Iwizadi to replace the council. They looked into the portal where they saw Umwahu on the inside of the Nightmare and laughed at him.

"Any last words?" Iwizadi asked Umwahu.

"If you can escape, so can I," he growled. Iwizadi laughed.

"I highly doubt that. You never had much imagination, other than your twisted delusions of family joy. I hope you enjoy being alone in darkness forever."

"Mark my words, I will get out of here. It might take a

long time, but I will escape. And when I do, I will come for you. The next time I see you, I will kill you like I wish I did when we were kids. I hope you enjoy waiting, never knowing when I might come. You will suffer like you made our mother suff-"

And the portal closed, leaving Iwizadi in the cave with his army still coming through his new portal. The last person through would close it, leaving Umwahu alone in the void with the creatures Iwizadi had created to serve him.

More and more people came out from the Nightmare and joined the celebration.

"Thank you all for choosing the right side of history," he addressed the growing crowd in the cave. "Today marks the first day of the rest of Libalele's history. Today we take the power that is ours, and make Libalele the magic city it should be. We will make a future for magic. We will make a future for us. Anyone who gets in the way will be removed."

There was a subdued cheer. The magic army were a solemn bunch, not given to wild shows of enthusiasm, but showed their devotion in serious action. They left the cave after Iwizadi and began moving down the stairway cut into the inside of the mountain.

"First, the council," Iwizadi whispered up the stair, more to himself than to anyone else. His voice echoed unnaturally. He had planned it this way, so that his eleven strongest supporters and magic users would be on the council. In the new Libalele, his vision revolved around a magicocracy. He wanted a society where the leaders were chosen based on their magic ability.

He entered the council chambers, which were empty at that time. The next meeting was scheduled for that evening. Iwizadi sat at the meeting table and invited his army to sit with him. They all filed into the room and for the first time, he could see them as they truly were, in space that he had not himself created, in time that flowed naturally. They were ordinary people, about forty of them. There was space for twelve to sit, and the rest stood around, waiting for their instructions.

"This is our city now," he said quietly. "I have been waiting a long time for this moment."

"What if they fight back?" someone asked.

"With what?" Iwizadi cackled. "You have magic. They have nothing. How can they fight you?" There were sounds of approval in the crowd.

"How should we tell them the good news?"

"Use your imagination."

Councillor Nekinso opened the door to come in and prepare for the next meeting, and froze when he saw the crowd.

"Councillor! Good to see you," Iwizadi greeted the man.

Nekinso recognised many of the faces and instantly knew that somehow, they had escaped from the Nightmare. His thick eyebrows raised high and his forehead wrinkled dramatically.

"Impossible…" he babbled. "How?"

"It was not easy," Iwizadi admitted, ushering Nekinso to a chair. He had discovered that he had a taste for theatrics. "But no prison is made perfect."

"What do you want?" Nekinso gathered the courage to ask.

"I want to thank you, Nekinso," Iwizadi said, taking the man by surprise. "Thanks to you, I have learned that there is no more magic, and the people are destroying the earth instead. Knowing this has given me a purpose."

"What purpose?" Nekinso found himself forced to ask, after Iwizadi dramatically paused.

"Well, what good is magic, if nobody uses it? What good is the earth, if you go around tearing it up? What good is a city, if its people are fools and its leaders are crowned fools for life? Starting today, Libalele will be ruled by its most magical citizens. There will be no restrictions on the use of magic. You are relieved of your position as councillor."

Nekinso knew he had made mistakes. He knew that allowing Umwahu to retain power was the wrong decision. He looked around at the people present, remembering some of the power he had seen them wielding before they were sent to the Nightmare.

"You are right," Nekinso bargained. "We have made some bad choices. Let me make it up to you. Let me join you. I can help you."

"What do you think, people?" Iwizadi asked the room. "Should we show him mercy and let him join us? Or should we make him an example and throw him in the Nightmare, like he did to so many of you?"

There were shouts of both 'mercy' and 'Nightmare'. Nekinso broke into a furious sweat and tried backing out of the door. Iwizadi flung him across the room and onto the table with a flick of his wrist. He looked around at their vengeful faces and knew he would not be leaving the room alive.

"The people are asking for both mercy and an example, councillor," Iwizadi said. "So, I will show you mercy, then make you an example. That sounds fair, doesn't it? Fairer than sending a six-year-old boy into the Nightmare?" The crowd made some jeers of approval. "I want you to help our cause by announcing to the city that we have taken control. That would be a great service, and maybe I can show you more mercy if you do it well."

The councillor felt every eye in the room staring at him

with hatred. He had sentenced at least half of them during his tenure. He had personally opened the portal to their prison. He believed strongly that magic was dangerous, and here was the proof that in the wrong hands it would be disastrous. But he saw no way out, his own command of magic being weak and rudimentary. After spending so long fearing it and working to eliminate it, he never tried to understand it.

"Of course, if you don't want to help, I can kill you here and now and make the announcement myself. Your choice."

Some choice. The councillor held Iwizadi's gaze, and saw a young man who had chosen the path of evil. His thirst for revenge had overcome him. There was no hope for him, and there was no hope for the city. Time in the Nightmare had changed him from an ordinary young boy into a monster.

Nekinso remained silent. If this was to be the end, so be it. No amount of bargaining could stop the crowd of magicians. They had come for revenge, and they would get it. Iwizadi might have started with another vision, but when a crowd of angry people demanded blood there was little that could stop them.

"Kill him!" someone yelled out.

"Is that what you want?" Iwizadi asked Nekinso, who refused to answer. The temperature was rising in the room that was not built for such a large crowd. Iwizadi asked the crowd next. "Should we kill him? Should we throw him in the Nightmare?" Nekinso shook his head furiously.

"Kill him! Kill him!" they began chanting. They were losing their usual calm demeanours as they became a mob. The noise was deafening, and with each chant, the temperature rose more and more. Nekinso had sweated through his clothes and there was a wet patch in the front of his trousers. The crowd was clapping in time with the chant, and it went on for what felt to Nekinso like an eternity – an eternity like what they had experienced in the Nightmare, shut away from time.

As the noise of the crowd grew to its climax, and the temperature in the room burned him ferociously from the inside, Nekinso's last thought was that the real nightmare was not the prison, it was the cruelty of man. Then he fell limp on the table in a puddle of his own sweat and urine, surrounded by the cheering and whooping and stomping and clapping of the murderous escapees, now completely given to their primal instincts. There would be no stopping their parade of violence now that they had tasted their first victory.

"Go and take the city!" Iwizadi roared maniacally above the noise, and they stormed out through the huge doorway and down the stairs towards the entrance to the mountain, shouting and laughing the whole way down.

Each person in the mob had their own personal grievances to settle. When they reached the base of the mountain and entered the city, they split up to find their own enemies. For most of them, that was the person or group who had played a role in sending them into the Nightmare.

Zenzele was convicted after using Water magic for illegal purposes. He burst through the door of his old friend's house and saw him recoil.

"Zenzele!" His voice trembled. "How? What are you doing here?"

"You think using magic to have fun is a crime?" He had been in the Nightmare only two months.

"I only followed the law."

"You were my friend." He sent little jets of water at his

friend. It wasn't dangerous at all, but playful, and a little menacing. They were brushed aside, but were just mildly annoying and continually splashed his face.

"I'm sorry," he managed to say through the jets continually bombarding his face. "I believe in the law."

"Did you consider that maybe the laws are not always just? I'm telling you now the law is changed. Magic is not a crime anymore. The council is finished. Iwizadi has taken control." The jets of water increased in volume and frequency. Zenzele could hear his old friend gasping for air in between them, but coughing and spluttering as he inhaled water. Just when he was about to pass out, Zenzele eased up and let his friend catch his breath. When he was somewhat recovered, Zenzele started again.

Meanwhile, other reunions were just as creative. Thukile was a woman convicted in one of the early purges against magic during Umwahu's campaign. Her crime was that she had convinced birds to favour her fruit trees over her neighbour's. Bird magic was already considered a barbarian act by then, a prehistoric leftover from a time before magic was civilised and society had rules. It was the magic of a lawless time, and Thukile had used it in lawless ways. No amount of argument could convince people that the birds had simply preferred her trees.

She went to visit her old neighbour. She expected to see her old trees and garden withered away, in favour of her neighbour's, but she was thrilled to see that hers continued to outshine all others. It seemed the birds had been loyal to her through the years.

"Themba, are you home? It's me, Thukile." She strode confidently to Themba's door, spitefully kicking a small herb growing by the path. The door opened tentatively.

"Thukile? What are you doing here? Go away."

Thukile pushed the door back forcefully with a burst of a magic unknown to Themba. She was knocked backwards and stumbled to regain her balance.

"What do you want?"

"I am pleased to see my garden is doing well." Thukile went inside and closed the door behind her. "Not like you though, how you've aged terribly."

"You witch. Those birds…you bewitched them, and now they behave in unnatural ways."

"I'd like you to know that that is no longer a crime."

"Good for you. Bad for everyone else."

"You wasted sixteen years of my life because you were jealous."

"Good riddance." Themba spat on the ground and touched her forehead then her sternum with her left thumb.

"But now I'm back." She stepped closer to Themba, then pushed past her and went to a window. She looked outside and called to some nearby birds. Themba watched, disgusted with the disgraceful and inelegant display of primitive magic. Thukile whispered some things to the birds and then made to leave the house.

"I hope you don't plan on going outside anytime soon," she threatened. Some crows had already positioned themselves in Themba's garden, staring menacingly at the door. Thukile danced out past the birds, praising them for their loyalty.

All that day, similar conversations took place. Some ended in violence and death. Iwizadi, who among the enraged had passed one of the longest sentences, strolled through the city, noting where it had changed, and revisiting places of old memories. Funny, he thought, they felt so distant like they belonged to someone else.

He saw the market, where he and Umwahu had bought

vegetables and fruits. It was bustling, as usual. It hadn't grown outwards, but seemed busier than ever. The sounds of haggling over prices and the smells of fresh produce were a welcome relief from the Nightmare, where there were no sounds or smells. At least, not until he created them from his own memory. The real thing was better.

He stood on the outer edge of the mass of humanity going about its daily routine and sneered. Their lives meant nothing to him. They were the people who allowed him to be imprisoned and had allowed the council to take their magic away from them. He recognised some of the sellers, even through the transformation of time. Some of them had been generous to him in the past, but when he was on trial, nobody spoke out against the harsh laws.

After watching the ordinary city life for some time, Iwizadi wandered down to the river. He found the place where he had caught the fish on the day that changed everything. He cursed the tree and its shade where Umwahu had slept, lazily taking credit for his hard work. He swung his arm out at the river, and several fish rose to the surface, dead. Umwahu had taken everything. All he had ever done was destroy.

Reports of the coup quickly reached the councillors, who managed to call an emergency meeting. They gathered in councillor Bhekis' home, rather than risk being captured trying to go to their usual chambers.

"Thank you all for coming," Bhekis began. "Before we begin, I would like to acknowledge councillor Nekinso, who we have learned has been murdered by this unlawful mob." The six people in the room bowed their heads. Not every councillor had come. Some hid in their own homes, not wanting to risk being taken hostage or killed on the way to the meeting.

"It seems they are visiting the people who sent them to the Nightmare," said councillor Sisa. "They seek revenge."

"I believe you are right. And that means that we too are in danger. It will not be long before they come to visit," said Bhekis. He stood leaning against a wall. The curtains were drawn across the window. The other people were scattered casually around the room, some sitting on the floor, others on chairs.

"How did they escape?" councillor Yabo lamented. "The Nightmare was built to be unbreakable."

"There is a rumour that Umwahu released them all unintentionally," Bhekis answered.

"Umwahu? What the hell was he doing up there? He knows that the cave is off limits unless we are delivering a new criminal." Yabo was furious. "And where is he now? I want answers!"

"They say he was tricked," Bhekis said. "Apparently Iwizadi is behind it all, and managed to trap Umwahu inside the Nightmare."

"I don't believe you," Sisa said. "It should not be possible. This is just another one of Umwahu's tricks to control us."

"Say what you will about Umwahu, but I don't believe this is his plan." Councillor Nomzamo was the oldest present. She had served on the council almost eight years and had hoped to see out her term with a minimum of effort.

"Whether it was his plan or not, by going up there – for whatever reason – he has caused this," said Yabo. Everyone nodded at this.

"Let us return to placing blame later," Bhekis suggested. "For now, we must decide on action. If it is true that these people are taking revenge on those who placed them in the Nightmare, then we are all in danger. I believe that if we are cornered, we should not be afraid to use the emergency plan. We know the Hymn."

"That's a very drastic action," Sisa argued.

"As a last resort only," Bhekis clarified.

"Even so…" Sisa trailed off. "Maybe we could start with an announcement."

"Announce what?" Yabo asked. "These people have killed Nekinso and declared themselves in charge. They do not respect us. We have no power anymore. No Authority. What would you say to placate them?"

"I believe they seek redress. An apology would be a good start," Nomzamo suggested.

"Councillor Nomzamo, we all respect your wisdom here, but can you really bring peace to an angry mob with an apology?" Bhekis wanted the others to take a stronger approach. Nomzamo shook her head sadly. "I suggest we consider magic."

"What magic?" Councillor Thokozi spoke for the first time during the meeting. Out of those present, he had been least in favour of the various magic reforms made over the years. "You know I have always opposed the harsher restrictions."

"We have the ancient spells taught to us to defend the city against invaders," Bhekis said. "The council was originally installed to protect the people."

"Today we have failed," Nomzamo whispered. There was a moment silence. Nobody knew how many deaths there had been to that point.

"I would suggest we start with the Incantation To The Wind To Remove Intruders," Sisa said. "Even though we are only six councillors, it should be strong enough against a few dozen attackers."

"It is a good place to start. If we are lucky, we will be able to stop the attacks right away," Yabo said.

"But if we are unlucky," Councillor Nkosi broke his silence. "It will only enrage them, and divide us."

"It is our best option so far, Nkosi," Bhekis replied. "History tells of the spell being successful with only two councillors. It is our obligation to protect this city by any means. I support Sisa's suggestion."

"Then let us begin. We have already lost a lot of time," Nkosi said.

The six councillors stood up and formed a circle, standing at evenly spaced intervals. Sisa began a soft chant, with words from a language not spoken anymore. The mood in the room immediately lifted, and they felt courageous. The other five joined in the chant, and the power in the room grew to something almost tangible.

In Sisa's mind's eye, she saw the city from above. She looked out at the chaos as if she were a huge eye on top of the mountain. The chanting pulsed through her and she looked down at the members of the angry mob, each taking revenge, each chasing down various people who had wronged them.

As the chanting continued, the winds through the city grew stronger. Some of the people stopped what they were doing when they felt the unnatural wind. It blew ferociously through the narrow streets, seeking out the attackers, driving them towards the city's edges. They heard voices in the wind, screaming at them to leave. A dozen of the mob were terrified enough to let themselves be driven out, and when they had left the city limits, they were relieved to feel the wind let up. Those who had fled the city looked back at it in confusion and saw that it was surrounded by swirling gusts and an impenetrable barrier of wind. They could not have re-entered if they wanted to.

Sisa saw that the spell had only partially worked, and cursed the cowardly councillors who had not come to the meeting. With the strength of the full council, they would have succeeded.

They had to stop casting the spell before it began to fight back. As with every type of magic, the secret councillors' spells also came with negative effects for the users.

"Only some of them are gone," said Sisa to the others.

"Then we will need a stronger spell. What is next?" Bhekis asked.

"Invocation Of The Gods Of The River," Thokozi answered.

While the councillors prepared for their next defensive spell, Iwizadi stood reflectively by the river, watching the magic wind that threatened his new reign weaken and die down. Presumably some of his group had been affected by the spell, but he wasn't worried. He admired the magical wind, watched its shape, adored the way it seemed human. It was a spell he desired to learn. Perhaps he should let the councillors live, just long enough to pass on their knowledge at least.

Thokozi took the lead in the next spell. It was a more destructive spell than the Incantation To The Wind, but used in more dire circumstances. The chanting was less fluid than the Incantation To The Wind, and felt much more angular. A few beads of sweat appeared on his bald scalp. When the other councillors joined in, he felt his awareness become one with the river. He knew every drop of water it contained, and he knew every living thing it sustained. The river surged, breaking its banks and flooding parts of the city. The water stormed through the streets, thrashing the buildings and any people unlucky enough to be outside. Gardens were destroyed. People were swept away, both guilty and innocent.

Iwizadi saw the surge approaching and marvelled at its magic. Yes, there was definitely still much for him to learn. His imagination was somewhat stunted in the Nightmare, after being deprived of all stimuli for so long. Nature, he thought, was the biggest inspiration of all. He missed it very much and made a promise to himself to spend as much time as possible learning from it.

Instead of being knocked out by the flash flood, Iwizadi was absorbed by it, and carried on walking beneath its surface as if nothing had happened. As he saw the wave approach, he reasoned that if he can survive without any matter around him as he did in the Nightmare, he could surely survive a change from air to water.

It was uncomfortable underwater though, and he conjured up an air pocket to surround him. The atmospheric weight of the water was too much to bear for a while, and the air was much better. He laughed, intensely enjoying the play with magic. It was the kind of fun he always wanted to have, but had been discouraged from. It was all a game to him.

Thokozi saw the movement of the water, and tried to ignore the casual destruction it caused on its way to fulfil its purpose. All but a handful of Iwizadi's followers were either drowned or swept away. But Thokozi could also feel something wrong. There was something tampering with the spell. He felt through all of the river, imploring the river god to lead him to the problem. The spell was going on for too long, and Bhekis opened his eyes. He saw that Thokozi was dripping wet, and panting hard, but Thokozi refused to let go of the spell until he knew what was disrupting it.

One by one the other councillors came to see that Thokozi was suffering. Sisa went to shake him, but he refused to be brought back to reality.

Thokozi finally saw that underneath the surface, a young man was laughing and dancing, safely encapsulated in an unnatural pocket of air.

Bhekis slapped Thokozi hard, and he opened his eyes. He coughed up a mouthful of water, and fell to the ground, gasping for air.

"We have failed," he said at last when he had recovered. Nomzamo was patting him dry with a towel. "There is one man whose power is greater than the river. I saw him, and I recognised him. It is Umwahu's brother, Iwizadi."

"The child?" Yabo asked incredulously. "How can a child overpower the river god?"

"He is no longer a small boy. He has grown to a man. Now I believe that he is capable of breaking from the Nightmare," Thokozi explained.

The river gradually flowed back into its normal place. It didn't like being out of its element, any more than the people didn't like it being in the city. Frightened citizens looked out their windows to see the water retreating. They came out to survey the damage. They were pleased to find that most of their attackers were missing.

Iwizadi was then back above the surface of the water. He assumed that unless his followers were smart enough to get out of the way of the river, they would be incapacitated. He decided that it was time to pay a visit to the councillors and gently persuade them to relinquish their magic. Earlier in the day, he had made up his mind to banish them to the Nightmare. It was not a particularly inventive punishment, but he felt that it would do justice, and satisfy his desire for revenge. It was more fun than killing them.

Unbeknownst to the councillors, their Invocation had revealed their position. Iwizadi was able to trace the source of the spell back to the house where Bekhis lived, and he began to go there.

"We have no choice," Bekhis argued. "He cannot be allowed to continue. He will kill us all."

"He might put us in the Nightmare," Sisa said.

"Would that suit you better?" asked Bekhis. Sisa did not answer. There was a sombre mood in the room as they thought about what Bekhis was proposing. As the last line of defence, the Hymn To The Mountain came with a tremendous cost. It was designed as a spell that would wipe clean the city and anyone in it, so that even if the attacker somehow managed to survive against all the forces of nature, there would be nothing left for them. In all of its history, no council had ever needed to use it, though there had been times when it was threatened.

The councillors were divided about the Hymn, and only Bekhis seemed to think it was the right thing to do.

"It is our only option. Would you prefer to let him take over our city and undo all the good that we have done for everyone? Everything that we have worked towards, and that our predecessors have done will be for nothing if he gets his way."

"But the Hymn will destroy us all," said Yabo simply. "That includes all our good work. And us."

"It is better than to let it be corrupted at the hands of a demon," said Thokozi, deciding that Bekhis was right. "I saw him defeat the river god. There will be no stopping him if he reaches us. He will destroy the world."

Iwizadi casually strolled through the city. He paused to examine the damage done to his family home by the wind and the water. His parents were long-dead, he knew. The news had been in Nekinso's mind once upon a time, when Umwahu had taken some time away from politics. It hadn't shocked Iwizadi. He felt nothing for them, after they had let him be taken away. They had not fought hard enough to save him.

On one side of the room stood Bekhis, Thokozi, Sisa and Yabo. Facing them stood Nomzamo and Nkosi. Bekhis knew they could begin the Hymn with four people, but he wanted the cooperation of the other two.

"We have already lost," Yabo argued, trying to convince the remaining two councillors. "Libalele will never be the same, even if by some miracle we can dispel him another way."

"And if he reaches us, our personal fate will be unthinkable," Thokozi said. "He is a devil. I have seen him laugh in the face of the river god."

"We will be remembered as heroes, the councillors who made the hard choice to protect Libalele at all costs," said Sisa.

"No one will remember you if we perform the Hymn," Nomzamo pointed out. "There will be nobody left to remember you."

"We are running out of time," Bekhis pushed. "We need to start. Surely, he is coming this way now. This is what our ancestors created the Hymn for."

Without waiting for Nkosi or Nomzamo to agree, he closed his eyes and began to sing. Nkosi stepped forward to push him over, to make him stop, but he was restrained by Sisa and Yabo on either side.

"You would rather kill us all, than have hope," Nkosi cried. Nomzamo shook her head slowly.

They ignored him, and joined in the singing. It was a mournful hymn that seemed to drain the fight out of those in the room. Nkosi felt his muscles weaken, and his motivation to fight Bekhis left him. He felt resigned all of a sudden and knew that it was too late. Bekhis was right. Nomzamo still shook her head slowly at the ground, fighting against the spell for as long as she could.

Thokozi joined in the song, which now penetrated all their bodies and souls. There was no thought in their minds that was not touched. Nkosi knew the words, and started by mouthing them. He didn't want to sing, and he tried to resist, but the pull of the destruction was too great. As the song worked its way into their ears, it searched every part of their minds, looking for that little piece of them that begged for death. In every mind, there was a hidden nugget of desire to watch things burn, and the Hymn knew how to find it.

The Hymn spread through the city and everyone heard it, and they started to panic. The ground shook beneath them, and the people began fighting. The Hymn was bringing out the destructive desires of everyone and everything. Iwizadi heard it as he approached Bekhis' house, and knew something was wrong. He kicked open the door, which splintered and came off its hinge, already feeling the effects of the Hymn. He saw the six councillors standing together and singing the song to destroy the city. He was filled with a violent rage as he had never felt before, not even when the Fire magic threatened to destroy him as a child. The Hymn was different. It contained a raw type of unrestrained destruction that could not be ignored.

"No!" he yelled at them, realising that they were going to ruin everything. If the city and its people were destroyed, there would be nothing for him to rule. His vision was crumbling apart. "Stop singing!"

They did not stop. The magic had already taken over them, and held onto their dangerous desires so tightly that there was only one way for it to end. Iwizadi shook Sisa, and got no reaction at all. Outside, he could hear shouting and various loud noises as property was damaged, and people set about tearing down buildings.

Iwizadi shook them harder and slapped Nkosi, resisting as hard as he could the Hymn's attempts to take control over his actions. He dreamed of rebuilding the city, but not this way. He wanted to take what was already there and re-shape it into something glorious, a city that would be his legacy, a grand symbol of prosperity and a beacon for all magic users. He needed a canvas to work with, and the Hymn was throwing it all away.

"Stop it!" He tried a spell of his own, to see into the minds of the councillors and make them stop. But when he saw into Bekhis' thoughts he knew there was no stopping. The Hymn would carry on destroying until there was nothing left. Everything he saw in Behkis' mind was consumed with rage, and a compulsion to destroy. There was no goodness left in him, the Hymn made sure of it.

Iwizadi released his spell and fought against the terrifying power of the Hymn. His misguided obsession to build something beautiful was strong enough to partially ward off its effect, but the more he looked at what was happening around him, the more futile he felt his efforts were.

He knew he had failed. The councillors would rather tear down everything than let him get his way.

There were still the people who had been forced out of the city by the wind, waiting on the outskirts and watching it tear itself apart. Iwizadi would go to them, and together start to rebuild his vision. He was not completely defeated, but he knew that his dream would not be as easy as he first thought.

Bekhis kept the councillors' book of spells hidden in his house. During his brief excursion into Bekhis' mind, Iwizadi saw it. On that day, he had witnessed three powerful spells that were beyond his imagination. He had to know how they were done. He shoved Bekhis to the floor, who remained in a trance, and went to the drawers in Bekhis' bedroom. Hidden in a false bottom was the councillors' book of spells, including instructions to perform each one. It would be very useful in the future, he was sure.

With the book tucked under one arm, he ran from the city, searching for his most loyal fans. They found him and were glad that he had not died in the flood or the rioting.

"They have made their message clear: 'over my dead body'," he said to the people who were left standing there with him. "Very well. We will make our own city, far from here, and it will be perfect. It will be a city made by magic, for magic. Are you coming with me?"

Thukile was the first to stand by him. She took his hand and he felt her admiration for him.

The city was torn to the ground, and everyone in it killed. Fires burned it down to ashes until there were just ruins and dust, smouldering in the shadow of the mountain. Ash lay on the soil, and no living thing would grow there.

The last survivors of Libalele agreed to follow him, wherever he went; to come to his side, whenever he called on them for help. It was their mission now to repopulate the world with magic.

Chapter 4

"I knew we couldn't trust her."

"She has betrayed us."

"She only does whatever he tells her."

"Why would she do it?"

"Bird magic never hurt anyone."

"It only protects the leaders. Not good for the people at all."

The criticisms were endless. Nobody had a good thing to say about Aisling or Iwizadi, and it was starting to affect Khuch. The other Khun bullied him and some blamed him for what Aisling did. He was just as surprised as they were when she announced that Bird magic would be made a crime. All in the name of solidarity. They were one people, she had said, and Bird magic created divisions. There was an outcry.

Maria was saddened, but since Orn's departure she had no need for Bird magic anymore. He was the only bird she wanted to talk to. She knew Aisling was making a foolish choice, that is if it was indeed hers and not Iwizadi's.

It had been a week since the announcement, and a few official warnings had been handed out. Iwizadi said that in his experience a firmer approach was more effective, but Aisling insisted on a system of warnings before more serious punishments were delivered.

She had not yet come to realise that the Khun in charge of the warnings were inclined to only offer 'first warnings', no matter how many times someone had actually broken the law. The public on the other hand, realised very quickly, and enjoyed the unique type of precarious protection afforded by the corruption of an unjust system.

But in spite of their tenuous safety against imprisonment, they were outraged by their leaders' decree. It didn't matter ultimately who made the decision – Aisling or Iwizadi – because they increasingly believed they were a population of prisoners.

A few nights after the new law came into effect, a meeting was held in the tavern; the same tavern where Khuch had overheard Ychir speaking out against Aisling. All Khun, even Khuch, were invited. Only Aisling, Maria and Iwizadi were explicitly banned. The tavern was the unofficial meeting place for all of Ychir's political gatherings. Its owners could hardly get enough stock to satisfy its growing clientele.

Khuch knew that he faced intense scrutiny as he walked inside and found a place on the edge of the room to listen in. But after Aisling's latest blunder with the ban on Bird magic, he felt he simply could not support her. The ban felt like an attack on Khun identity and based entirely on fear rather than reason. Maria told him to be patient with Aisling, that she would make mistakes on her way to becoming a good leader. But he could not keep his thoughts to himself, and he needed somewhere to voice his concerns.

He remembered how he had blown up at Maria when he discovered Substance M. She was working for the Capital when they developed the false magic that subverted nature and stole the essence of the Khun. Ever since leaving the refugee camp in the forest, he had been assaulted with one injustice after another. Was there no limit to the suffering that his people had to endure? The whole world was against them, and now so was his own wife.

They had barely spoken since the ban. He made sure not to be in the same place as her.

"Ladies and gentlemen, we have a special guest here tonight," Ychir said loudly to be heard above the crowded room. He stood on a table. "You all know young Khuch Chaddhal."

Ychir gestured at Khuch with an open palm, and took a swig of beer with his other hand. The crowd turned to face Khuch, whose plan to listen quietly had been thwarted. He awkwardly raised a hand while pushing his back to the wall.

"I must say, you were the last person I expected to come," Ychir joked. "Trouble in paradise? Married life not all you hoped it would be?" There was laughter and Khuch stared angrily at Ychir, his face not expressing much, but his posture defiant.

"Enough teasing, Ychir. Get on with it," someone called out. A chorus of agreement rang out.

"Fine. Well, you all know why we are here. This meeting tonight is to discuss what we should do about the new injustices we face. It starts with Bird magic, but pretty soon it will be more. I guarantee that when they start to take away our freedoms, they will not stop at one." The crowd roared in approval and there was much toasting of glasses. Somebody coughed deeply and had to go outside so as not to disturb the meeting.

Khuch enjoyed hearing Ychir speak out loud the feelings he had been hiding. It was comforting to know that he was not alone.

"But freedoms are just the beginning!" Ychir was on a roll

now, and had a lot to say on the issue. "We know that Khun are unique in the world. We are a people of magic, and it is part of who we are. Magic is our lifestyle. Magic is our identity! Magic is who we are! If they remove the magic, what is there remaining? What are the Khun without magic?"

The crowd was getting rowdier and cheering loudly. Khuch hung onto every word. He felt as if Ychir had taken the words from his soul. He clapped and cheered with everyone else and got swept up in their enthusiasm. The meeting was a dramatic contrast to the solemn discussions he was used to and had always assumed all Khun took part in. Growing up in a small refugee camp, there was no need for this kind of meeting. Chuluun kept strictly to old-fashioned traditions and was the voice of his family. Ychir was there and often angry, but Khuch never knew he could be so persuasive. This was what Khuch had been missing; a way for him to give voice to his concerns. He missed his father, but right there in the room of angry Khun, hearing Ychir's angry speech, he felt for the first time like he had stepped out of Chuluun's shadow.

Ychir saw Khuch clapping and decided to single him out again.

"Khuch Chaddhal, what do you think of all this? We know you are in bed with our enemy, so perhaps you would like to enlighten us: what are their next moves?"

Khuch was prodded by several hands, who guided him towards a table and helped him get up. He had never spoken before so many people and it was terrifying.

"I agree," he started weakly, not knowing what else to say. The crowd waited for him to say more, and Ychir pushed him further.

"What do you think of the ban on Bird magic?"

"I use Bird magic often. The decision affects me personally." He started to feel more confident and discovered that he could talk directly to Ychir and ignore the other faces in the room. "The birds have been warning me that they were uneasy recently. Losing Bird magic is like losing part of myself."

The crowd seemed happy to hear that, and Ychir continued preaching.

"Ladies and gentlemen, even the biggest fan of our *benevolent* leaders opposes their decisions." The way he sarcastically stretched out the word 'benevolent' made some people laugh. Khuch felt angry at being called Aisling's biggest fan. "So, you have lost part of yourself. How much more are you willing to give away? Will you continue to love our leaders until there is nothing Khun left about you?"

Khuch stood there on show for everyone, feeling angrier and angrier the more Ychir spoke. It was anger towards Aisling and Iwizadi that until now he had buried and refused to admit. He said nothing and Ychir went on:

"I have always said that our leaders are not Khun no matter how they pretend. And now we have the proof. They are willing to strip away our culture. And what authority do they have? An old man threatening us with cheap tricks!" Ychir laughed forcefully and dramatically, guffawing insultingly. As Ychir drained his beer, Khuch was again swept up in the rhetoric and clapped approvingly. Mechanically, Ychir's empty cup was replaced with a full one, which he raised above his head carelessly, splashing those around him. With every punctuation mark, the crowd responded with a cheer.

"Well, I say: no more! They have gotten away with it five weeks too long! Taking away our magic is the final insult! This must end now before it's too late!"

It dawned on Khuch that Aisling had gotten what she wanted. The public was indeed united: united against her. Solidarity.

While this was all happening, Aisling was with Maria at home. It was a tense mood between them, but they acted polite to each other. Maria felt horribly lost without her friend Orn visiting daily. Aisling could see that her mother was lonely and tried to spend more time with her. She knew that her decision had caused more harm than good, but it was too soon for her to go back on her word. It would send a poor message if laws were introduced and repealed at random.

It was a warm night and Maria sat next to an open window. She never grew tired of how impressive the stars were on Gazar compared to in the Capital. Since Orn left, she had been thinking often about their plan to see inside Iwizadi's mind. She knew he was right, that it was the only way to know his intentions, but she also questioned her own motives. Why did she need to know? What was it about her that she couldn't just let it go? She couldn't get the thoughts out of her head, and she stressed day and night, putting off the moment when she finally decided to act. When she stressed, she wished she had Orn, and felt even worse knowing that he was not there with her.

Aisling often entertained herself at night with reading. There were some interesting books about history kept in the palace. Maria had read them all, and sometimes they discussed them together. Now, Aisling had a copy of the *Buteelin Domog* in front of her. She wanted to ask Maria about some of the things in it, but communication had been very bad between them since the ban on Bird magic. Instead, she stared at the open page, her mind elsewhere.

As they sat in the same room, not talking, Aisling was

unaware that Maria had literally taken her mind and placed it in her own. She was looking for an understanding of why Aisling had decided to ban magic, suspecting that Iwizadi was behind it all along. She felt some guilt at what she was doing, and thought about retreating, but she came from a place of love, and also thought she might uncover that it was one of Iwizadi's decisions.

She wanted to help her daughter with whatever she was going through, if only she would tell her. Amidst the turbulent visions of Aisling's thoughts, Maria saw Khuch. Though he too was swirling unpredictably, he seemed to be the most persistent thought in her mind. But he was disappearing into the storm. Her daughter, just metres away was experiencing a storm inside. Compared to the last time she read a mind – Orn's – Aisling's had nothing stable to anchor her position.

What Maria saw gave her a new perspective on Aisling's leadership. She saw that Aisling regretted the ban on Bird magic and wanted to know how to make things right with the people again. Like anyone with a bad habit, she thought that Iwizadi could help her. She kept returning to the source of the problems, thinking that next time would be different. Maria pushed deeper into Aisling's mind, trying to find a reason for the ban. She knew that Mind magic could be bad for her, but it was an addiction, it was a compulsion, she felt useless when the only thoughts she could hear were her own.

Iwizadi was there, but he wasn't fully to blame. Maria watched Aisling's memory of the decision-making, and came to understand that her daughter was more mature than anyone gave her credit for. She was willing to make herself hated and feared, if it meant the Khun were safe.

But safe from what? Maria couldn't quite work it out, and

knew that Aisling herself didn't know. Whatever Iwizadi told her, it must have been a serious threat. Were other nations threatening to invade again? Umwahu's name was floating around, but the thoughts were incoherent and vague.

Maria released her spell. She was so well practiced at Mind magic, that nobody watching her would have known that she was doing anything wrong. Recently her Mind magic had become so powerful that the thoughts of others sometimes unintentionally bled into hers as they passed in the street. It was as if her mind acted as a magnet for stray thoughts. When it started, she was alarmed, but over time it became normal for her. She knew better than anyone the way that the Khun thought about Aisling. She wanted to help.

"I'm tired, I think I'll go to bed." She got up and kissed Aisling on the head.

"Goodnight," came her daughter's flat response.

"Goodnight." Maria shut herself in her bedroom and sat on the bed. She felt disgusted at herself for violating her daughter. She wanted to be sick with the feeling of guilt, and knowing that Iwizadi had said something to spook Aisling into making choices that would sacrifice her own safety.

Aisling sat in silence for a while longer, thinking about her mistakes. She would go to Iwizadi in the morning and push him for more information about Umwahu. She needed to know when he was coming and what else she could do to prepare the Khun.

Khuch came inside and went straight to her. She saw that he had a strange look on his face. It was something like anger mixed with loyalty and remorse, and he was a bit out of breath.

"Aisling, go to the mountain now. I came ahead of them,

but they will be here any minute." He had left the tavern before anyone else, after the crowd had eventually taken him down from the table. While Ychir was delivering another passionate speech, Khuch snuck out. Thinking about the reasoning behind the ban, he wanted to believe that she had done it for a good reason. But why? Despite the anger he felt at their situation, he also remembered the love he felt for Aisling. It was a lifetime of love, and though the mood in the tavern was powerful, its toxicity could not erode his devotion to her. He was angry at himself for getting sucked into Ychir's words. He needed to know why she did it.

Aisling grabbed a few bits of clothing and she was ready to go. Khuch knocked on Maria's door and told her to get ready too.

They left through the back door, and could hear loud voices approaching from a few streets away. Some of Khuch's louder thoughts reached Maria, and she was scared. Not just for their immediate safety, but for the greater implications of the unrest.

"I hate to admit it, but we need his protection right now," Khuch whispered as they briskly walked to the mountain.

"Tell me what's happening, *Tsenkher*," Aisling held his hand while they moved. He stopped to tell her as quickly as possible.

"Ychir. They want you out. They want him to lead. They say taking away magic was an attack on what it means to be Khun."

Maria heard his thoughts and she trusted him less. *They think? Or you think?* They started walking again, with Khuch leading them urgently.

"I know I made a mistake," Aisling admitted. "And I want to make it right. I'm just trying to be a good leader, like Chuluun."

It was the first time she had admitted to others that she was wrong, and rather than gloat about it, Khuch stopped and picked her up in a hug. She was lighter than ever. He couldn't help but kiss her, despite their rush. She jumped up and wrapped her legs around him, and imagined how happy their lives could have been if they were allowed time to enjoy being a couple. She felt the Love magic come from him like she hadn't felt in a long time. That was the Love magic she had been trying to copy and spread through the city. How did he do it? Did he feel it from her too?

"I am sorry for doubting you," he said.

"It's okay, we can talk it through later."

"I thought we were in a hurry," Maria coughed at them, secretly pleased to see them make up.

They reached the entry to the mountain a few minutes later, the loud voices not far behind. Aisling told the guards to let her family in with her, and they didn't bother arguing. It was Iwizadi's rule, not theirs, who was allowed in and out. Hopefully the guards would buy them time and not join in with the rebellion.

Aisling told Khuch and Maria to wait in one of the rooms on the lower level while she went up to see Iwizadi. With some argument, they agreed to wait, and she raced up the stairs. In the heat of the moment, a foolish decision can seem wise, and frightened people can be convinced of anything. Aisling convinced them not to follow her, but in hindsight she would have liked them to be with her, to protect her from the poisonous words of Iwizadi.

Maria wanted to talk to Khuch. She wanted to tell him everything she had seen in Aisling, and about her own plan to uncover Iwizadi's thoughts. She wanted just one more voice of reassurance before she went ahead with it. She wanted to tell him what she heard from Khun in the street when their thoughts screamed at her, but she knew that he already knew, because she had heard it from his mind too.

The room they were waiting in had a wooden table taking up most of the floorspace. Around the edges of the room there was a fireplace and a window. There were few decorations, and it looked like the room was not often used. Khuch sat on one of the chairs at the table opposite the fireplace. It creaked loudly and he guessed it was very old. The ceiling was high enough to dispel any claustrophobic sensations. Maria paced uncomfortably.

More than anything, she wanted to thank him for what he did that night, for putting love and the bigger picture ahead of his own anger. For choosing Aisling. For choosing to be a good man to the people in his life. So, she started with that and her words came out almost as fast as she could think them.

She talked the whole time they were waiting for Aisling to return. She told him all the things she wished she could tell Orn.

She told him about her affinity for Mind magic, and how recently it was getting so strong that she felt its effects even without explicitly casting.

"It sort of sounds like the first stages of mastery," he told her. "I saw it with Tesver. When the magic chose him, it visited him all the time, even when he wasn't trying to cast it."

Not wanting to become a master yet, Maria shivered. She told Khuch about what she overheard from the Khun's thoughts, and he shifted uncomfortably, assuming that she included him. Tactfully, she never directly accused him of the sort of negativity she frequently heard.

But she stopped short of telling him that she had been inside Aisling's mind. It was something she decided should never be known, and she promised herself never to do it again on purpose. She debated with herself whether or not to tell him that there appeared to be a good reason for the magic ban, even if it was too vague to understand. In the end she decided it could wait.

Finally, she told him about her plans with Orn to uncover what she could about Iwizadi's motives. Khuch was not as enthusiastic as Orn had been. He considered the risks too high, despite Maria's obvious talents.

"I would like to support you because I am also curious. But I worry that you could make things worse for us all, if anything goes wrong."

"I know," she paced the room anxiously. "This is why I haven't done anything yet. I wish I knew when I would be ready."

"Nobody ever knows when they are ready," Khuch said, trying to console her. "When my father convinced us that it was time to return home from exile, we were frightened the whole way, until we were inside our homes. We were away for sixteen years, and still not ready."

"That's true." She sat down and flung her arms out onto the table in front of her. Khuch thought in many ways she had the same mannerisms as Aisling, and sometimes it was amusing when he saw the similarities.

"Everything you've told me about your power of Mind magic tells me you are ready. But if you want one more practice to convince you, maybe you can tell me what Ychir is really planning." Khuch wanted to know more about him. He had been a thorn in his father's side during the entirety of their time in hiding. There was a long history of aggression, and after the meeting in the tavern, Khuch realised he did not trust Ychir at all. For all his bold talk and rabble rousing, there was something ingenuine about him.

"Ychir?" Maria asked, but did not need an answer. Khuch's misgivings leaked from him and she could tell immediately.

"He will be leading the pack out there."

"Let me try to find him. It will be good practice to cast over a distance."

She relaxed back into the chair with her arms on her lap and sent her mind searching. An invisible tentacle of smoke snaked its way from her head and out the door. It made its way down the stairway and through the entrance hall. When it came closer to the main entry, she felt the presence of consciousnesses on the other side. The tentacle dissipated into an amorphous fog and snuck underneath the door. Instinctively, it picked out Ychir, who was arguing with four of the guards at the door. He was backed by about twenty others. In sheer numbers they could have overpowered the guards and come inside, but a rumour that the guards were given enhanced magic ability from Iwizadi stalled them.

The invisible smoke reformed into a long cord, and wrapped itself around Ychir's leg, slowly binding him, absorbing his essence, until it reached his head. It snuck into his ear and Maria felt a slight tickle, knowing she had found her target.

From Khuch's perspective, he saw Maria sit quietly with her eyes half-closed. A few seconds later she inhaled sharply, and was quiet again.

Maria gave time for Ychir's thoughts to settle into place before exploring them. The first thing she noticed was the anger. He was a man consumed with anger. It was plastered over everything she could see. There wasn't a single thought that was not built on a foundation of it. She felt unsafe. He was dangerous.

In the middle of his thoughts were the same things she

had been hearing from Khun all over the city, but they were more frantic. He wanted to get rid of Iwizadi and Aisling and her. Even Chuluun he thought was too progressive. Ychir wanted nothing to do with foreigners at all.

But there was something else. There was a small kernel of conflict. Maria waded through the maze of knotted anger, trying to get a better view of the contradiction. The further she delved, the more compact the thoughts became and the tougher it was to move on.

It was the book. She found the book and swept aside the layers of anger covering it, like one would brush off cobwebs. Ychir wanted to steal the book. It made sense, being the Khun's holy book. But Maria saw that that wasn't everything. She pushed even deeper into his mind, past swirling torrents of thoughts. Rarely had she pushed this deeply into anyone before.

At last, she came to Ychir's most secret thoughts. There were the usual places of lust and violence that were in every mind she explored, but Ychir had another secret place devoted to betrayal.

She fought her way inside, and a deep feeling of dread overcame her. The realisation that she was not the first to be there made her recoil in fear. She considered abandoning the mission, but there had been no signs yet that Ychir was cognizant of her presence, and she continued, despite her fear. Maybe she was mistaken. Maybe it was just nerves getting the better of her. Who else could have been there before? Only Iwizadi was powerful enough.

There was a memory, tucked away where she could have easily missed it. Ychir wanted to keep it secret, even from himself, and she knelt down to dig it out. She looked closer, and her mouth fell open. She felt a terrifying tug at the world around her, as if she had been standing on a rug and it was being pulled away from beneath her. There was someone else trying to visit. That's when she knew it was time to go. There was no point staying any longer than necessary in someone's mind. Hijacking their thoughts was dangerous even without competition. As he was putting Ychir's thoughts back in place, she caught a glimpse of the intruder. She gasped and fled, away from Ychir and all his anger.

Khuch watching, noted that the whole thing had taken less than a minute. Maria blinked and flexed her wrists.

"Ychir plans to steal the book," she told Khuch.

"The book of Boloi? Iwizadi's book?"

"Yes, but not for himself."

"What? For whom then?"

"The Capital."

"That's not possible. What do you mean?"

"I wasn't alone in there."

"Who was it? Was it Iwizadi?"

"No," Maria did not want to admit it. "It was someone I used to know. General Osbourne. He was in charge of the Blue Unit back when I was at the Capital."

The Blue Unit was a secret operation belonging to the Department. It consisted of one leader and a dozen soldiers, all trained in magic and equipped with Substance M.

"The same Blue Unit that attacked Khot last month?"

"Yes."

"Why would Ychir ever work with them?" Khuch thought that was very unlikely, considering all the things Ychir talked about.

"The book," Maria thought out loud. "It must be very valuable. The General will give Ychir anything he asks in return." Was this what Aisling was trying to unite the Khun against? An invasion from the Capital? Maria dreaded the thought of another attack from Blue Unit, and doubted if the Khun could survive, let alone fend them off. They would rather fight to the death this time than flee back into hiding.

"And we know what Ychir wants. He wants help removing Iwizadi and Aisling. He wants the Capital's army."

"Yes, there is no doubt about that. He has no secrets in that regard. He wants all foreigners out. He believes in the cause out there, no matter what other intentions the Capital has for him."

Khuch thought long and hard about the information. On the one hand, Ychir could help to remove Iwizadi. If he had the support of the Capital, he might be able to do it. That would probably be a good outcome for all the Khun.

But it would mean the loss of their holy book. And in turn, Ychir would insist that Aisling and Maria leave too. No matter, thought Khuch, he would go with them.

Maria deliberately blocked Khuch's loud thoughts from her mind. She didn't want to be constantly harangued by the thoughts of others.

And it would mean the Capital would have the book, which was worse than simply losing it. If it meant so much to them, it could not possibly end well for the Khun. The Capital must not be allowed to see its spells. Maria wished she could have properly seen Aisling's motivation.

"As much as I want Iwizadi gone, and Khun to lead Khun," he slowly said, formulating his thoughts as he went, choosing words carefully. "With the book in the hands of the Capital, we will be in constant danger."

"I don't think Ychir realises," Maria agreed. "He is short-sighted. He is blind to their intentions. His own motives occupy all his thoughts."

"If the Capital gets the book and studies the magic in it, we will lose what makes us unique. They will come back with stronger magic than before."

"Ychir sees the Khun as a special race. A chosen people."

"It is not just him. Everyone at the tavern tonight feels the same."

"He does not realise that he is being taken advantage of. He thinks he is leading the revolution, but really, he is being played. This isn't a fight between the Khun and their right to leadership-"

"It's a fight between Khun and their right to survive."

"He must be stopped at any cost."

"Could Ychir be convinced to betray Osbourne?"

"Perhaps," Maria considered the idea, leaning on her elbows, slumped in pessimism. "But it looks like the only thing that will convince him is Iwizadi giving up and leaving."

"And that's not going to happen."

"There has to be something we can do."

"We need my dad back. People always listened to him."

"It is no coincidence that he is the one Iwizadi sent away."

As Maria and Khuch discussed their options, Aisling was high in the mountain, in Iwizadi's study, where she was learning that he already knew about the violent mob at his doorstep.

"I remember our last chat," he said, looking out the window. He could not see the base of the mountain of course, but Aisling somehow felt that he was watching the scene unfold down there. "We expected that there would be resistance to the ban."

"Yes. We knew it was going to be dangerous for us... and now I need your help fighting them off. I believe you that we can't let Ychir take control." She slumped into a chair, leaning forwards as far as she could with her head hanging low.

"You know, I think you can handle this crowd on your own." He didn't bother looking at her, and focused on something outside.

"Are you serious?" She sprung upright. "I thought we were in this together! Remember how you said we are alone in this place? Just the two of us from our people?"

"Are you sure? Did I ever say that?" His voice was dreamy and lazy, which threw Aisling off guard when her confrontational attitude wasn't matched.

"You said-" She started moving towards him but was interrupted.

"I said many things. I also said 'show them they have a good leader'. Have you done that?" He was still looking out the window.

"No, I've made things worse."

"Things often get worse before they get better."

"But what should I do now? Ychir is leading a revolt right now."

"Like I told you last time, 'be strong and they will follow you'."

"But now I've united them all against me, just like we knew would happen. I'm the last person they want to follow."

"Do you know why I am unchallenged and yet they came for you?" He turned around to face her, and she saw that there were dark circles under his eyes.

"No." She was strangely concerned by his sickly appearance.

"I have shown them reason to hesitate."

"They are afraid of you…"

"Exactly."

"I want to be a good leader. A fair leader. I don't want to threaten them the way you did. I can't hurt them."

"Aisling, can you argue with results? They think you are weak and yet they leave me alone."

"No…"

"It is better to lead with fear than with love."

"Why?" She didn't want it to be true, but she remembered the Leader in the Capital. There was no love for him either.

"Because when people are afraid, you can lead them to safety. You can put ideas in their heads that you are the way to that safety. But when people are in love, they don't listen, because love is a type of madness. They come up with their own stupid ideas about how to live." He concluded his speech by bursting into a coughing fit. Aisling had never seen him show any sign of weakness before. It was the first time he seemed human. He wiped his hand on a tissue and she saw little red spots.

"But," she reflected on her own feelings. She had many times felt both fear and love at the same time. It was sometimes hard to tell which one was driving her decisions. "What about when they are afraid to lose love?"

"There is still fear there, is there not, guiding them through their woes?"

"I suppose so."

"Listen, I told you last time 'if you give an inch, they will take a mile'. As their leader, you don't have to give anything. You need to take, and take, until they have nothing left to oppose you with."

"The ban didn't work. Nobody was afraid. There were no punishments." He sat down and nodded.

"In my experience, warnings do nothing. Swift action is required. But did it not create a feeling of community among them? I mean, look out there at what you've created. That team of angry Khun is because of the ban. It's what you wanted, right?"

"Maybe that's true… but what should I do now that they're out there and they've come for me? They were supposed to unite against Umwahu."

"Well, he's not here yet, is he? The ban achieved its purpose, reverse it now if you want. You knew it was going to make you unpopular, that was the whole point. But it doesn't matter. The Khun are not the original magical people of this land. Whether or not they use magic is unimportant. Our people matter most. Chuluun should be more than halfway to them by now."

"Reverse the ban?" She sat in silence and thought about it for a moment. "It will make me look like an idiot."

"You are," he said bluntly. She felt insulted. "And they believe it. But you won't always be."

"So, I will go down to meet them, and tell them that the ban was a mistake, and everyone will go home happy." She could not hide the dissatisfied sarcasm in her tone.

"Whatever decision you take as a leader, you should be firm with it. Show them that you are the way to safety."

"Should I tell them about Umwahu coming?"

"No. I still do not know enough about his plan. When I find out more, you can tell them. But until then, they must believe that they can live in peace."

"And what if the soldiers come back?"

"I have turned them away from this island before, and I can do it again. Trust me, they don't need to know that soldiers *might* decide to come back one day. I can deal with that when it happens."

"When it happens?" She glared at him. "You know something, don't you? You already know what the soldiers are planning. Tell me!"

"It's not important."

"Yes, it is!" Her voice was louder than she knew it could

be. It was the first time she had really stood up to Iwizadi, and she was surprised by her confidence. "If my people are in danger, I need to know!"

"You will lower your voice." He stood up to his full height and leaned forward on the desk menacingly. He didn't look sick anymore and she was afraid. "You will go down now and show them that you are not a leader to be taken lightly. You are a leader to be feared, and Ychir will discover that the hard way. The next time we talk I hope to have more answers about Umwahu and any other threats that might be coming."

She was furious, but knew there was no arguing with him. Underneath his angry façade was simple ignorance. He didn't know something. And he didn't want to admit it. She stormed out of the room and told herself to be brave. She could talk to the angry Khun from the window on the first floor in the room where Khuch and Maria were waiting, that way she wouldn't be within reach of any potential outbursts.

When she entered the room, Khuch and Maria were sitting awkwardly, silently and tensely. Aisling didn't have time to ask what they were talking about. She assumed it was to do with the situation outside. She went straight to the window, opened it and poked her head outside. Immediately, the crowd saw her, and the guards were relieved to have the attention taken off them.

"Why are you hiding up there?" Ychir called up to her, trying to provoke a reaction. "We want to talk to our brave and wise leader."

"Hello Ychir, and hello to all who have come here," she stalled, still not sure how to say what she wanted. "I want to say straight away that I was wrong about the ban on Bird magic."

Maria and Khuch exchanged panicked looks, knowing

how Aisling might be perceived as weak and ineffective. Maria felt that there was more to it and felt frustrated trying to figure it out. Aisling pressed on, struggling to be heard above some shouts from down below.

"I was wrong to think that was ever an option. You know that I only have the best interests of Gazar in mind."

"Do you?" Ychir taunted. "Or do you have *your* best interests in mind?"

"I really do want to do good for Gazar and Khun," she protested. But her words were met with a derisive snort from those listening. Even one of the guards rolled his eyes. She decided that Iwizadi's approach to leadership was too heavy handed for her liking, and wanted to try things her way first: with justice and diplomacy. "I want to listen to you and work together. Ychir, would you like to come in and talk?"

Not expecting an invitation, Ychir was momentarily taken aback. Khuch could sense that it was a bad idea and started to say something, but Aisling turned to him as if to say 'trust me', and Maria shushed him.

"Just me? Or will you listen to all of us?"

"For now, just you Ychir. You are clearly the leader of your party and they trust you to do what is right for them." Aisling had to be delicate in getting him alone. She had to provide a reason for refusing the others, not just say they were an angry mob and she was scared. Ychir turned to his party and said some quiet words.

"I will come with two witnesses," he said.

A minute later, they were at the door to the room, escorted by two of the guards. Ychir sneered, and showed off his lopsided mouth filled with poorly maintained teeth.

"I would be careful with this one, Aisling," he said, pointing his chin towards Khuch. "We don't know whose side he is on."

"I support Aisling," Khuch said.

"Could have fooled me," Ychir arrogantly said slowly, walking confidently into the room and roughly pulling up a chair. "Everyone at the tavern tonight enjoyed your speech."

"Whatever you're trying to do, it won't work," Maria said as calmly as possible, trying to ignore what she knew about Ychir's thoughts. His mind screamed loudly into the room, drowning out the other stray thoughts and disorienting her. Something felt wrong. "Can we please focus on why we are here?"

"I don't know about you," Ychir drew out his words. "But I am here to throw out those who claim ownership of the Khun."

Without warning, his two supporters disabled the guards with a spell that paralysed them.

"I thought this was going to be a peaceful discussion!" Aisling exclaimed. Ychir had no fear.

"There is no peace in Gazar, so long as you claim to be our leader." She knew it was her fault. She had done it on purpose. But it was harder than she ever expected and she wished she could tell him that there was a reason for it all.

It had been a long time coming. She had wrestled with it for a long time, and never accepted her position. She had always imagined Chuluun taking over when he finally returned, and she was just trying to keep things together until then.

"Alright! Lead us if you want! I'll step down! I didn't want this at all. I only did it because Iwizadi made me, like how he made Chuluun leave." The mention of Chuluun made Ychir roll his eyes. "I tried my best to unite you and you still hate me. I look out there at all of you together, working towards a future, and I think that I helped strengthen those bonds." It was better to be feared than loved, Iwizadi's philosophy rang through her thoughts.

"You strengthened them, that's true." Ychir arrogantly stretched his arms above his head and flexed his fingers back. "We are all bonded strongly against you since you tried to make Bird magic a crime."

Maria heard the rising shouts from within Aisling's mind. *Please, don't.* She tried to tell her, but was drowned out by the flurry of clashing noises coming from Aisling and Ychir.

"It is time for the Khun to have one of their own as their leader. You say you will step down. For that, I thank you for coming to your senses." Ychir stood up and went to the window. He raised his hands in victory, but before his celebration could be met, he felt a pressure closing in around his throat. He made as if to free himself, but nothing was touching him.

"I told you, I am Khun," Aisling spat at him through gritted teeth, stepping towards him. Fear. Lead them through fear. Ychir's eyes widened, realising that her magic was far beyond his, admitting to himself that despite his posturing and machismo, he was weak. Maria and Khuch watched stunned, each yelling at her to stop what she was doing. Ychir's men released the guards, and together watched as Ychir was lifted off his feet and through the window. He dangled above the crowd, gasping for each breath. Although they were not high off the ground, he was afraid. The Khun below were ready to catch him, but more than falling, the fear of magic was in him. He had felt this power once before, when Iwizadi had first claimed Khot for himself, but did not expect Aisling to share his power. He was being humiliated in front of his people and could never regain their trust in him.

"Are you ready to talk properly?" she asked. He nodded, and was carried back in through the window. The spell holding his throat softened and after a few seconds he could no longer feel where it held him. "What exactly do you want?"

"We-" he interrupted himself to cough. He sat down, his legs taking up a lot of room. "We want the same thing we always have. To live here, without anyone else in charge. No foreigners." He looked at Maria while saying this.

"I am no foreigner," Aisling said. "You helped raise me."

"You are," Ychir could not be convinced. "And so is *he*. As long as he is here, we will not rest. As long as you refuse to admit that you do not belong here, we will be a constant threat to you."

"How exactly will you threaten me? It wasn't hard to overpower you before." She smirked, surprised to find that she was enjoying the feeling of being in command. *Make them afraid of you.* The others in the room were quiet while the two leaders fought. Khuch felt torn again. He fully believed Aisling was Khun, and couldn't see why anyone who knew her would argue otherwise. He also felt the same ambition to get rid of Iwizadi. He knew that there must be a way to reach a compromise, even if they couldn't see it yet. They had not been able to devise a way to turn Ychir to their side before Aisling returned. He felt trapped in between two opposing forces that were gradually crushing him.

Fear.

Ychir realised at that moment that he had made a huge mistake. He had underestimated his opponent.

"We will always be watching you," he came out with, trying to retain some of his shattered dignity. "Maybe you don't fear me, and maybe you can overpower me. But would you be threatened by an army? How many Khun would it take before you take me seriously? How many would you be willing to subdue? You say you are one of us, but you would just as easily turn on us."

Aisling refused to answer the questions and instead stared him down.

Maria heard something between his words that the others did not: Ychir had plans to bring in backup. He had connections to an army in the Capital, and all he needed was to steal the book. They had to prevent that from happening at all costs. Should she warn Iwizadi? Or should she steal the book herself?

Ychir got up to leave without waiting for a reply. He preferred to leave Aisling to think about his words, because it was the best threat he could come up with: wait and see. He left the room with his two supporters, thinking that Aisling would be asking herself those questions late into the night. The two guards left with them, making sure the visitors left the palace and didn't wander around inside causing trouble. The last thing they wanted was for uninvited guests going to see Iwizadi.

"Aisling," Khuch went to her and put an arm around her shoulders. She held him around the waist. "We believe you are as much Khun as anyone here. But threatening him was a bad idea."

"I know," she said, looking up into his face. "But I was so angry with him, I had to remind him who is in charge." She was thinking about the impending threats that Iwizadi had alluded to, and Maria caught some of her thoughts as they dangled from her head. It wasn't enough for her to piece together the full story, though.

"Some men are incapable of seeing reason without violence," Maria said to them. She turned her attention directly to Khuch. "He provoked Aisling and left her with no choice. I have met men just like him in the Capital. It never ends well for them, but there is always a struggle, and other people suffer."

"Why can't he see that I'm trying to do good?"

"There is too much anger in his mind. It obstructs his vision," Maria said. She paused, before deciding to describe to Aisling what else she saw in Ychir's mind.

When she had finished explaining the complication, Aisling went to the window and looked out at the party dispersing into the city. She turned back to face Khuch and Maria.

"He can't be allowed to steal it."

"We know," Maria said.

"Even if we have to assume that the Capital will keep their end of the deal, if he gets his hands on the book, it will be the end for us. We will have to run."

"You are right to have misgivings about the Capital. Osbourne, especially," Maria said. "Playing fair has never been their preferred way of doing things. It could be that they have no intention of helping Ychir once they get their way."

"Do you think Ychir would fall for a trick like that?" Khuch asked.

"Maybe. He is obsessed with his vision, and he can't think very far in advance," Maria answered. The air had turned cold as the night settled in and the wind picked up. Aisling closed the window, which instantly made the room feel small and stuffy.

"Whether they help him or not, the outcome is bad for us," Aisling concluded. "If they do hold up their end, then Ychir gets the Capital forces to help him fight us and Iwizadi. And I expect Iwizadi will easily fight them off. And if they don't, then Ychir will be angrier than ever and feel even more justified in his quest to throw us out. He will fight more fiercely and so will his supporters, and in the end, Iwizadi will have to fight them off."

Khuch and Maria were impressed. Aisling hadn't shown such clear thinking in a long time. Maria loved that she kept her dad's spontaneity, but often thought it was a bad quality for a leader. Now, she saw her daughter showing signs that she was maturing as a leader and learning to slow down her thoughts.

"I am impressed with you Aisling," she said to her daughter. Khuch nodded in agreement.

"Why? All I've done is let people down. And now I somehow have to stop Ychir stealing from Iwizadi without either of them knowing that I know anything." Maria knew exactly what that felt like, but said nothing.

"You are thinking things through. Like my dad would do," Khuch answered for Maria. "Isn't that what you always talk about? Leading like he would?"

Aisling didn't say anything, and she nodded slowly. Khuch had explained it in a way that made sense. Maybe being a leader had less to do with choosing between terrible options, than it had to do with choosing them well, the least bad option, by thinking things through.

"What should we do about Ychir?" she asked. "I think we should keep an eye on him. Khuch, maybe earlier I would have said to go to his meetings, but he doesn't trust you now. Mum, maybe you could help us with your Mind magic. You can do it better than anyone else."

"I can do that," Maria nodded. "At least then we can know if he makes any plans."

"And when it comes time to stop him-"

"We will stop him before he even begins," Khuch said hopefully.

Iwizadi's words swirled around Aisling's mind. Fear. Love. She had tried to show the Khun love until now, and it had led them to a crisis. She would lead through fear. She would make Ychir afraid to steal the book.

As Aisling, Khuch and Maria were talking in the mountain, Ychir went back to his party and told them that no decision was reached. He told them to go home. Some of them criticised him for not following through, but they had all seen him held captive over the window ledge by Aisling's spell. He told them that he met her threat with his own, that she would always have to live with the knowledge that at any moment they could bring the fight to her. It seemed to satisfy some of them.

They did not have the slightest awareness of Ychir's deal to get the Capital forces on their side. They thought he was all bark and no bite, but did not know that he had a real plan, and a real army waiting.

A few weeks earlier, he had felt his mind rattle during the night, as if someone was shaking him awake. But nobody was there. Traditional Khun lore holds that ghosts can make physical appearances when needed, and at first, he thought that's what he felt. It was nothing special and he tried to go back to sleep.

But then a voice spoke to him in his mind and he knew that it was a very powerful magic, not just a ghost.

The voice said it hadn't looked for him specifically, but that it wanted to talk to one of the Khun in charge. He instantly said that he was in charge and could talk on everyone's behalf.

Over the course of their conversation, Ychir learned that he was talking to a man in the Capital named Osbourne, and that he was in charge of the men who had attacked them with false magic. Ychir was indignant and wanted nothing more to do with him, but Osbourne insisted.

"What if you had those men on your side?"

And then Ychir was interested, because like all violent men, he craved more power. They struck up a deal. Osbourne knew about Iwizadi's book somehow. Ychir was reluctant at first to agree to help him, since the book was an important part of Khun identity, but Osbourne reminded him of the power he was offering. Ychir wanted that power so that he might finally kick out the foreigners who had taken control of Gazar and take it for himself.

Osbourne persisted, and gradually Ychir's resistance to him faded away. Osbourne thought maybe it had been too easy, and that Ychir's single-minded ambition had made him an easy prey. After talking for some time, Ychir was convinced that in return for the book, he could rely on Osbourne's help when it came time for the Khun to rise up. It would be my pleasure, Osbourne said.

Ychir didn't question it at the time, but he later began to wonder what the true value of the book was. For him, and for every other Khun, it was a symbolic book with some spells described inside. It was full of arcane text that few people could read. He supposed that Osbourne wanted to know more about magic so that he could do it the natural way and he didn't have to rely on injecting himself with Substance M. Why else would he want a stupid old book? Ychir wondered.

As he walked back to the tavern with his group, some of its members branched off and went home, their spirits dampened after being so hopeful earlier in the night that the revolution had begun. Next time, he promised them. When they reached the tavern, there were only a handful in the group. These were the most loyal to the cause, and Ychir trusted them the most.

He told them of his plan to steal the book, but in a way that made it seem as though he was rescuing an important cultural artifact from the filthy foreigners' hands. They admired his courage and planning ability.

When eventually the tavern owner wanted to close the shop and turn in for the night, Ychir and his friends were just about passed out on the table. One of them was slurring a story about his old house on the night the war had come. None of them would remember how they got home when they woke up the next day.

Maria didn't dare enter the tavern and face a pack of angry nationalists, drunk as they were, so she found a dark place nearby and began to cast her mind inside. For the second time that evening, she sent a smoky finger dancing into Ychir's brain and waited until she was ready to explore.

He was very drunk, and unable to feel anything. Unlike earlier, when he was ready for action and his ethnic pride was behind every thought, this time his mind was a mess of incoherent, half-formed sentences and sentiments.

Maria was looking for any plans to steal the book. But even though just an hour earlier, he had told all his pals about it, the alcohol had made his thoughts completely unintelligible, and Maria reluctantly and quickly abandoned her mission for the evening. She would have to try again when he was sober. To try when he was in such a state would be futile.

In the morning, she went to visit her friend Sanakh. There was something on her mind; something that could not be easily digested. She needed a Khun perspective, even though she had already talked to Khuch about it. She didn't want to press the issue with him, and didn't want to raise it at all with Aisling. Especially Aisling, after what had happened to Peter.

She said goodbye to Aisling, noticing how well-rested she looked compared to recently. Her skin looked firmer and more radiant, like Maria's did when she was younger, and she seemed more energetic. In spite of this however, there was something like a cloud of defeat casting a shadow over her. Her growth as a leader had given her wisdom. And with that wisdom had come both confidence and a troubled mind.

Maria found Sanakh tending her garden at the front of the house and they went inside together for tea. One of the most luxurious things about the Khun, Maria thought, was that they had a lot of time for socialising and gardening. A lot of the labour that went into producing food was performed by magic, so compared to other peoples, they had lots of spare time. Maria also thought it was curious how their excess time notwithstanding, they rarely chose to focus on creative pursuits. It seemed like a cultural blockage on imagination.

"The house is looking beautiful, and your garden very nice," Maria knew the standard ways of greeting and complimenting Khun. At first, she thought they were simple people, but quickly learned that they had a depth and a highly nuanced culture that wasn't immediately apparent.

"Thank you, my friend," Sanakh poured them both cups and set up the pieces on a chess board. Though neither of them played, it was polite to offer a game. "There is something troubling you. I can see it."

"I want to ask what you know about mastery," Maria said. For all their social rituals, the Khun were very direct in approaching a topic. Sanakh raised her eyebrows and examined her friend's face. Maria had a distracted look about her.

"Is this to do with Peter?"

"I just want to understand more about it. How does it begin? How does a master know when it is happening?"

"I cannot tell you about Peter, because I was not there to witness it," Sanakh explained. "But it came as no surprise when I heard about it."

"Why is that?"

"You know, each magic draws on some part of the human emotions," Sanakh began. "Fire is rooted in anger. And it was fire that chose Peter."

Maria looked into her cup and moved it from one hand to another. She hated hearing that Peter was unhappy. Any time someone talked about him that way she was riddled with guilt.

"He lived well, and he loved well, but underneath it all he was angry. And the Fire magic knew it. It was his strongest, by far. We could all see that it chose him from the beginning. But it is a mystery why magic will sometimes choose to absorb the power of one man, while destroying another."

"What about the other recent master? You told me about Tesver. What was his experience?"

"In a similar way, it was the Bird magic that found him and called on him to change. He had always lived his life balancing hope and fear in the way that birds do. At first, there were small changes to him. You know that all magic carries risks and consequences. So, we thought nothing of it when as he grew stronger in Bird magic, his appearance began to resemble a tree. But very rapidly, he became more of a tree than a man, and the announcement was made that he was being called to mastery. Within only days from then, his spirit had been absorbed by Bird magic, and his body was replaced with a tree."

"So, it begins with the side-effects of the magic?"

"For Tesver, yes. The usual risks from Bird magic began

to form part of his ordinary existence."

"And then the side-effects get stronger until the final transformation is rapid."

"That's what we saw happen."

"Sanakh," Maria felt the words pile up in her throat. "What are the risks of Mind magic?"

Knowing that her friend felt great affinity for Mind magic, Sanakh was able to read between the lines.

"If you are feeling this sort of thing happen to you, you can either choose to trust the magic or not. You might not have proof that it will absorb you instead of destroy you, but it will be something you feel. Only you can be the judge."

"I am scared, Sanakh. I don't want it to happen to me," Maria looked sad, as if hoping her friend could make it stop.

"You know that it is a great honour to be called by the magic to mastery. I do not know of any Khun who tried to resist the pull, so I cannot say if you will suffer any negative effects from doing so."

"I'm not ready to be a master. I don't want to transform, even if it's such a great honour. I want to be here with my daughter. She's going to think it's just me leaving her again."

"But last time was not your fault. Nor is it your fault if you are to be transformed. It simply is. This is the way of the universe."

"I always thought I could be in charge of my own destiny," Maria said, but saw Sanakh shake her head. "I chose to leave the Capital and my unhappy family when I was young. Peter and I ran from all of that and started our own life. When I was back in the Capital later, I didn't believe in destiny at all. But all of the things that have happened to me in my life are not the results of my own choices. I've had to accept that."

"You said Iwizadi helped you find your memories, and he

helped you to find Aisling."

"He did," Maria reflected. "I have him to thank for that. It doesn't mean I trust him any differently, though. He made it clear that he did those things for himself, for whatever plan he has for this city."

"So, his actions influenced your destiny."

"They did."

"Do you think your actions could influence his destiny too?"

Maria thought about her plan to explore his mind and realised Sanakh was right. Maybe she did not have control over her own destiny, and when Mind magic was ready it would take her. Maybe her timeline was soon to reach its end, and there was little she could change. Like how a string tied tightly on a post can be pulled in this way and that on one end, but the closer one goes to its knot, the tighter its motion is controlled, until there is no slackness left in the string at all, and one can only feel the knot.

But her actions would still have consequences for others. The things she uncovered in Iwizadi's mind might still cast wide ripples in the tides of others' fates.

"Thank you, Sanakh. I was so worried about myself, I forgot about the good I can still do for others."

"You know it is exceedingly rare for magic to call a master?" Sanakh said esoterically. "For both you and your husband to be called is extraordinary."

"Promise me something," Maria said quietly. "If it happens, if I let the magic transform me, promise you'll look after Aisling."

"Maria, you know there is not much she needs me for. She is a strong woman with a strong husband."

"Promise me."

"Okay, I promise. There you go making choices that

affect other people's destinies again." They laughed at that, and Maria was happy knowing that her friend was there with her, even if underneath her happiness there was a rising tide of anxiety.

Chapter 5

After three days and nights of difficult trekking and sleeping both poorly and not enough, Zaria and Rainer saw the outline of a town in the distance.

"I think that must be Posyelok, or at least a small village attached to it," Rainer deduced from how far he estimated they had travelled and their rough direction. "The convoy would have passed through here the day after we were taken."

"Do you think we can find a car? Or a bike?" Maria asked. "Even a donkey would be nice." She relied on Rainer's knowledge more than she would have liked to admit and often dressed up her serious questions in sarcasm. He sometimes laughed a little chuckle, but more often than not he ignored her jokes.

"That is going to be hard to answer, Zaria. It is yes and no." They continued sneaking through the underbrush, aware that any obvious paths could be tracked by Nyikan spies in the night.

"What do you mean?" She had improved at treading lightly through the dense growth and moved much more confidently than before. She was beginning to tire of the smell of moss however, and caught herself missing the pungent stink of the swamp she knew best.

"You insisted that we do not report to the army."

"So?"

"If we go into the town asking for vehicles, people will ask what we are doing and where we are from."

"I didn't think about that," Zaria realised with a heavy heart that things were still looking very challenging. Movement through Naha had been restricted since the time of Danika the Bright. Maybe she was better off just reporting back to the army, she thought. At least then she could get a vehicle to Blue Island, even if it cost her freedom.

"So, if you want your donkey, we might have to get creative." Rainer was starting to like Zaria and her strong personality. At first, his sense of duty was all he could think about, and his mission was to take them both back to the army. Even if he said otherwise. But he found that over the days, the more she talked about freedom and being in charge of her own life, the more he started to agree with her. Like many others in the army, he found its structures of control to be oppressive, and the best part about joining was being able to see more of the country.

"Well, a donkey was my third preference. A car would be much nicer."

"But with a car, we are limited to travelling by road."

"And roads have checkpoints…"

"Exactly. At least as far as Zenetz Province. That is where the wild west begins. It might be a good place for you, lady who so loves to be free."

"So, you say we shouldn't get a car."

"Since neither of us have any documents to say why we are travelling alone, we should find horses and avoid the towns."

"But out in the wilderness we could be attacked by

Nyikans."

"But if we are caught by Nahans, you will be dragged back to your castle, and I will be court marshalled for desertion. Probably they will put me in the castle dungeon with other political prisoners."

"I don't want that to happen to you."

"It's not too late for me to report back. This is our first sign of Nahan civilisation, after all."

"Would you risk your life for freedom?"

"I have until we reach that town to decide."

As much as Zaria didn't like that answer, she didn't push him any further. She knew that he had softened towards her radical ideas, but she felt that if she pushed him about it, he could just as easily decide to turn them in out of spite. She admired his devotion to duty and thought it was both his best and worst quality.

They moved through the wild territory, well-practised at not disturbing any animals. They left the plants as they found them and trod lightly.

"I've seen him too," she said. They had reached an open space where wild wheat was growing all around them. The smell was overpowering and Zaria felt she might be allergic to it. The sun was beating down in the hottest part of the day. It seemed like an age since the cold night in the mountain pass.

"Who?"

"The man in your dreams."

Rainer stopped moving and looked at her for an explanation. They had not talked about the dreams since leaving the castle.

"What did you see?"

"The room you described. The man."

"What about the destruction?"

"No. Not in my dreams."

"Dreams? More than one?"

"Many." They started walking again. Zaria had never told anyone this before and she felt vulnerable. "He has talked to me before."

"What did he say?"

"He told me he has the cure to the illness. He wants me to come to him and get it."

"The illness? The one that's spreading through the country, killing people?"

"Yes."

"If I had not myself seen him, and seen the effect he has on entire armies, I would say you are crazy." Rainer nearly stepped into a little trickle of water, but instead crouched down and splashed some water on his face and neck. It was very refreshing. Handfuls of dirt came away as he wiped his skin.

"Do you believe me?"

"Yes." Zaria couldn't control her relief, and while Rainer was still squatting by the water, she launched at him and drew him into a big hug. He nearly toppled over by the sudden shift in weight.

"That means you must believe me about the dreams we had too." He shook her off, and in spite of himself he laughed and smiled at her child-like spirit. He might have felt too old for such exuberant displays of affection, but she didn't.

"I do," she confessed. "But what I don't understand is why the same man would want you to go and me to come."

Maybe it has something to do with magic, she thought. He wants my magic on the island and he wants the soldiers out.

"I don't understand either." Rainer started walking again.

"But I know that he holds a power greater than we can understand, and I know that I cannot trust a man like that."

"I agree." Zaria kept up with Rainer's pace easily, since his stolen boots fitted him poorly too. Even still, the heat of the day made her sweaty. "But I would like to understand it. I have to try to see if he does have the cure."

After another hour of walking, they were close enough to the town to see it in more detail. They hid on a nearby hill and examined it. It looked to be a town of about a thousand people, judging by its size. There was the usual army checkpoint at its main gate, but no real protections such as walls or patrols. It seemed to have no real plan, and was very much just a loose collection of buildings where people lived and worked. There was no trace of the King's money, as even the small number of soldiers at the gate looked downtrodden.

There were some paddocks with horses on the south side of the city.

"Looks like the decision has been made for us," Rainer said, patting Zaria on the shoulder. "There is no station here to report to. Looks like you will be getting your donkey after all."

"Really? And will you be coming with me?"

"I see two horses." Rainer expected the hug this time. He was a man not used to receiving affection. Military men rarely were. But he stiffly returned the hug and smiled woodenly. After a second Zaria released him. "I think my time in the army is over. I have devoted my life to service, but I realised this week that it is not devoted to me. My progress can be stripped away at any moment the King wants, because he doesn't accept the truth. You don't know how demoralising it is to work for something for a lifetime, and be told to start again. I will help you reach the island, but then I will leave you and make my own life in the Zenetz Province."

"That makes me so happy to hear."

"So, let's wait until dark, then go steal some horses. They will probably think it was just Nyikan bandits when they wake up in the morning and realise."

When nightfall came, they silently approached the paddocks. There were two horses grazing peacefully, and were easily led away from their stables without argument. They were clearly very used to humans. No lights were lit in any of the buildings nearby and by the time morning had come, Rainer and Zaria were miles away to the west, still travelling over the wild country, avoiding the roads. It was freedom at last.

They rode for days and days together, and as the country got wilder and their supplies got lower, they decided it was time to risk visiting a town. By this time, they were so far from the castle that the towns didn't bother checking documentation and there was a lot more freedom of movement. The next province to the west, and the largest of Naha was Zenetz. As Rainer liked to say about Zenetz, 'laws there are nothing but words'. Zaria was never so excited in her life, but it was the nervous excitement that comes with venturing into the unknown.

Zaria named her horse Chesna because he was so gentle. Rainer named his Vasiliy after the general as a joke, because he said he could see a resemblance.

They rode in a westerly direction for the next few weeks together. Though Zenetz took up nearly half of Naha's territory, only a small proportion of its people lived there. It was largely wild and empty, the perfect place for someone to hide. But it was also dangerous and lawless, and its towns were stricken by poverty. There was a general resentment of the King and the royal family, and Rainer advised that it was best to say they were from one of the other neighbouring provinces if anyone asked.

As anxious as she was about the dangers of nature and lawless people, Zaria enjoyed the trip. With Rainer's experience of outdoor adventure, they moved safely, sleeping hidden amongst boulders, cliffs, or sometimes in trees. As they got to know each other better, Zaria felt a tugging at her spirit. In the whole time since they had been moving, Rainer had not once asked her about her magic. She was sure that he would have been curious about it, just as she was curious about him and his life. She learned that he was married once, years ago, but he lost his wife while on tour. Not being allowed to return home for her last days was just another thing he resented the army for. They had no children.

She thought maybe she should bring up the magic with him, but then thought maybe it would be a bad idea. His silence made it pretty clear that he did not want to know about it. It was hard for her not to talk about it, though, and her thoughts went in circles as she tried to decide whether or not to bring it up.

Along the way, they stopped in various small villages for supplies. Nobody seemed to care who they were or where they were going, and it was a pleasant change from the constant demands that people faced back in the east. Even though the locals weren't too curious, they were friendly and hospitable, and shared the little that they had.

In every village they stopped in, there was the trace of the disease. It had spread unbelievably widely, to even the most remote places in Naha, bringing death and sadness with it everywhere it went. There had to be a cure.

Eventually one day, they stopped to rest when they saw

the coast. The ocean opened in front of them only a few hours away, and despite the overcast weather, it was spectacular. Zaria was familiar with the sea on the east side of the continent near the castle, but there it was a place where the muddy swamp poured into the abyss, and dirty ships polluted the harbour. Here on the west coast was different. The land sloped gently down into the water, and there were golden beaches as far as she could see.

"It's beautiful," she gasped, and Rainer laughed.

"It gets better every time I see it," he agreed. He was looking livelier each day. He pointed towards the right side of the beach, to the north. "Do you see that tiny shadow, way over there in the distance? That's the army's coastal base. They call it Blue Base."

Zaria squinted and still could not see anything. He must have very good eyes, she thought.

"How are we going to get across to the island?"

"Further to the south of here, away from Blue Base, is the point where Blue Island is closest to this land. Unfortunately, we will have to cross into Nyika briefly."

"Nyika! Will we be alright? Is it safe?"

"Yes, we will be fine," Rainer said light-heartedly. "You have your abilities, remember? Besides, Nyika is the only other place within a month of travel where we can hitch a lift to the island."

It was the first time since they started their adventure that Rainer had mentioned magic. Zaria took it as a good sign that he trusted her.

That night, they set up camp near the beach. The gentle lapping of the waves on the shore helped Zaria relax, and the horses seemed at ease too. She had never seen anything like the way the sun set over the ocean.

In the morning, Rainer was first up as usual, and went a

short way into the water to catch a fish. Zaria tried the water and was surprised to find that it was freezing cold. How Rainer could stay out there with water up to his chest was beyond her. Throughout the journey, she was constantly amazed by his way of doing difficult things with ease and simply getting on with the job. Maybe that's what the army had taught him, she thought. Maybe that was just him. Would Iskander have withstood the icy water for half an hour to get her breakfast?

"Why is the water so cold?" she asked later, while they were eating. "I thought it would be warm like on the east coast."

"There is a current that takes all the frozen water from Arazi down past here," Rainer answered. "We have to be careful with it, because it can drag a boat off course."

"I never realised Arazi had such a big effect on us"

"The world is just nature with people in it," Rainer said. "All of these countries, these borders, kings and queens, this war for the island… all of it is bullshit."

"And they made you a general in the army?" They both laughed.

"It was their choice, not mine," he shrugged "I kept doing the things they wanted".

Back in the east, saying that sort of thing could get a man locked up. But here, alone on the west coast, with nothing but nature to hear them, they could say whatever they wanted. She realised she agreed with him.

"What if I stayed with you?" she asked. "What if I don't go the island, and instead, you and I live here in nature, away from all that bullshit?"

Rainer just shook his head.

"No. You have your mission to finish. You have to see if there is a cure. Your destiny leads towards more bullshit, but mine has led me here to nature."

"What about after I finish on the island?" But she knew that he was right. She had chosen to come this way so that she could stop the disease from killing people in her home. She still had to go home to cure it. "What if my destiny is like yours, but I have to do this one thing first?"

"Then you should do it with all your heart, and when the future becomes clear, you should go to it without hesitation."

"Even if it's bullshit?"

"Yes."

"Well then, what's the point of that?" She was angry. Not at him, but at herself, for having believed for just a second that she had control over her own life. She stood up from where they were having breakfast and brushed the sand off her clothes.

"Zaria-"

"Let's just go. I have a job to do, and you have a life to live." She climbed onto Chesna and started riding south along the beach away from him. She didn't want Rainer to see her cry. She didn't want to lose him either, but she had to accept that their paths would diverge eventually. That was always the plan, she knew, and she cursed herself for getting too attached to him.

Later that day, they crossed a small stream. It bubbled around some pebbles and was cool and fresh to taste.

"We are now in Nyikan territory," Rainer said.

"It looks just the same. How do you know?"

"That stream is the boundary."

"Really? It's so…understated."

"What did you expect? Walls the whole way around our country?"

"Well, kind of, yeah." Zaria felt pretty silly admitting it.

There was a lot of the world that she didn't know about.

"Tomorrow we should reach a small fishing village, there we can get a lift."

"Your Nyikan is that fluent?"

"No," he laughed. "And just so you know, the towns out here barely speak it either. They have a whole range of other languages here, almost one per valley. You would have noticed in the villages we passed through."

"I thought it was just their accent. You mean they weren't even speaking Nahan?" She was incredulous. Rainer nodded. "Then how are we supposed to hire a boat if we can't understand each other?"

"Money talks. Same as it has for our whole journey." He made the international gesture for money by rubbing his thumb back and forth over his index finger.

That night they sat quietly. While normally they would be making jokes or playing cards together, they sat staring at their campfire. Zaria knew then that Rainer felt the same as she did about it being the last night of their adventure together.

"How do you do it?" she asked him.

"Do what?" he looked up, curious. Across the fire, her face was floating like a ghost, surrounded by darkness.

"In the army, you know that every night might be your last with someone. People you know and trust and love might be gone for good the next day." They sat silently while Rainer thought of what to say.

"In the army, you have no time to think about these things. Every moment of the day is filled with routine and sometimes pointless tasks. Yes, you might lose a friend in the night, or in a battle, but your days are always moving forward."

"That doesn't really answer it. How do you stop yourself

from looking at someone and thinking about how they won't be there anymore?"

"I guess you don't want my army answer."

"I'm going to miss you after tomorrow."

"I will miss you too."

"Then come with me to Blue Island," she felt her voice getting desperate. "Or wait for me to come back to you."

"No," he said softly to his feet. "You know I can't go there. And you don't belong here. Besides, isn't there someone else who should be waiting for you?"

Iskander. Would he have looked for her? Would he have waited for her?

"It isn't the same."

"It never is." He thought about people he had met on tour; people he would see for one night and move forward. Friendly locals, affectionate women. "But it gets easier to say goodbye."

"If it gets easier, does it mean people mean less to you?"

"No. It just gets easier the more you do it." His answer sounded so sad, and his posture had nothing of its normal strength. He leaned on his knees, sitting on a large rock. Zaria crossed the fire to where he was sitting, and sat next to him, pushing him across so she had enough room. She took his hand and laced their fingers together and rested her head on his shoulder. His hand felt limp, like he had no will left in him. Like his endless energy had finally decided to leave him.

"I've wasted my life in the army," he croaked. "I missed everything important. My wife died and I wasn't anywhere near her. I missed the funeral, stuck on the other side of the country. I said it gets easier, but it doesn't. Every single goodbye is still with me, I just try to ignore them."

"Then tell me it isn't going to be goodbye," she

whispered. "Promise we'll see each other again."

"I can't."

"Just promise."

They sat motionless watching the fire put itself out.

"There will be no more chances to say goodbye, living out here on my own," Rainer said.

"I get it," Zaria said. "I understand you. But you know, there are no goodbyes without hellos."

"I know."

Zaria picked her head up from his shoulder and turned to face him. He didn't budge, so she took her free hand and turned his face to hers.

"Don't run from your own life. All you'll do is keep missing out on all the things the army took from you. I don't want to say goodbye to you, but I'm happy to have the opportunity to. This has been the best time of my life and it's thanks to you."

She tried not to cry and forced herself to smile while letting her feelings out. But when she saw Rainer's face soften and his eyes moisten, she had to turn away and wipe her nose and eyes.

"Mine too. Thank you, Zaria," he said. "I promise this is not our last goodbye."

They slept well and, in the morning, made their way to the small unnamed fishing village, where they hoped to find a helpful fisherman willing to take a passenger. They arrived around midday.

Rainer was quick to find a man with a boat, and through broken Nyikan, a series of gestures and showing him some money, the man understood that Zaria wanted to go to the island. He managed to make it known that it was too late in the day already and they could go early the next morning.

They had some time to spare, and after exploring the tiny

village, they thought it would be alright to spend the afternoon in the pub with some fisherman. They both wanted to delay the moment when they went their separate ways. They stabled the horses for a cheap price compared to the city. Rainer would keep Chesna, they agreed.

There was a tiny pub next to the wharf, around which the town was centred. Fishing was the life of the town. Inside, the pub had room for three small tables with just a few chairs around each. A narrow staircase at the back of the room led to accommodation. The bar was tended by a short woman who was covered in tattoos in the style of the south Nyikan coast. Rainer hit his head on one of the low beams holding up the ceiling. The other patrons laughed at him. They were a group of three young sailors – likely pirates, Rainer warned Zaria – enjoying a free afternoon and getting drunk, and when they saw Rainer and Zaria enter, they stood up and greeted them warmly. Strangers were a real novelty, and they were eager to know about them.

One of the sailors was from a larger city on the south coast of Nyika, and spoke passable Nahan. He made friendly conversation with the bartender. The other two were from somewhere in the north where the border with Arazi was meaningless and the two countries blurred together. They chatted to each other in Arazi but could get the gist of the conversation in Nahan. Unlike Nyikan, Arazi was a language completely unlike Nahan. Some people described it as sweet-sounding, but others thought it was harsh.

"From Naha?" the Nyikan man asked as a way of chatting. There was no sense of being interrogated, whereas back in the east, being born in the wrong place was a crime.

"Yes." Zaria decided she got a good feeling from him. He reminded her of Vasiliy, even though they were from different parts of the continent.

"Where you going?" Again, the question was just for curiosity.

"Blue Island."

"You need boat?" Zaria thought he was being generous, but Rainer thought there was reason to suspect his offer.

"No, thank you. A man out there will help us tomorrow." Rainer butted in, smiling charmingly, thinking it wise to decline such an offer before Zaria did anything stupid. Not that she would, of course. He knew she had a good sense of when to trust people. Even still, he had to be careful.

"Grigor. He says Blue Island fish taste better," the sailor said, nodding sagely.

"That's good. Maybe I can try one," Zaria kept the conversation light.

"Why you come here though? This is Nyika you know. There is perfectly good Naha port just up the coast." This time the question felt laced with a hint of mistrust, like the man knew there was a good reason that Zaria and Rainer had chosen an enemy land over their own compatriots.

"This town is very friendly. The one over there is an army base." Rainer wanted to keep the reason very superficial.

"You in army?"

"No." Zaria shook her head. Rainer said nothing and drank some beer. It was watery and flat, but it was his first beer in months and he loved it.

"He is in army. Now I know why you come here. Is okay. I say nothing. I dodge draft too." The man was smiling broadly, as if he had found a new friend and offered his hand to Rainer. They shook, and Rainer felt there was nothing sinister in it. The man was telling his story plainly and had not lied. Rainer relaxed, but still chose not to reveal too much about himself. Even an itinerant Nyikan sailor and his Arazi pirate buddies couldn't know that he had abandoned the army. If anybody at all found out, the army could come looking for him.

"What your name?"

"Iskander," said Rainer, as it was the first name that came to mind. Zaria felt a pang of guilt. Why was he thinking about Iskander?

"I am Gabi. And you?" He held out his hand for Zaria and began shaking it before waiting for an answer.

"Danika," she said pleasantly. It was very common for people her age to be named after the queen. "Very nice to meet you."

"You know, last week we came down coast from north. Went past army base." He leaned across the table and raised an eyebrow while looking at them in turn. He lowered his voice conspiratorially. "Many people are sick. More sick than other places. No boats coming and no boats going. Better for you to come here."

As the afternoon became evening, and the evening got late, the sailors continued drinking at an unmatchable pace. Zaria and Rainer had some drinks too, but not nearly as many as their new friends. They sang all kind of songs in different languages that Zaria didn't recognise, and the mood was very good. Rainer paid for a room for the night.

It turned out they were in fact pirates. They had their own boat and felt no allegiance to any specific country. Their home was in money, and the things it could buy. Their duty was to get more, by means that Gabi didn't explain in detail.

When it came time to retire, they bid the pirates goodnight, and went upstairs to their room.

"You are always welcome to make party with us, Iskander and Danika," Gabi called out with surprising lucidity.

"People in the west are so much friendlier than in the

east," Zaria said, tripping up the uneven stairs.

They went into their rented room and saw just one double bed.

"She told me it was two beds," Rainer said. Not wanting to go back downstairs, he added: "You take it, I'll sleep on the floor."

"Don't be stupid," Zaria said. "You think I care about sharing a bed after camping with you for a month?"

They cleaned up by splashing some water on their faces. Zaria took off her clothes and lay down on the bed. It was the most comfortable thing she had seen since leaving the castle. Rainer also undressed and got under the covers. He was asleep before they could say another word.

What else could they say? Everything they were sad about had been expressed the night before. Zaria felt embarrassed that she had started to grieve their friendship before she even left. She got up to turn off the light, then fumbled through the dark room to find the bed. When she got under the covers and closed her eyes, her mind wouldn't let her sleep.

She wanted to wake him and tell him she loved him, but instead she pulled in close to him and put his arm around her and nestled her head against his chest. That's how she stayed until her wild thoughts eventually settled and she let the luxury of the mattress and the alcohol send her to a heavy sleep.

When morning came, neither of them had moved. Whoever woke up first didn't matter, because neither of them risked disturbing the other.

"Good morning," Rainer croaked when he noticed Zaria was awake. She turned her head up to him but stayed close.

"Like a young couple in love!" she joked, and they both laughed. Rainer wanted to be young and in love, but he was neither.

"More like an old married couple," he said. They separated and got up and got dressed. Rainer desperately needed to pee, feeling that the beer had washed through him now, and hurried to the toilet. Zaria sat on the end of the bed and watched as he left. She sighed. Why did he have to say his name was Iskander? And she wondered if maybe he had Iskander's youth there could have been more chemistry between them. Or if Iskander had the quiet confidence and wisdom of Rainer maybe she would love Iskander. She was sure she didn't now, like she thought she might have the last time they were together. It would be impossible for any man to compare to Rainer the way she knew him now. But Rainer had no room in his heart for romance, she knew, and she wasn't going to wait for him to make room.

Rainer came back to collect his things.

"Are you ready to go? Grigori won't wait for us."

"Us?" Her hopes rose that maybe he changed his mind.

"I mean you," he replied awkwardly, realising the mistake. She felt foolish.

"You're right, I should hurry."

Soon after leaving the pub and buying some food for the journey, they were standing on the dock while Grigori made some preparations on his boat.

"I guess I'm going now," she said, wishing she wasn't.

"I guess so." Grigori called out to them impatiently and gestured that it was time to go. Zaria took a deep breath in and kissed Rainer on the cheek.

"Go," he said. "Do what you need to do."

"Remember your promise."

"I will."

"Thank you."

"Thank you too."

He stood on the dock, watching Grigori's boat drift across the sea until he could no longer see it. Zaria watched the shore until she could no longer see Rainer, then she sat down and cried silently until Grigori came to her with a bucket, thinking she must be either seasick or hungover.

Gabi swaggered up to where Rainer was standing, his eyes bleary with the aftermath of his party.

"Always good women leave us." And then he vomited into the water.

"Where are you going next?" Rainer asked, still unsure of his own moves.

"I am going to the pub."

***

The sea was quite rough, and Zaria was relieved when in the early afternoon they reached calmer waters near the shore, and Grigori prepared to let her off at a collection of ramshackle wooden buildings. She later learned that it was a small group of fishing families originally from the same town they came from, as well as a few local Khun. It was comforting to know that she would not be immediately alone.

She looked around at the landscape. The water seemed bluer than any she had ever seen before, and it was teeming with fish. No wonder Grigori chose to do his work here. Behind the buildings, a ridge of mountain peaks rose sharply, and there appeared to be very little land for farming. Zaria couldn't make out any path into the mountains. The trees and grasses looked different to anything she had seen before. The grass was thicker and was dotted with small white flowers. The trees were a kind of palm, similar to the ones she had seen on the west coast over the last few days, and they grew in thick bunches out of every surface at all kinds of angles.

Grigori said something to a tiny woman in an apron, who Zaria assumed was his wife or daughter. Then he cheerfully waved her goodbye and set off to catch fish. The woman took Zaria into her house and prepared tea and snacks, most of which involved fish.

"Nahan?" Zaria asked, trying to find a common language. The woman shook her head. "Nyikan?" She bobbed her head side to side as if to indicate 'a little bit'. That was good enough for Zaria. "I am Zaria."

"I am Michaela," she said in a heavy accent. "Wait." She left the house and returned a moment later with one of the locals.

"She said you speak Nahan?" the local man asked, not without judgement. Zaria was glad to hear her own language. He must have learned from the soldiers, and spoke with a very formal accent. He looked Zaria up and down as if sizing up an opponent. "What are you doing here?"

"I came looking for someone," she answered. Rainer taught her never to play all her cards at once. The man was still as a statue, and his wide, wrinkly face betrayed no intention.

"Who?" he asked. Zaria tried to remember what Athena had told her about the Khun all those weeks earlier. *They are very direct people. They don't have the same rules of etiquette that we do.*

"A man I saw in a dream." *They are very superstitious and believe in witchcraft.* The man looked at Michaela, who was eating a fish snack, ignoring the conversation she couldn't understand.

"Soldiers here saw a man in their dream, and they ran away. But you saw a man in a dream and came looking," his voice rumbled deeply. Then he burst into laughter. "You are braver than the whole army!"

Zaria let out a cautious laugh too, as did Michaela, who had no idea what was so funny.

"Come to my house, I want to talk more to you," he offered, and Zaria thanked him. She thanked Michaela and shook her hand, like she had been taught was polite. Michaela didn't seem to care for politeness, but she nodded slightly before continuing with her day, seemingly relieved not to have to deal with the stranger any longer.

"My name is Amitan," the man said as he showed Zaria into his home. It was like Michaela's wooden shack, but with more of the native style: Amitan had tried to make it rounder. Zaria saw a dusty old Noi generator that looked like it had hardly been touched. He closed the door behind them. "Tell me, who is the man of your dreams?"

His phrasing was peculiar and she couldn't help but picture Rainer and Iskander. Zaria weighed up whether or not to tell Amitan about her dreams. She had made it this far, and she would need help finding him.

"He never said his name," she said. Amitan looked at her expectantly to explain. "I think he is the wizard Iwizadi."

Amitan nodded, and Zaria didn't know if that meant he believed her, or understood. Athena didn't say if the Khun told the Iwizadi story or not.

"Why did you come looking?" he asked, without giving away anything of what he was thinking. He gestured to her to sit down and he began making tea. She noted a chess board was set up on a table.

"The people in my country are sick," she said. "He promised me a cure."

"People are sick here too," he said with sadness, nodding. "I'm sorry."

"You trust him?"

"I risked my life to come here to find a cure."

"He is here," Amitan told her. Zaria smiled broadly and started to formulate questions about how she could meet him, but Amitan kept talking. "You should know that we do not trust him. I worry for you, that he has no cure to give. Because he has not cured us."

"What do you mean?" Zaria's smile was wiped away and she felt a sense of failure wash over her. Surely if Iwizadi had a cure he would have helped the Khun by now.

"It is a bad time for Khun here on Gazar." *Gazar. That's the local name for the island.* "He lives in the sacred mountain in Khot. When the army left, he came and took control. We are not free. There is strong evil magic in him."

"How do I get there?" Zaria asked, ignoring the comments about magic on purpose. "And what do you mean by 'bad time'? Is it dangerous for me to be here?"

"It is always dangerous," Amitan sighed. "But he wants you here, so he will keep you safe." He sat down opposite her and studied her face with interest.

Zaria felt an uneasy sense of violation, as if her life was not hers to control. The same anger at having her destiny written for her flared up like it did when she was with Rainer on the beach, and she fought to keep it under control.

"We Khun want him to go. We want him to leave us and take his foreigners with him. They have taken control. You should be careful of Khun who will resort to violence before discussion."

"Which foreigners are with him?" Zaria was interested to know which country had stepped in to fill the void left by the Nahan and Nyikan armies retreating.

"There is a woman in charge named Aisling. She was born in the Capital country and raised with Khun in exile. Iwizadi claims she represents Halasat, and she is one of the original people of Gazar. He put her in charge of Khot. We want her and her mother the evil witch to leave. But she is married to Khun, speaks our language and uses our magic. It makes the situation harder. Some of us believe she has a right to be here." He looked at Zaria and she thought it wise not to bring up her own country's history on the island.

"What is Halasat?" Zaria had never heard of the place where Iwizadi and his followers had settled after losing Libalele.

"Small nation of magic people, it is at the western edge of the world. Chuluun the traitor is going there now to bring its people back here. That is Iwizadi's plan."

"Why have I never heard of Halasat?" she asked. He shrugged his broad shoulders and took a loud slurp of tea.

"Nobody ever heard of them before Iwizadi came." She looked around awkwardly at Amitan's home. He didn't have many usable things, but every side of the room was covered in pieces of wood and other scraps.

"So how do I get there, to the sacred mountain?" She was not going to reveal her own magic ability. It was her last secret.

"If you really must go, there are two ways. You can sail west from here to where the mouth of the river Gol empties to the sea. Then sail upstream."

"Sail upstream? How?"

"Iwizadi summoned you, so the river will take you." *What kind of man controls a river?* Zaria gulped nervously as it dawned on her the immense power that Iwizadi yielded. What had she gotten herself into? Maybe it would be better to avoid making an entrance, since the locals were so opposed to foreigners anyway.

She also didn't want to draw attention from the Nahan army. They had probably arrived long before her and if they came into contact she would lose her freedom again.

"What is the other way?"

"Path over the mountains. When you cross, you will see Khot in the valley on the other side. It is only a day from there."

"I think I will go that way."

"Then I will show you where to start. But it is a hard climb, I warn you."

They finished their tea hurriedly and silently. Zaria could tell Amitan was keen to be rid of her.

When they exited his house, Amitan led the way north to where the mountains began. He pointed out a small track hidden amongst shrubs and overgrown with weeds and grasses.

"Nobody uses this track anymore. Good luck." He shook her hand in the Nahan way. She felt that the soldiers had left a lasting impression on the locals, and it embarrassed her to see their influence creeping into even the most basic interactions. "I hope you find your cure and leave quickly. This island is not good for you, and we don't want you here."

His hostility was delivered so casually that Zaria had to think about his words before feeling them. Was the anti-foreigner sentiment really so strong? It made sense to her. Stories the soldiers told from the occupation were often interlaced with a brutality that made her feel sick. It was no wonder the locals had fled. No surprise that they felt the way they did. She agreed that she didn't plan to stay any longer than necessary. She had a job to do. And she had to get back to Rainer somehow, she had decided, just as soon as she was finished.

"Thank you, Amitan. I promise to leave as quickly as possible," she said as she started the steep climb over the mountain ridge that drowned the village in shadows. He didn't wave. He stood watching for a minute until the overgrown flora had hidden her from view.

Zaria discovered that the track was reasonably well-defined, despite being in a state of neglect. She was able to make good progress that afternoon, and as it was getting late, she stumbled across a good place to make camp for the night. It would be uncomfortable compared to the night in the pub. And lonely, without Rainer. The silence bothered her more than it should have. She found her own thoughts to be terrible company.

The next morning, she reached the highest point of the track, which passed through a trough between two peaks. From there she could see the immense valley stretch out before her. The range she was on encircled the valley neatly, and in the centre, she could see the city, the river, and the one mysterious peak sticking out like a pimple. She thanked Amitan, hoping that all the locals were honest people like him. She could at least deal with hostility if they were honest.

She looked back in the direction from which she came. The village was barely visible down below, hidden behind trees. But it was the sea that stole her attention. It stretched as far as she could see, and it was hard to believe that only a day before, she had been on the other side. The salty sea breeze still reached her up in the mountain pass.

Being day time, she missed out on seeing the majestic spread of glowflowers in the valley below.

She decided that it would be foolish to walk straight into the city and demand to speak to Iwizadi. After hearing what Amitan had said about the local tensions, it would have been suicide to go and announce herself as Iwizadi's ally. Instead, she wanted to find a place to hide out and think.

By the afternoon she had descended the mountains and

decided to set up camp amongst some boulders where she could at least be somewhat protected if anyone came that way. She decided that without Rainer to judge her, she could use magic without fear, and spent the night in the warm glow of a magical fire.

That night she had her first sight of the glowing fields, and it was magical in a whole new way to her. Everything that troubled her was forgotten in an instant, and she understood why wars were fought over this land.

Zaria's luck was about to change however, as Khuch Chaddhal was walking nearby early the next morning.

She saw him first from a distance, from where she was still hidden between her rocks. He wore a traditional costume: loose fitting trousers and a shirt, and a colourful poncho. But he also wore army-style boots that he must have picked up from a Nahan soldier at some point in time. Some tiny birds flitted around and landed in front of him. He seemed to be talking to them. The birds zipped away in every direction, and he began walking directly to where Zaria was watching. She ducked behind a boulder, and hoped that he would miss her.

But a few minutes later, she heard his voice call out in the local language, then in the language of the Capital. She knew she couldn't hide forever, and stepped out bravely to where he could see her.

He was surprised to see her standing there, and for a moment, neither of them did or said anything. Slowly, she raised a hand to wave. He did the same, and said something to her that she didn't understand. She said something back in her own language, but he shook his head. She tried to remember what she had learned of the Capital back in school, but it was so long ago. She remembered when delegates from the Capital came to visit her father, they usually communicated with difficulty, even with an interpreter.

She hadn't planned for this.

Khuch didn't know what to do. He was on one of his normal hikes out to where he used to speak with Haforn before leaving on his quest with Orn, when a group of birds told him there was a foreigner just a few hundred metres out of his way.

And they were right. There she was: a beautiful young woman, brave and strong, and completely unable to communicate with him. He understood that she was Nahan from her appearance and her first choice of language, but he had no idea what she was doing there.

The most suspicious thing about her was that there was no evidence of a campfire. Unless she spent the night in the cold and darkness, she should have had to make a fire. He tried miming his thoughts about the campfire, and after some struggle, she understood.

Then Khuch was forced to admit to himself that magic was not a uniquely Khun trait. Zaria, already knowing the Khun belief in magic thanks to Athena's lengthy briefing, risked showing Khuch a magic fire.

For a moment, Zaria thought that she had made a mistake. Khuch had a shocked expression on his face, which she thought might have been a result of having seen magic for the first time. Instead, he produced the same magic in return.

She had the answer at last. They were not a primitive people like Athena had said. They had no need for Noi because they had magic.

He had a bright idea, and called out to the birds to join them. He asked them if they could talk to the mysterious stranger. Zaria saw him talking to them, and although she had never spoken to birds in her life, she knew that it was what she must do.

The birds finished listening to Khuch and flitted over to Zaria, chirping and singing.

At first, she didn't understand them, and Khuch thought that his plan had failed. But then, Zaria felt her mind opening to more magic. Already since being on the island, she felt that her magic was stronger and easier than ever before. The noises from the birds started to take shape and she could understand the individual sounds that make up words, then the words that make up sentences, then the meanings of each word, then the meaning of the whole sentences, then she heard what they were saying.

Through the medium of the birds, Khuch and Zaria were able to hold a conversation.

"Who are you?" he asked. "How do you know how to use magic?"

"My name is Zaria. I come from Naha," she figured she might as well explain her magic, seeing as he was a fellow user. "I have been able to do these things since I was a little girl."

"This is the first time I have heard of any foreigner born with magic," Khuch scratched his head. "It should only be possible for Khun and the people who live in Halasat."

"But here I am," Zaria said. "And you are the first person I've ever met who can do it too."

"Yes, you are here," Khuch said. "Why?"

"I am looking for someone," she answered.

"Who?"

"Iwizadi." Khuch turned away.

"I should have known." He turned and started walking away slowly. "Ever since he came, things have been going wrong. First, he turned us against each other by putting

Aisling in charge – not that it was her fault after seeing the way he threatened us all – and now I guess he's inviting random people from around the world."

"Hey!" Zaria called after him and jogged to catch up, careful not to twist her ankle on the loose rocks. The birds went with them. "I met another Khun yesterday. Amitan. He told me that foreigners aren't welcome. I know all that already. I just want to find Iwizadi so I can get the cure and go home."

"Cure?" He stopped and studied her face. She squinted in the bright sun. "For what?"

"For the disease spreading through my country. He told me in a dream that he knows what to do about it. Please, show me how to find him."

Whatever Zaria expected, it wasn't laughter.

"You believed him?" Khuch started walking again. "All he does is keep secrets and lie. I'm sorry for your trouble, but you should have stayed home. There is nothing for you here."

"Stayed home?" Zaria pushed him on the shoulder and he was momentarily thrown off balance. "You don't know my home. Even if you're right and it turns out to be a lie, risking my life to come here was the best thing I ever did. My home is a prison, where the inmates think they're free. So, I'm asking you again, please take me to him."

Khuch recognised something of Aisling in Zaria's stubbornness and persistence, and it touched a soft spot in his heart. She bore a faint resemblance, the way her cheek bones shaped her face. And the shape of her hairline was similar. The way she talked about being a prisoner made him reconsider.

"Fine," he agreed. "I can take you to him, but you will have to pretend I have captured you and you are a spy.

Seeing as you come from Naha, the other Khun will believe it. But I don't know about Aisling. She might suspect there is more to the story."

"Thank you," she said.

"Don't thank me yet. This might end badly."

And so Khuch began to lead Zaria back to the city and to the mountain where Iwizadi lived. On the way, he learned that it was Iwizadi himself who had sent nightmares to all the soldiers, resulting in them fleeing in a panic. That changed his opinion of the wizard slightly. If the other Khun knew that, maybe they wouldn't be so eager to see him leave.

"But you say they plan to come back?" he asked. That was a strange thing for Zaria to hear. It meant that they had not yet arrived. It added up with what Gabi had told her and Rainer back in Nyika about the base being out of action recently. Zaria put two and two together and understood that she had somehow beaten the army to Gazar. That made her life a little easier, but she still wanted to leave before they arrived.

"Yes. They are close – just across the water." Khuch gulped but said nothing. Seeing his anxiety, she added: "But their base is stricken with the disease and they are unable to come here while dying. I have heard from a sailor that there are no ships going in or out of the base."

"You know, you are a spy after all." Zaria looked at Khuch strangely.

"No, I'm-"

"A spy for us," he cut off her objection. She blushed and looked ashamed of herself. She so readily gave away their military movements! Had she been enlisted, that was an offence that carried prison time. "Thank you for letting us know about the upcoming invasion. Our benevolent leader

Iwizadi has managed to keep it a secret from us."

Zaria was starting to understand why the Khun wanted Iwizadi gone. He was capable of telling them of the Nahan army's movements but neglected to.

"Unless he knows they'll never make it…" she thought out loud. Khuch grunted but added nothing.

Khuch led them directly to the mountain, taking the shortest possible route through the city. It was best if nobody saw Zaria, and he hurried her along. But it was the middle of the day, and plenty of people stopped what they were doing to watch him walk a foreigner straight to their sacred mountain.

"I caught a spy," he explained to some people he passed, knowing that they would gossip and spread the word. Zaria kept her head down after seeing the looks of fear and anger on the locals' faces.

As the rumours quickly spread, Ychir came running to see for himself. He blocked their path and examined Zaria carefully, getting uncomfortably close to her face. She could smell the fish from his lunch. Ychir jolted his head towards Khuch.

"So, young Khuch Chaddhal, the lover of all things foreign, the son of Chuluun the traitor, has caught a spy," he jeered. "Tell me how you know?"

"I found her hiding in the foothills to the south of here. She only speaks Nahan and Nyikan, the languages of our enemies. I am taking her to the leadership directly." He desperately wanted to tell Ychir about the Nahan army amassing just one day from Gazar, but to do so would be to reveal Zaria's magic ability. It was prudent to keep that hidden for now.

"You think it's wise to take a foreign spy to our foreign leaders? Why not bring her to us locals and let us decide what to do with her?" Ychir was making a scene, and unfortunately for Khuch and Zaria, he had plenty of support from the people gathering to watch. Since the incident at the mountain, he had been slowly regaining the respect of his old mob. "Does anybody here speak Nahan or Nyikan?" He spat out the names of the languages like he had eaten sand. A few hands rose, and some people volunteered. The occupation really had had a lasting impact on the Khun.

"You, Yardag, come here." Ychir pointed at a very short, fat man with glasses. "Interpret."

"Alright." He pushed his glasses up his nose.

Two large Khun held Zaria in place.

"Why are you here?" Ychir asked through Yardag. Zaria, knowing what little she did about the politics of Gazar, and not having followed the conversation up until then, was scared. A captured spy in the presence of nationalists was like a delicious roast dinner for starving athletes. She would stall as long as possible and hope beyond hope that Iwizadi, or at least the infamous Aisling would appear and stop the crowd.

"I got lost on my way to the Capital lands on the western continent." When Yardag had relayed he message, there was booing and hissing from the ever-growing crowd.

"Where were you coming from?"

"Naha."

"Why?"

"To visit," she paused, trying to remember the leader of the Capital's name. "Abe…Brown. On official business."

"Did your official business involve scouting our land?"

"No! I got lost on the way!"

"It just seems a little farfetched," Ychir growled at her. "Why would Naha send you alone to the Capital?"

"I took the initiative."

"You have an answer for everything!" He laughed and some others did too when they heard him. Khuch was standing anxiously beside her the whole time. She realised that he risked his own safety for her. Why would he do that? "I don't believe Naha would send one woman alone on a diplomatic mission. Everything they do is with the army."

"But you believe they would send one woman alone to spy on you?" Some people nodded and accepted she made a good point. *Please Iwizadi, Aisling.* A group of swallows flew near her and seeing them, she felt strangely confident.

"Don't-" Ychir slammed a fist into her abdomen, and she doubled over in pain. She was winded and couldn't breathe. Her face turned red and thick strands of saliva dripped from her open mouth as she struggled to breathe again. "Don't make a fool of me. Now, I have another question for you, spy. How is it, that the great nation of Naha does not know that Abe Brown died nearly three months ago?"

Zaria regained her breath and managed to stand up, or rather was dragged upright by the goons keeping her in place. She met Ychir's fierce gaze and while she was thinking of another excuse, she noticed the crowd behind him on the road to the mountain parting. She recognised the old man at the front, and guessed that the young lady with him was Aisling. She was amazed by how similar she looked to herself, though Aisling had more of a hopelessly naïve look about her. The two big Khun holding her arms released her.

Ychir heard murmuring behind him and turned around to see Iwizadi standing barely out of arm's reach. Zaria saw Ychir flinch almost imperceptibly, but he stood his ground. Athena's information was far too basic to capture the nuances of Khun life and politics, Zaria thought. It wasn't even close. Athena painted a picture of disorganised beasts incapable of thought. Here Zaria was witnessing a people with allegiances and factions on the verge of a coup. How had Athena gotten it so wrong? Was it intentional? Was it personal?

"Ychir, you will stand aside," said Iwizadi in barely a whisper. Yet his voice crept up alongside Zaria and made her shiver and the hairs on her neck stand tall. This was humiliating for Ychir. No wonder he hated him. "Don't make me make you."

After a few seconds standing off, Ychir reluctantly moved out of the way, and Zaria saw the wizard approach her.

"I thought you might never make it, Zaria," he said in the same calm whisper. "Please come with me, and excuse our friends for their warm welcome."

There were murmurs all around, but the crowd slowly dispersed, as Iwizadi showed Zaria the way to the mountain. Khuch and Aisling followed together, equally anxious and confused, and relieved that Iwizadi intervened when he did.

"I need to tell you something, but I don't know how," Khuch said to Aisling. They held hands and he sent Love magic flowing through her to calm her after the tense and confusing scene they had witnessed. For the first time, she tried sending it back, and saw the look of surprise on his face when he realised what she was doing. "Since when could you do that?"

"I've been practicing. I wanted to surprise you," she answered. She could tell she had succeeded and it made her happy.

The four of them entered the mountain and Iwizadi led them into his study at the top of the stairs. Zaria admired the construction on their way up in the same way Aisling had done not long before, when it was her first time. Nobody said a word as they climbed the stairway.

Iwizadi closed the door behind them when they had all entered. Aisling saw the look on Zaria's face and knew that she had seen the room before. Aisling understood then that Zaria was not just any random stranger. Iwizadi had been in contact with her.

"You know this place?" Aisling asked, before anyone else could take the lead. It was not so much a question for Zaria as an accusation towards Iwizadi and a declaration of her growing mistrust.

"She won't understand," Khuch informed Aisling. "But we can communicate through birds."

"Inefficient," Iwizadi interrupted. "It works, but it is an inelegant solution. With a little Mind magic, we can eliminate the need for it." He swung his arms in a circle energetically, over and over for a few seconds until suddenly, he stopped. Aisling thought nothing had happened, but then Iwizadi spoke directly to Zaria. "Welcome, princess."

To the amazement of everyone else, Zaria understood and answered. His spell had removed the language barrier between them, and though each still spoke their native tongue, they were understood.

"Thank you, Iwizadi." She turned to Khuch next. "And thank you, sir, for everything you have done today. You took a huge risk to bring me here." Khuch bowed his head slightly and Zaria turned to Aisling. "You must be Aisling. My name is Zaria. I am the daughter of the king of Naha."

Iwizadi sat down and watched them chat. Aisling extended a hand for Zaria to shake. They shook professionally and with suspicion, like any good diplomat would do. Zaria was no stranger to politics.

"Pleased to meet you, Zaria." She looked at Iwizadi sitting comfortably. "From the way you looked when you came in, you have seen this room before."

"Yes," Zaria admitted, also looking at Iwizadi. "I have visited this place in my dreams."

"And what exactly were those dreams about, if I may ask?" Aisling asked. Zaria took the hint that Iwizadi was taking on the role of spectator and followed Aisling's lead not to involve him. She did not understand why, but she could always find out later.

"There is a sickness in my country," she explained. Aisling looked nervous. Khuch had leaned against a wall to watch the meeting unfold. Iwizadi was like a statue. "It is spreading. When people fall ill, they cough until they bleed, and their spirit leaves their body. People are dying and we don't know how to stop it. In my dreams I heard that a cure exists. I journeyed here at great personal risk to find it and bring it home."

"I'm sure that you have not had an easy trip," Aisling replied. She stood about a half a metre away from Zaria, and was not sure what to do with her arms. They hung weirdly by her sides until she remembered them, and awkwardly put her hands together in front of her. "From the little that I know about your secretive country, it can't have been as simple as choosing to walk here. But I hate to tell you that we do not have a cure either. People here are also suffering from the disease."

Zaria felt her face go hot and red, and she was very angry with Iwizadi. She turned to him and took a breath in order to yell at him, but he interrupted before she began.

"I am glad you made it here in one piece, Zaria. Please all of you sit down. You are making me uncomfortable." They were compelled to find seats. "You are no doubt thinking I lied about the cure. You are half right: I do not have it *yet*. But I will have it soon."

"When?" Zaria was pissed off about being misled, and cut straight to the chase. Aisling was impressed and decided she like this new woman. Iwizadi however, laughed softly. Was his voice weaker than usual? Aisling wondered.

"When Chuluun returns with the Halasetters," he answered. Seeing their confused faces, he explained further. "I know how to make the cure, but I need additional power from more magic users. That is one reason I have summoned you, Zaria."

"So, I help you with additional power, then you give me the cure, then I can go home?" she asked directly. Iwizadi nodded, but Aisling, who was the only person in the room unaware of Zaria's ability, was surprised.

"You have magic?" she asked. Like Khuch had been earlier that day, she thought that nobody in the eastern continent had magic.

"Yes," Zaria answered. "Since I was young."

"How can it be? I thought the Khun and Halasetters were the only magical peoples," she asked Iwizadi.

"Well, there's your answer," he replied. "In Zaria's lineage there is Halasat blood."

"No, that's not true," Zaria butted in. "As a member of the royal family, I can safely say that my family history can be accurately traced back to ancient days. Way back, to the time when the provinces of Naha were united."

"How long ago was that?" Iwizadi pressed her.

"Almost nine hundred years ago."

"Is it not at all possible that in all that time, just one of your ancestors could have been one of the descendants of Halasat? Or that there could be an ancestor from before that time?"

"Our family records are perfect."

"Then I suggest you study them closer." He did not care

that he had insulted her. "You have an ancestor who is descended from me. The royal blood in Naha is magic blood."

"It's nonsense," Zaria said. Aisling and Khuch watched in surprise. "If the royal family is magical, why am I the only one who can do it? Why does our history never mention magic? Why can't we win the stupid war with Nyika?"

"Think about it, Zaria," Iwizadi affected a rare patience that Aisling thought sinister. He was never so patient with her. "You have always felt like you were different to those around you. Like they lack imagination." She nodded, but retained her fierce expression. "Imagination is the key to magic. It is, in a way, its own kind of magic. For generations, Nahan adults have had only the war on their minds, unable to think of anything else. But you were unique in giving your imagination attention. You gave it space to grow, and when you did that, you allowed your magic a place to develop."

"You're saying that for our entire history, the Nahan royal family has lacked imagination and sacrificed its magic?"

"Exactly that, yes. It is a good summary."

"I don't believe you."

"You will." His confidence was off-putting, as he casually leaned back in his chair. "Now that you are here, you might as well give Aisling some help with leading the city while we wait for our other magical friends and family to arrive. You have experience with leadership do you not?"

"I don't think so," Zaria shook her head and stood up to leave. "I don't trust you. Sorry, Aisling, I can't help you. I'm going home."

"It is a shame," he tutted. "I really could use your help in developing the cure when the others arrive." She hesitated at the door, remembering the reason she had come. She also remembered Rainer and her promise to herself, and put a hand on the doorknob. She was never again to be a victim of destiny.

"Please stay, Zaria." Aisling took Zaria's hand and looked imploringly into her eyes. She sent a tiny pulse of Love magic into the stranger. Her eyes were a very dark blue, and up close, Aisling recognised a faint similarity in their features. Maybe Iwizadi was right, and they were descended from the same people. "At least, please stay awhile and we can try to build a relationship between our countries. I have so many questions about Naha, and I'm sure you have questions about the Khun. I can share what I know about the western continent too."

Maybe Zaria recognised the similarities too. Either that, or it was Aisling's transparent honesty that was enough to convince Zaria that she still could gain a lot from her time on Gazar. She decided to stay. It would be interesting to see the ways they use magic.

"You are welcome to stay with us in our home while you are here," Khuch offered. Aisling nodded enthusiastically.

"Thank you," Zaria said, "But what about the people who think I am a spy? Your friends in the city were not happy about my presence. Maybe I would be safer staying here in the mountain." She looked at Iwizadi, but he had stopped paying attention to the conversation. He wasn't interested in the trivial details about where Zaria stayed. She felt a flash of anger again when she saw his arrogance. He didn't care about her. She still wasn't sure why he made her come. He knew something about the disease that he wasn't telling them.

"We can handle them," Aisling said confidently. "Ychir knows he can't win a fight against me."

Zaria laughed a little because she imagined Ychir's massive bulk losing a fight with Aisling's thin and tiny frame, but quickly stopped when she saw that no one else was laughing.

"You're serious?"

"You're safe with me."

"How will you convince them I'm not a spy?"

"How do I know you aren't?"

The two women smiled at each other, recognising that they had a lot in common.

"Iwizadi," Zaria addressed the wizard again without trying to disguise her distaste for him. "When were you going to tell Aisling and the people here that there is a Nahan army gathered just across the sea to the east?" Aisling's jaw fell open and she glared at Iwizadi. He glanced up at Zaria lazily.

"They aren't going to be a problem."

"What?" Aisling demanded.

"They are sick. They won't try to invade for a long time."

"We still have a right to know!"

"Why worry about something that doesn't matter?"

"It matters to us!" Aisling shouted. Zaria had to agree. There was something about Iwizadi that didn't sit well with her. The way he kept things hidden.

"Then why didn't you find out yourself?"

"I-"

"I am not here to run Libalele for you."

"Then what the hell are you here for?" Zaria butted in. "You don't do anything but keep secrets and lure foreign women to you with lies."

Everyone was silent after hearing that. Even Iwizadi was taken aback with Zaria's brutal appraisal. Aisling felt a great admiration for her, and decided she wanted her to stay as long as possible.

"You will leave my office now," he said patiently. "My

life's work is too complicated to explain. When Chuluun returns we will create the cure, and you can go home."

Deeply unsatisfied, but unwilling to argue further, Zaria and Aisling left the mountain with Khuch in tow. Their energies matched well and they quickly got along and began talking about their own lands. They made their way back home, leaving Iwizadi to be alone, engrossed in his self-indulgence. Aisling was happy to answer any questions about Gazar, and Khuch helped clarify things when she needed him. Zaria was especially interested in magic, because she had never been able to discuss it with anyone before. She thought smugly and with disgust that Athena would be able to find some way of turning such beautiful power into propaganda, or justification for the invasion.

Zaria also had a million questions about Iwizadi and on their first day, Aisling barely had any opportunity to ask her own questions about Naha.

As they walked from the mountain to their home, Zaria noticed the hard stares they received from various people along the way. She had seen that type of stare before from people in her own city as they watched guards bring Nyikan prisoners to the castle dungeon. Zaria thought Aisling must be either very brave or very stupid to have such confidence in her own magic that she could be her own bodyguard. But not having seen her strength, she also wondered if there might be a reason for her confidence. They did not see Ychir, but Zaria recognised his interpreter from during the interrogation. He froze where he was walking in the street and stared at her with mistrust. Aisling met his gaze and he then bore a look of wounded pride. Only Khuch kept his head down. His shame was on full display.

"It must be hard for you, Khuch, to be a bridge between cultures." She put a hand on his forearm and he lifted his head. Aisling wished she had been the one to comfort Khuch instead and felt a pang of jealousy, but realised she was being stupid. There was no reason to be jealous. Khuch nodded and made nothing of the possibly flirtatious touch.

"Hard for both of us," he said. Zaria was very interested. She imagined it would be like a Nahan man marrying a Nyikan woman. It seemed impossible. "Aisling was not born Khun, but grew up with us and knows our culture."

"Why did that happen? Where were you from originally?"

"I was born in Capital country, but when I was five, my dad and I moved in with a group of Khun that he knew."

"Why did he do that?"

"He kind of hated the government we had over there. He said living with the Khun was much better. He was right, it was a very good place to grow up. After knowing about magic, I can't imagine trying to live without it." She remembered the frustration she felt when she was kept prisoner in an anti-magic building. Not knowing how to use the Noi-powered technology was horrible.

"He sounds like he had a point," Zaria said, thinking about how many times she had wanted to run from her own government and live where nobody could find her. It would have been a huge scandal though, for the princess and heir to the Nahan throne to disappear. She wondered what they were saying about her now. "Where is he now?"

"A few months ago, he became a Fire master," Aisling said, feeling the same pain she always did when talking about Peter. "He is in every Fire spell we use."

"What is a master?" Zaria asked.

"Sometimes, magic chooses a user more strongly. When it happens, they escape death and become part of the magic itself," explained Aisling.

"It is a great honour in our culture. It is very rare," Khuch added. Zaria was mystified. Athena's teachings had been completely inadequate and inaccurate. She was expecting to meet cavemen living in flimsy wooden shelters, but here she saw an advanced society with culture and violence and a vision for their future.

When she was in the western provinces with Rainer it was the same feeling. Seeing that the toxic atmosphere of violence in the castle did not extend to the friendly towns they passed through, she had to wonder if her perception of other peoples had been tainted. Did her dad know the truth about people too?

But master or not, Aisling had lost her father. Even coming from a nation of war, Zaria felt sorry for her.

"I'm sorry for your loss," she offered a token phrase and touched her arm lightly.

"Thank you." Aisling put a hand on Zaria's, and in an instant, they both felt a spark of recognition. Though neither of them could name the feeling, they both knew that some ancient forces had conspired for them to meet.

On the way home, Aisling and Khuch explained to Zaria how Iwizadi had seized power through violence, after the Khun had returned home and fought off the soldiers from the Capital. They told her how easy it was for him to overpower the whole population on his own. They didn't tell her about Substance M, and how the Capital was distilling the essence of magic into an injectable supplement for its army.

They reached their home and went inside, closing the door behind them. Khuch started to prepare tea in the hospitable way he had been taught. Aisling and Zaria sat at the table and chatted. Maria wasn't home. They didn't know where she was, but guessed she was probably with her friend Sanakh.

"You said Chuluun left two months ago?" Zaria asked.

"That's right," Aisling answered. "About that long ago. Maybe a bit more or less, it's hard to keep track of time. He ought to be at Halasat by now."

"And when he comes back, he will bring more magic people with him?"

"That was Iwizadi's plan," Aisling said, looking at her hands. Her discomfort was obvious to Zaria. Khuch's too. "Then when they get here, apparently Iwizadi can use all their magic together to cure the disease. I don't know if I believe it."

"After what I've heard about him, neither do I," Zaria said. "But surely when these people arrive, the Khun will be unhappy?"

"Exactly right," Aisling said. "That's why they hate him. He says the city belongs to them, and he will simply allow the Khun to live here. They want him gone. He is just another invader to them."

"And to you?"

"I think maybe he has caused more harm than good."

"But you listen to him?"

"I need help," Aisling admitted. "He put me in charge of running the city, just because he says we're related. I didn't want it! But I couldn't let him threaten the people again, so I agreed. Chuluun would have been a much better choice, but instead he's been sent on a stupid mission that will ultimately force the Khun from their homes again!"

"And the Khun still don't accept you?"

"Some do and some don't. Most of the ones who I grew up with know that I'm just like them. But there are lots more who think I'm just another foreign invader. Ychir is their leader. I've already had to use force to make him back down. I worry there will be a more organised assault soon. I don't want to have to force him again, or worse, if I have to force a group of them."

Zaria nodded slowly and remembered the growing uneasiness she felt back home. There were the people who felt bold enough to criticise the king and the war at their own risk. There were the voices of those who said that the government was their enemy, not the Nyikans. Rainer agreed that the people could revolt at any time with the right provocation. She saw the same conditions taking place on the island. The difference was, Aisling wanted to help the people whereas her father didn't care. What the hell did Iwizadi want?

"Some people in Naha also think the government is illegitimate," she spoke up. "Maybe I can help you. But I don't know what I can do." Khuch laid out a pot of fragrant tea and some snacks made from local foods. Zaria looked at the food and realised Athena had said nothing about what the Khun eat. It was all propaganda. Athena must have known and deliberately didn't include it in her history.

"Would you really?" Aisling took Zaria's hand over the table. "Thank you."

"Don't thank me yet. I haven't done anything." She picked up a small biscuit piled with a slimy green thing. It looked awful but smelt very good. "I think I have a lot to learn too. And a lot to unlearn." She put the biscuit in her mouth and chewed, slowly at first. Then her eyes widened in surprise and she ate another one. It tasted vaguely like sweet mustard and had a spongy texture. It was very nice, but unlike anything she had ever tried.

"Unlearn?"

"Where I'm from, all the information is controlled by the government. Everything is only half true at best." She saw Khuch looking on approvingly as she decided which food to try next and had a feeling that the basic rules of hospitality were pretty much the same all over the world.

"That sounds like Iwizadi." Aisling ate a piece of a hard crumbly cheese made from the milk of a local creature that was similar to the goats she knew from where she grew up. Zaria nodded. Khuch was silent through the conversation. He had always preferred to listen to others than to talk. "And the Capital. My dad used to complain about the news being propaganda, even before I knew what that meant. There's nothing new about it."

"It seems like Ychir knows how to use it too," Zaria said. "He's convinced people that you don't deserve to be here, even if you do belong here and fought to save it from the Capital." Aisling remembered with regret that it had been her plan to manipulate Ychir and use his influence to turn the people against her.

"I keep trying to tell them I'm one of them. But I don't want to deliver my own propaganda. It feels wrong to tell half the truth."

"It might be the only way to get people on your side."

"But if the people are with me, then Iwizadi will be against me. That's the only way to get them on my side: to join them against him. And if I do any work with him, then Ychir just tells everyone that it proves his point about me. I'm stuck."

"Let me think about it overnight. I might remember some more examples from my father's time as king."

"Thank you again."

The conversation lightened somewhat after that, and Zaria was happy to share information about Naha. Aisling and Khuch were curious about such mundane things like what people wore and what they ate, and most importantly how they lived without magic. Aisling and Khuch knew how things worked with a heavy reliance on Noi in the Capital, but they were surprised to learn that Naha was not as technologically advanced as the Capital. They had only recently invented Noi-powered transportation, and a lot of people still relied on communal batteries, whereas in the Capital, most homes had a personal power supply. Yet the Nahans claimed they were on top of the world. They made noise like they were the biggest, the strongest, and the best. And they always wanted more.

The three of them talked and ate until it became dark, and Khuch set up a makeshift bed, saying he would find or build a proper one in the morning. Maria still had not come home, which was unusual, but not a cause for concern. Khuch went outside and called to a local owl, asking it to return any news of Maria.

They all went to bed happy. Khuch fell asleep quickly as usual, while Aisling lay awake next to him. But instead of her mind being occupied by stress as it had been every night recently, she was thinking about how nice it was to have Zaria stay with her. It was nice to have a friend.

In the next room, Zaria was thinking the same thing about Aisling. But she was also thinking about Rainer. Since parting ways, he kept coming into her thoughts when there was a quiet moment with nothing else to occupy her mind. She thought about what he said about destiny, and what it meant that she would be staying on the island longer while waiting for Chuluun to return. Wasn't that what she wanted all along? To stay and learn about magic with the Khun? But since Rainer entered her life, she felt like destiny was pulling her towards him, and that the island might be just a distraction, or a way to him. Or maybe she was destined to be unhappy.

The owl began its nightly rounds, hiding camouflaged in

trees and hunting a few mice from the grasses in the valley. It had promised to wake Khuch if it saw Maria anywhere. Shortly after midnight, it rapped on Khuch's window and told him that Maria was with Sanakh, and she was okay.

The owl had little interest in human affairs. It cared about feeding and finding a mate, and that was it.

Though it was past midnight, Maria was awake in Sanakh's home. It was a cool night and the house smelt of garlic from their meal earlier. Since confiding in Sanakh her worries about mastery, Maria had spent more and more time with her friend. It was a difficult time, and the effects of Mind magic were getting stronger with every day. Maria could hardly sleep, and when she did, her dreams were not her own. Nobody warned her that transitioning to mastery would be so uncomfortable. They only ever talked about it as a good thing.

She wished it would either go faster or leave her alone. It was torturous to suffer under a barrage of alien thoughts. But Sanakh was kind and helpful, and kept Maria's secret.

That night as she lay awake, Maria decided it was now or never. She thought she might not have the strength of will the next day to perform the dreaded task she had been putting off since Orn left.

While Sanakh slept, Maria felt her dreams. Not by choice, but because her Mind magic was insatiably hungry for the thoughts of others. It was spreading further and further, and she often was faced with the thoughts of more than one other person. It became difficult to prise them apart, they all bled into one.

Sanakh's dreams were peaceful. That night she dreamt of a simpler time from before the war. She dreamt of Chuluun, too, and Maria had her suspicions confirmed that Sanakh was in love with him.

It was difficult to concentrate under the constant inflow of various thoughts, but Maria sat still and tried her best to empty her mind. Then just as she had done a hundred times before, she began to send a searching plume of smoke out towards her target. She didn't feel worried about the distance between her and the mountain anymore. The Mind magic that was slowly taking over her existence transcended the limitations of space. She felt she could travel the world through others' thoughts.

Iwizadi was awake, too. There was no evidence that he ever slept.

She found him in his study as usual, writing in his book, and without hesitating, she attached her mind to his. His thoughts began to fill the space she had emptied for them in her mind. She felt no bump this time, just a completely smooth transition.

And she saw into his mind.

At first glance, it was similar to any other that she had visited. He had all the landmarks that would help her if she got lost. He had all the same emotions as anyone else. For the first time, he seemed human to her, and not like a supernatural being.

But his mind was neither tormented nor calm. Instead, it was in a state that Maria did not recognise. She saw his thoughts swirling all towards a central place. Everywhere she looked, every thought was directed at one thing. There were traces of it in everything. Most minds were a jumble of random thoughts, but Iwizadi's was an organised funnel, all pointing to one thing.

His was a mind consumed with obsession.

But in the place where his thoughts converged, occupying the centre of his mind, there was a confusing blob. Impossible to make out what it represented from the outside. Maria knew she had to push through to see it from the inside, to find out what it was that Iwizadi was obsessed with.

She hesitated for a moment, fearing that he could discover her. But there were no signs that he knew about her intrusion, so she approached his central thoughts, and peered inside beyond the curtain of chaotic convergence.

Maria, like every other child in the world, had grown up with a local fairy tale. She had heard the story of Iwizadi the rebel, told by all parents in the Capital. That was all she knew of his life. Half a truth, diluted by centuries of retellings and forgetting.

When she first saw inside his obsession, she was amazed by its simplicity. For all the power of the mind outside directing its entire being into a singularity, the obsession itself was remarkably calm. Maria could easily see what it was about and begin to trace its origins.

But she did not lose sight of her mission to discover his motives and future plans.

She saw that despite Iwizadi's plotting and threats, he wanted one thing, and one thing only: To transform Libalele – Khot – into a glorious city of magic, and to live as its leader until the day he died.

"Why?" she said to herself. "Why hide behind violence and treachery? Why not just tell the truth and ask for help?"

She started to look further back in time and look for reasons, for answers to her questions. And when she did so, she ran into the name Umwahu in many threads of his obsession. Umwahu, she knew was his brother's name, but why was he so important to Iwizadi's vision?

As she continued to search for answers and trace the various threads to their sources, she ignored other things along the way. Hidden doors leading to doubts. It wasn't what she had come to see, but it was interesting to see that they were there. Iwizadi was just a man, after all.

There were old thoughts of Khun, too, stretching back a very long way. But Maria chose not to investigate their origins. She was looking for his plans.

One of the threads of Umwahu led to a memory of two young boys fighting. Like Peter and Jack. Maria couldn't help making a comparison to her husband and his brother. He was just a man.

Many more threads led to childhood memories, but many others led to a complete nothingness that was accompanied by the word Nightmare. Maria dared not continue a thread when it led there. Some things were supposed to be private, even from oneself.

He was sick, and he was hiding it from everyone. He was suffering from the same disease that affected half of Gazar. It was making him frail and cough blood. And he knew he couldn't hide it forever. Maria felt a sting of pity for him, knowing that he was sick and dying, and working tirelessly towards an obsession. He was just a sick old man.

Then by luck, one of the memories of Umwahu ended at the emptiness of the Nightmare. Maria watched a scene unfold, and she saw the complete memory of the day that Libalele was destroyed. She cried as she watched Iwizadi murder councillor Nekinso in the chambers that she had spent many days in. She cried watching the prisoners run loose through the city and take revenge on their friends and neighbours. She cried as Iwizadi burst in on the councillors performing the Hymn to the Mountain and causing the city to tear itself apart. The sound of the song was still there in Iwizadi's memory.

Maria pulled herself away from the terrible memory. She had never in her life thought such destruction and cruelty was possible. She was in a place of hate and wanted to leave.

Returning to the centre of the obsession, she turned another direction and followed a different thread with Umwahu's name. This time, she found herself looking at the vagaries of the mind. She recognised this as a section of the mind that contained plans and futures. This was what she hoped to find.

But it was unclear what she was looking at. There was Umwahu and Nightmare everywhere. And magic. And when she passed through a darkness and emerged on the other side, she was surrounded by a proud city. There, she could see no more mention of Umwahu or Nightmare.

He was dreaming of a future with neither, but there was still a part of his plan missing. Maria felt as though she had failed Orn, unable to see a complete view of what Iwizadi wanted.

But it was better than nothing.

Suddenly there was a rumble.

The mind shifted around her, and Maria heard a voice say: "Who are you?"

It had never happened before, but she had always known that it could happen. She was discovered. She had spent too long looking at his thoughts and digging up deep, old memories and he had figured it out.

"Who are you?" he repeated. All the thoughts of his mind turned to uncovering the identity of the intruder, and Maria saw herself everywhere she looked. He knew. "What are you doing?" But he thought to himself, shielding this doubt from Maria: *You aren't the same one as last time.*

Maria regretted not having done this earlier. As powerful as her Mind magic was getting, receiving random passing thoughts of people in the city, it must have been easy for Iwizadi to detect.

"You know, Maria." His thoughts felt like they were crushing her. "You should trust me more. You are one of the chosen people." It was deafening to be surrounded by such concentration and she fell to the ground.

"I have to go. I'm going now." She tried to crawl towards the point where she had entered the obsession. She tried to remember how to get there, but it all looked different now.

"No," he told her. "You aren't going. Why would I let you leave?"

"Let me help you destroy them," she bargained.

"What would you know?" But he understood that she probably learned all she needed already.

"You want a future without Umwahu." She was trying hard to find something he could use. "But you don't know how to do it yet. Let me help you create the future for the city that you dream about." She felt the crushing pressure of his focus relent a little, and she stood up.

"The future of the city is the future of all magic, and Umwahu threatens my vision," he said. "He will soon have broken free from the Nightmare, and he will come for me. There will be no future for magic unless I destroy the Nightmare with him inside. I have the Khun to help, and our people are on their way. They are all I need to destroy him."

So that was it. That was what Iwizadi wanted all along. That was what Aisling was trying to do by turning the Khun against her. It wasn't about politics or a chosen race. It was personal. It was just like Peter versus Jack. In their battle, nobody won, Maria thought. Peter became Fire, Jack was murdered, and everyone who loved them had to live with loss. It was Iwizadi versus Umwahu, and nobody was going to win.

"Your fight with Umwahu will make us all losers." When

she spoke, every surface of his obsession became a catastrophic maelstrom of anger and self-righteous arrogance.

"You don't know him at all! There is no way for you to help me!" The pressure of his concentration returned and Maria felt like all of her body was deep underwater and she couldn't move. "He is pure destruction. If I don't stop him, he will destroy everything."

"Stop! You're hurting me." She gasped for air, feeling that her lungs could explode from the effort.

And that's when it happened. Maria was no longer there in Iwizadi's mind. Distantly in Sanakh's house, Maria's body sat still, radiating Mind magic strong enough to wake Sanakh. She could not be shaken from her trance, and Sanakh realised that the moment had arrived for her transformation.

Iwizadi was furious and his mind raged.

Maria felt it.

She felt every mind.

She was every mind.

Sanakh watched as Maria's body melted away into a shimmering reflection of itself, and disappeared into a memory. She felt sad for losing her friend, but forced herself to see the positive side of the transformation. The world had gained another master. Mind magic had gained the power of Maria. She would always be there in every spell.

Chapter 6

After the fiasco that was Operation Blue, the Capital was forced to rethink its approach. Unfortunately, days after the failed attempt to steal the book, Leader Abe Brown had overdosed on Substance M, leaving a power vacuum in the most technologically advanced nation on the planet.

Abe's secretary had been the first to find him, collapsed on the floor of his office. He was unable to move, but his pupils were enormous and he had an expression of bliss on his face. He told her it was wonderful, then he stopped breathing.

For those few who knew about Substance M, it was no secret that it was dangerously addictive. Nor was it a secret that Abe was fond of it, or that Jack Hargreaves – the Department director and Peter's brother – was Abe's personal supplier. Nobody knew what had happened to Jack, other than he had never returned from Blue Island. He was presumed dead.

When Abe heard that Jack was missing after the ill-fated Operation Blue, like any addict he panicked about how he could maintain his habit. Sure, the Department was still operational, but Jack had been the one who turned a blind eye to the occasional missing vial. He would have requested Miss Morris continue Jack's vital work, but she had strangely gone missing too, and there were rumours that she had helped two Participants escape. That was a serious crime if it were true.

Everything was falling apart for Abe. He weighed up his options. The Capital was a grand city and held a large territory rich with resources, but the people were unhappy. No matter what he tried, they couldn't be pleased. He tried giving them jobs and they just demanded more money. He tried giving them more Noi, but they complained it was too expensive. There were rumours of police and military disobedience in some of the smaller towns.

There was no pleasing everybody.

Abe opened a small back zippered case that contained all his remaining Substance M. Four vials. He had taken two on occasion, and felt like a wounded god. What would four be like? He didn't care for consequences at that moment, staring greedily at the shiny equipment. The Capital would be fine without him. The people didn't care for him or any of the things he had given them. It didn't mean anything anymore. The only thing that mattered was that he had four vials in his hand.

The first one felt the same as it always did. He enjoyed the initial discomfort as it entered his bloodstream, and the powerful surge of magic overtaking his being. This time though, he didn't play with magic the way he normally did. He was consumed with his own thoughts and was ready to continue. He waited until he had passed the discomfort and was feeling powerful.

A few minutes later, the second dose sent him into ecstasy. He could barely see for a minute, and felt as if he might float away, or like his head might lift off from his shoulders. Not even the soldiers in Blue Unit had taken this much during the assault on Gazar. He felt invincible. Maybe they should have had more, he thought. Maybe then they could have won.

But there would be nothing left for him when he came down. He had to take it all and he hoped never to come back. What a way to go, he thought. I wouldn't want to die any other way.

He used magic to prepare the third dose. With the magic effects of the drug pulsating through his body, he played with making the objects move in the air without touching them. Three was the most he had ever taken, and the shock of it nearly knocked him out. He could feel his neck straining and his veins and tendons all sticking out. It was tremendous. It was uncomfortable. It was exactly what he wanted. He flew across the room and looked out the window at the city below him. Even in the daylight, the blue glow of Noi illuminated the vista as far as he could see.

Marvellous progress. Noi is the future.

The third dose felt so fantastic that he nearly forgot he was trying to kill himself. He wanted nothing more than to feel that way forever. But he remembered the withdrawal was proportionate to the high. He had to continue. If Substance M didn't kill him, surely the aftermath would. If only there was a way to keep this high and never come down.

He barely registered the fourth dose. It crept up on him and surprised him. He saw that a needle was in his arm, then he saw that it wasn't. He felt like his veins would explode. His heart was pounding in his chest and beating fast. Time seemed to slow down. He felt unimaginably good.

Until he didn't.

He got what he wanted, and when he was found shortly thereafter, he passed from the world in a state so altered it might have been a dream.

But Abe wasn't dead. He didn't know the culture of magic, and nor did anybody in the Capital know that in exceptional circumstances, magic could create a master. On the other hand, the Khun had no idea that Substance M could pump so much concentrated magic into a person as to actually induce mastery.

But mastery of what?

His secretary backed away quickly when she saw him rise. He had no breath left in him, but somehow, he was upright, floating a little off the ground. He opened his eyes, and they glowed with the blue of Noi. The terrified secretary could not turn away, though she wanted to run. Her legs were paralysed with fear. She didn't know what she was looking at. A moment earlier, Abe Brown, Leader of the Capital, had been dead in her arms. Now, he – or a spirit that looked like him – floated serenely in front of her. She always knew they were developing unnatural things in the building, but not like this.

Shortly after the shocking reanimation, Abe's body and spirit were absorbed by the magic force that runs through the world. Not having been called by any particular magic, he couldn't be called a master technically. But nor was he dead. He was something else not alive, not dead, and not in a state of mastery, and for that reason, a debate raged in the Capital as to whether he could be allowed to continue ruling them.

Abe himself took no part in the debate, and was instead occupied with more spiritual matters. He enjoyed being a creature of magic much more than a human, but it came with the irritating side effect of not being able to communicate with humans in the usual way or interact with physical objects. He was something like a ghost, in the sense that the older, more superstitious generation in the Capital might have imagined them.

And while the elite of the Capital argued endlessly about what should happen to them, Abe used his newfound freedoms to explore the world and play with magic. He got what he wanted: the perpetual magical feeling of Substance M, and he was happy to watch the Capital fall apart. He didn't care about it anymore. It wasn't his problem.

He discovered he could connect his mind with other people and not only see their thoughts, but put his own thoughts in their heads. Maybe, he thought, he could finish what he started. Maybe then, the arguing would stop.

He set about exploring the world by sending his thoughts into other people. It was easy enough to do, being made of magic as he was, and each time he jumped between skulls he felt like he was driving through a tunnel very fast. It was not unpleasant. But rather than risk being found out, he pretended he was General Osbourne, the same bellicose, irritating, belligerent, undisciplined man in charge of Blue Unit. Serves him right, he thought, to have his reputation dragged through the mud.

Abe found his way to Gazar and explored the minds of some of the people he found there. There was a common theme occupying many thoughts and he quickly pieced together the events of Operation Blue. He learned why it had failed, and he learned about Iwizadi and Aisling. He learned how Jack had been tricked and killed by his own spell. That was true magic power, he thought. That was what he wanted. And he still could get it, he thought, if he could somehow steal the book containing all the magic knowledge ever recorded; the book Iwizadi was writing in. With the book, he might be able to transform himself into something even more magical and alive.

He quickly learned that an oafish Khun named Ychir was

leading the dissent, and he was an easy target. He began planting thoughts in Ychir's mind, and they started communicating from time to time. Abe convinced Ychir that they wanted the same thing. Abe would help depose Iwizadi by supplying troops, as long as Ychir helped steal the book first.

At first Ychir was reluctant, because the book was an important cultural artefact, but Abe wore down his resistance. Ychir made a deal with the voice in his head.

It was too easy, Abe thought.

After the failed negotiations the night Ychir and his supporters marched to the mountain, Abe made contact again. Ychir was embarrassed and worried that Abe would pull out of the deal if he didn't hurry up and steal the book. But Ychir also argued that the mountain was too heavily guarded and he needed Abe's soldiers to help. He needed the soldiers first in order to steal the book.

Abe said he would think about it, remembering that such a strategy had recently failed. Maybe he would have to think about a different way of getting to the book.

He tried searching Iwizadi's mind for details of its pages, but it was too hard to find any useful information in there. Everywhere he looked was about Umwahu and the Nightmare, and Abe gave up, just as Iwizadi began to notice him.

The news of Abe's disappearance was kept quiet for a time, but eventually the elite stopped arguing and put a woman named Alvilda in charge of a temporary government to at least keep the Capital operating as normally as possible, until a permanent leader could be established. Some people thought it was a good time to do away with the old laws of hereditary, lifelong leadership.

After Alvilda had been officially recognised as provisional

leader, she sent messages to the three nations on the eastern continent. With some deliberation, she chose to send a message to Blue Island too. If that pathetic little nation could finally establish itself, they would stop flooding the Capital with refugees, and that would be good for the people. They might be able to establish more naturalistic magic research on the island itself if relations were good.

The Kingdom of Arazi did not really care about the Capital. It was perpetually embroiled in civil war over petty territory disputes, and the occasional clash with Naha and Nyika. It sent a short message in reply, congratulating Alvilda.

Diplomacy done, she thought.

Nyika and Naha, on the other hand were very interested in the message. They both saw immediately that a change in the government in the west was an opportunity to gain the upper hand in their war. An ally as powerful as the Capital would be enough to win. Both nations wasted no time in sending a party of diplomats to meet and schmooze with the temporary government and win Alvilda's favour.

There were no permanent missions in the Capital. There had been none permitted since the time of Abe's father. That was a time of dramatic social change and technological advances, in which the Capital shut out contact with the rest of the world. Abe never bothered to reinstate diplomacy.

Alvilda however had been one of Abe's advisors for many years and an expert in international affairs. It was her job to know what other nations were doing and give Abe information to keep him ahead of the pack. He never listened of course. He never wanted to be leader, but it was Capital law that he inherit the post from his late father. He left all of the work to a team of ministers.

The parties from Naha and Nyika arrived on the same

day. They had both sailed from their respective seats far over on the east coast of their continent and were glad to see land. With their available technology, the trip took over four weeks. With Capital technology, it would have taken three days by air and sea. Alvilda was pleased to see their awestruck faces admire her nation's technology.

Though their route took them nowhere near Blue Island, the party from Naha would have liked to see how their army was faring at the naval base. Rumours were that over a third of them had died from the disease and they had never made it to the island.

In a show designed to intimidate, the parties were met at the docks and flown to the Capital in the latest model Noicraft. Neither Naha nor Nyika had invented safe air travel yet, and they were amazed by it. To further solidify the Capital's position in the meetings, Alvilda insisted that both parties be transported in the one Noicraft. It would send a message to them that they were the same to her.

"Welcome to Capital country," an official greeted the two waiting parties at the dock after disembarking from the craft. It was drizzling slightly, and they were standing under shelters on opposite sides of the dock. The Nahans had sent four diplomats. The Nyikans had sent three. They were to go to the Capital while their ships' crews remained in the hotel near the dock. All seven wore uniforms of high-ranking soldiers and had the looks of people who had witnessed combat, participated in its violence, and given orders to commit inhuman acts. The Capital official wanted to laugh at their backward, warmongering ways but thought better of it. He shook all of their hands.

"My name is Padraig. I represent the Capital government and have been sent to fly you to the city. This way please." He led them all to the Noicraft. They had seen it gracefully land and were greedily thinking of how they could make their own back home. None of their spies had done justice to the elegance of the machinery. They had imagined Noicraft to be loud and clunky, unsafe and gimmicky. But as they boarded now, they were bewildered by its smooth design and quiet engines. They did not even notice taking off until the official informed them that they would arrive within an hour.

"We have been locked out of diplomacy here for just one generation, and look what we have missed out on," whispered one of the Nahan representatives to his party. His name was Jan, and had served in the army for nearly twenty-five years. He was retired from active service due to an injury and had been pestering King Timofea for years to increase Naha's espionage capabilities.

"I see you all admiring the Noicraft," Padraig said. "It's our latest model. It uses a newly patented conversion engine. Barely feel a thing, but if you look out the window, you'll see just how fast we are moving." He spoke his own language. Both the Nyikan and Nahan parties were trained in it, but not yet fluent. They would be by the time their mission was over. The Capital did not bother to provide interpreters. It was another way of showing their dominance.

"What type of Noi engines do you use in your countries?" Padraig asked. "I'm ashamed to admit that we have little information about your technologies." He was lying. The Capital knew perfectly well that its guests had no aircraft. It had spies everywhere. He was trying to force them to feel ashamed of themselves.

"Our fleet uses another engine adapted from the navy," said one of the Nyikans, Lazor. The others nodded in agreement, not wanting to lose face in front of their potential new ally, while also boasting in front of their perennial enemy.

"Interesting," Padraig said, nodding sagely. "What kind of efficiency do you get?"

"It depends," answered Lazor evasively. He leaned back against the wall and folded his arms. His sleeves were rolled up, revealing immensely muscular forearms covered in elaborate swirling tattoos.

"On the extraction quality, of course." Padraig winked at him, knowing full well that Nyika was a land of scarce Noi deposits. That was why they wanted Blue Island. He had toyed with his guests enough for now, and didn't need to insult them openly before they even arrived at the city.

"Exactly," Lazor grunted, nodding. He glanced over at the Nahan delegation to see if there were any signs that they had believed him.

Realising that they could not bluff their way through technical discussions, the Nahans and Nyikans declined to talk any more about Noicraft for the remainder of the journey, and did their best to not look impressed.

But their eyes were glued to the windows when the city came into view. They had never seen such a huge expanse of manmade structures. Nor had they seen proof of the Capital's Noi wealth: the entire city was lit up and it was an imposing feat of architectural and technological opulence. For all of them it was like stepping into the future. Lazor and Jan shared a look that for a brief moment transcended their ancient feud and instead recognised their collective inadequacy. That look then turned to rivalry, for they both knew they had to be the one to gain the Capital's partnership. The race had begun.

"Quite a view, isn't it?" Padraig said. "No matter how many times I make this flight, it still takes my breath away.

See that tall building there? That's where we're headed."

In just a few more minutes they had landed on the roof of the Capital headquarters building. Alvilda and a small group of officials were there waiting to greet them. As they stepped out of the craft and onto the roof, Jan remembered to thank the pilot, and the Nyikans all rushed to follow suit, not wanting to seem like the ruder of the two nations. Instead, they just looked clumsy. The pilot smiled politely at them. After they had left, he burst out laughing.

"Welcome to the Capital," Alvilda said warmly. "I suppose you are all tired after your long journey. We will show you to your rooms and dinner will be served at eight. Tomorrow we can start formal meetings. For today, get some rest and enjoy the views of our spectacular city."

"Leader Alvilda," said one of the Nahan crew named Emil. "On behalf of all Naha, we thank you for your generous offer of hospitality and we hope that in the coming days we can work together to re-establish a friendly relationship between our nations. It has been far too long since we have welcomed each other." He tipped his head deferentially, and produced a bouquet of Nahan swampbush flowers. He presented it to her, and one of the other officials stepped forward to receive it. "This flower is the symbol of our nation. It grows beautifully while surrounded by ugliness."

"Thank you kindly," Alvilda replied. She grimaced, looking at the hideous flowers and hearing Emil's explanation.

Not to be outdone, one of the Nyikans, a man named Dmitri stepped forward with his own gift: a wreath of Nyikan vines.

"Leader Alvilda, on behalf of the great progressive nation of Nyika, we humbly thank you for your invitation. We hope that Nyika and the Capital can solidify our productive and friendly relationship, so that all the world benefits. These vines are our nation's pride. They grow uniquely on our slopes when the southerly wind sprays them with seawater."

Each of the delegates had their own room in the building. They were all on the same floor. Though none of them would ever admit it, the Nyikans and Nahans felt more similar than different compared to their Capital hosts.

"It's all Noi," Jan said to his party while they were meeting before dinner. "Everything they have is Noi. That's why we must secure the island. Naha could have all this."

They were in a meeting room in the building that had been set aside for the visiting delegation. There were comfortable chairs and an informal atmosphere. A tray of spirits was available, and they had each taken some shots of a local clear spirit. It had a flavour like blackberry but warmed their throats and bellies as it went down. Jan made a mental note that he must bring some back home.

"Yes, we know this," said Emil. "My question is what kind of deal we can strike with the Capital. Back when Nyika and Naha mined the island together and fought against Arazi, our deal was unfavourable. Can we get a better proportion if we work with the Capital instead? They already have so much Noi here, I think we should push for at least seventy percent."

"So, they do all the heavy lifting and we take the reward?" laughed Jan. "I think they will refuse. A country does not get this rich by giving away its prizes."

"My goal is for Nyika to get nothing," said Agnes, one of the other two members. "If we get something and they get nothing, the king should be happy."

"He would be happier if we get everything and defeat Nyika into the ground." Emil paced back and forth. The bullet wound in his cheek gave him a permanent scowl.

"Whatever we negotiate for ourselves doesn't matter, our first priority should be to ensure that Nyika walks away with nothing," said Ivan. He was the highest ranked of the group, and the others considered what he said. He sniffed back some mucus. Many of the crew had contracted colds while at sea. "When we are sure that they will not be supported by the Capital, we can start to negotiate our terms."

"But there is a risk of a bidding war," Jan said thoughtfully. "If we ask for seventy percent, they will say sixty. Our first priority should be to win the Capital's favour. Then we can negotiate our terms."

"And how will we do that?" Agnes asked. "They can't even tell us apart."

"Exactly. We will show them that we are more worthy. Show them that we are more capable of wielding technology, and more ready to live in this modern world. Show them that the Nyikans are not ready, and they are still cavemen." Jan answered passionately.

"It is a devious plan," admitted Ivan. He poured the group another round of shots. "Perhaps it is wise for us to listen first to the Capital's suggestions, and second to the Nyikan requests. Then we can think of the best arguments to offer in order to upstage them. Yes, Jan, you are right. We will show them that there is no point in arming Nyika and supplying them with technology. A toast!" They raised their glasses and banged them down on the table before drinking the contents.

In an identical meeting room at the other end of the building, the Nyikan trio were having the exact same conversation. They boasted about how they came to Naha's rescue back in the day when the Arazi pirates threatened to take over Blue Island, and had their own toasts to celebrate.

Lazor thought the drink reminded him of the medicine used to treat gangrene in the army.

"I think if we are ever to win the war against Naha, we will need the Capital as our ally. Before coming here, we underestimated their power. With them on our side, Naha will be forced to admit defeat," Lazor argued. He refilled their glasses.

"So let them do what they want on the island, as long as we are supplied with weapons and training." Dmitri gave Lazor a hard stare. He had bright blue eyes and a powerful jawline. Lazor could not tell if he was agreeing or being sarcastic.

"The island is not the main focus of the war. We want to crush Naha into dust and claim its land for Nyika. With Capital weaponry, we can defeat them before they have a chance to benefit from the Noi on the island."

"What do you think, Bogdan?" Dmitri turned to face the third man. He was leaning against the wall, and was tall and thin. He had a very plain face, and his expression was very private. In spite of his recognisable height, he had worked as a spy in the Nahan army for many years before retiring to his current ministerial career. Lazor and Dmitri both considered his opinion to be final, and respected his extensive experience.

"A swift attack will not be expected," he intoned. Maybe it was his boring way of speaking that helped him in espionage. People could easily lose interest in him if he wanted them to. "I think it is a reasonable, yet daring, approach to victory. Depending what the Nahan pigs want from the Capital, it could work."

"I expect they will be focused on the island and Noi production," said Lazor.

"I agree. We should let them think they are getting the

better deal by us negotiating poorly for control over the island, but make a deal separately to benefit our army at home."

The Nyikans finished their first bottle of spirits with endless toasting. They saw that there was plenty of time before dinner and opened another.

In the room that used to be Abe's office, Alvilda was holding an impromptu meeting with the senior officials. Abe was not there. He was somewhere stuck between the magical and physical worlds, travelling through the minds of others and enjoying freedoms he never knew possible.

"I assume that they are both here to win their war," she lounged back in Abe's chair with her feet up on the desk. The other officials were relaxing around the room very casually too. A few were smoking huge cigars. "Each one will be trying to drag us into their problems. It should be amusing to watch."

"Remind us why you invited them?" A man in a double-breasted jacket with a combover asked. His name was Dara, and he had previously been an advisor to Abe. His specialty was gauging the volatility of labour unions and public sentiment. Dara was thin and balding and ageing, but pretended he wasn't. Before working in government, he had been in the construction industry. After losing a finger on a worksite, he began campaigning for workers' rights to safety. He was then picked up by the government and turned into an industrial spy, allowed to continue his work with the unions as long as he gave insider information in return. He saw nothing wrong with that.

"Because we can use them. This country has been closed to the world for decades. With a change in leadership, it is a good time to start afresh and join in with the rest of the world." Alvilda was pleased to find that her commitment to learning about the world's political systems had finally paid off in power and respect. Powerful men were listening to her expertise. It was a nice feeling. She was aware that she was the only woman in the room.

"It is pleasing to see how backward they are compared to us." Dara sat on a leather armchair, sprawled out with one leg resting high on an arm. His gangly limbs took up a lot of space and he looked like a giant spider.

"Yes. But there is much more to it than that. By re-opening our country, we are going to look like the type of country that people wouldn't mind having as a world leader. We can show them that we are and always will be on top of the world." She gesticulated enthusiastically with her cigar but her tone was flat and driven by facts and logic.

"So, it benefits us beyond mere diplomatic relations."

"There is much more."

"What then?"

"We all agree that the Capital is the clear leader of this world. In terms of money, power, technology, labour laws… you name it, we are the best." There was general approval around the room. "So, I say we are not ambitious enough. Under Abe Brown's leadership this country stagnated. It lost all the momentum it had gained under the previous leader. I want to bring that momentum back. The Capital deserves more territory."

"As much as I agree with you, how does it help us to treat the representatives from Naha and Nyika like partners rather than subjects? What's stopping us from simply conquering them? The old-fashioned way," asked another man sitting on a sofa at the back of the room. His name was Sean and he was average in every way imaginable. He was the minister for energy, a post he had gained through unwavering dedication and regular attendance.

"I have given it a lot of thought, and there are very good reasons. You need to think more long-term. You're right, we *could* simply walk all over them with our army, but in the long term that will create resentment among them towards us. Ten, maybe twenty years later they will organise a revolt."

"So, we make them like us first?" Sean was not a shrewd politician like the others. His specialty was Noi and how to dig it out of the earth.

"Exactly. But there is still more to it. What is it that they are fighting over? Does anyone know?" The officials looked around at each other for confirmation. They shrugged and shook their heads. "Nobody knows. I doubt they do either. Their war has gone on for so long that they've all forgotten what it's about. That's the level of intelligence we're dealing with," she laughed and pulled on her cigar. The others all laughed too. She blew out a huge cloud of smoke. "But one thing we do know, is that for nearly twenty years now, they have been trying to take control of Blue Island." *And we benefited*, she thought, considering the influx of refugees that had led to the development of Substance M and the discovery of magic. She couldn't say it out loud because not everyone knew about magic yet.

"Blue Island is our leverage, then? We can help them get something they want. But don't we want the Noi on the island too?" Sean asked.

"Yes. But think more broadly. If they are at war with each other, we have less work to do. They can continue tearing each other apart until one day we walk in as their 'friend and ally', and end the war. And we can do that in such a way that we install our own 'peacekeeping' institutions and they will be grateful to us." It dawned on the officials that with a little patience, the Capital could be able to double its territory with very little effort. They all became very excited. "We have so much Noi here we can afford to wait. We let them fight over Blue Island to the death, then we walk in and take it."

"That's a very sneaky plan. So, you intend to prolong their war? How exactly will we do that?" Dara asked.

"We will have to wait to find out how they try to negotiate tomorrow. They will reveal what they want. I expect they will try to betray each other in some way, or outbid each other in private meetings with us." Through the large windows they could see the sun setting and the colours of daylight changed to an ethereal mixture of reds from the sky and blues from the Noi.

"That sounds fair."

"In practical measures, they will likely ask us for military or financial or technological support. What they do with these, I don't really care. Give them outdated Noi weapons. It will still be an advancement over what they currently have. Watch them go wild and decimate their own populations." She got up and inspected Abe's liquor cabinet. She pulled out an aged bottle of unopened whisky. Eyeing it with approval, she showed it to the room and they nodded enthusiastically. It let out a strong oaky smell when she opened it and poured a few glasses and handed them out. She sat back down and put her feet up again, took another pull of the cigar, then sipped at the whisky while the smoke remained in her mouth. She swallowed and then exhaled a great thick cloud with pleasure.

"Is there a risk of them reverse engineering the technology? Or using it against us? I'm trying to think long-term, as you say." Dara was still sprawled out, now with a glass in one hand, waving around for emphasis. Instead of a spider, now he looked like a marionette controlled by an inexperienced puppeteer and its strings tangled.

"Yes, of course there is a risk. We can't meddle in international affairs without some risk to ourselves. But there is so much to gain, remember. There are things that mitigate the risk, however. First and most importantly, we have to remember that their lands are not as rich in Noi as ours is, and they don't even know how to extract it properly. Even if they could reverse engineer our tech, they wouldn't be able to generate enough power to mass produce them. Second, over the long-term, our country will have established and maintained friendly relations with both, and they will feel gratitude to us for helping them in their war. They will not turn against us if they think we treat them right."

It was cunning and devious, and a defining moment in Alvilda's career. She was absolutely certain that it would work, and would be exactly what she needed to convince the officials that she should be elected Leader permanently, not just temporarily.

"I agree with the plan," Dara said, fiddling with his combover while taking a drink from his glass. He still had one leg draped leisurely over the arm of the chair, while the other tapped out a rhythm to a tune he remembered from the morning. All of his limbs moved independently, but his words were focused and accurate. "A distraction like Blue Island and the stupid Nahan-Nyikan war is perfect. We have things they want. We make them feel like they are gaining power from us, but we orchestrate it so that ultimately, they both lose, and we win their lands."

"What about the local population on Blue Island? Or the Arazi?" asked another attendee, Rory. He had been silent until then, smoking cigarettes continually. When he wasn't allowed to smoke, he chewed gum, and he constantly smelled of tobacco. His eyes had huge drooping bags under them and he always had a thick layer of stubble and a greasy appearance. People tended to avoid him, but he was one of the Capital's most respected engineers and led the team that developed the latest model Noicraft using a design he stole from Peter.

"What about them?" Alvilda asked shortly. "The Khun are a primitive people and the Arazi are disorganised barbarians. They pose us no threat. All we will do with them is keep them on their own land and prevent any more refugees from reaching us."

"Threat to us or not, you should remember the parts they have played in the war on Blue Island. They are wild cards, both of them. Maybe the Khun are harmless as you say, but are they not currently back on the island after having won some disastrous battle against us? And the Arazi have been known to hijack boats and blow up our ports. And for a long time, the Nahan and Nyikan armies actually teamed up against their hold on the Noi on the island."

"Then we use them. They will probably try similar things again in the future, but by that stage we will be able to install some of our own troops on Blue Island. The Arazi wouldn't dare attack us. They might be impulsive and ignorant, but they are not suicidal. Things will continue the way we plan them."

"Perhaps you are right." His voice was gravelly and he had too much mucus in his throat that he constantly tried to clear. Alvilda wished he wouldn't talk. "What if one of our enemies decides to arm the Khun? There are a great many of them, all with a land to defend."

"The Nahans and Nyikans are too stupid to do that. They only care about their war, and they see the Khun as just another inconvenience."

"I think it's worth considering, no matter how unlikely." Rory had the attention of the room, and begrudgingly Alvilda agreed.

"Okay then, let's say hypothetically that Naha manages to organise the Khun into an armed force. How would they be able to convince them of that without any risk to themselves? The Nahans and Nyikans want the Khun marginalised and out of the way."

"Then what if Arazi steps in and offers to make a deal with the Khun to drive out their invaders in return for Noi?"

"Arazi scum and the primitive Khun, working together to defeat a combined Nyikan and Nahan army?" Alvilda laughed loudly. "Think about what you're saying."

Though Rory was laughed into complacency, he stewed over the remote possibilities. In engineering Noicraft, not one single possibility could be ignored, else they risked explosion or malfunction. Alvilda was too cocky, he thought. She acted as though she had all the answers, but she refused to look at every possible outcome. *If she was on my team, I would have sent her back to school.*

Dara and Sean both agreed with Alvilda that such an outcome was so unlikely as to be not worth considering. At eight o'clock they all made their way to the official welcome dinner for the guests. Rory trailed behind his colleagues, gloomily considering the possibility that he was right. The Khun were an unknown player in the game. What bothered him most was not knowing how they had managed to reclaim their land and overpower a unit of highly trained Capital soldiers equipped with the most modern technology? How had they known that the other armies had left Blue Island. Why did the Nyikans and Nahans leave in the first place? Rory was deeply troubled by all this, and by Alvilda's refusal to acknowledge the gravity of his doubts.

Her plan had holes that she arrogantly overlooked.

The dinner was served with a jovial atmosphere, and all three parties were friendly. Everyone was feeling some effect of alcohol from their informal gatherings, but they were all there to play politics, not to start arguments. That could wait for the more formal meetings the next day.

Members of all groups attempted small talk and humour, although they found that their jokes did not easily translate across culture. Lazor was very proud of his joke about a Nahan farmer, but while his compatriots hooted in laughter, the Nahans were disgusted and offended, and the Capital team were bewildered. Jan hissed something at Lazor in his own language and the mood became very tense until Alvilda poured more drinks and offered cigars around. Nobody attempted any more jokes after that.

The formal meetings hadn't yet begun, but all the guests were eager to get started. All through dinner they kept trying to start discussions about what they each wanted from the Capital, but were shut down each time with a reminder to be patient. Alvilda assured them that when the time came, they would have their concerns taken seriously.

That night, Jan went back to his room quite drunk. He was excited to start work the next day and prayed that the Capital would be fair and reasonable. The Nyikans he could count on being brash and tactless, and he promised that no matter what was agreed, he would leave with his pride intact and a reputation that outshone his belligerent neighbours.

Like most of the men in Naha, he had grown up indoctrinated under the dominant ideology. He learned that the war with Nyika had started way back during the reign of Bogdan the third. He was told that the Nyikans were the primary aggressors in the war and it was his duty to keep them out of Naha at all costs. The Nahan army was trying to reclaim territory it had once owned in the distant past, he was told. He knew all the stories about the atrocities committed by Nyikan soldiers, and he had devoted his life to the war effort.

Now as he lay in bed awake, after spending more time with them in one day than he had in his whole life, he wondered if perhaps some of the stories had been exaggerated. They seemed like regular people, just like him.

While the Capital slept, Abe Brown set about to mischief far away on Blue Island. He was enjoying his new state of being, as it allowed him to not only travel the world through minds, but also to eavesdrop. He listened in as Alvilda and her team talked through their plans. The only sensible voice in the room was the man with the disgusting phlegmy voice, Rory. Abe didn't like Alvilda's excessive ambition and her unwillingness to consider things that could go wrong. He thought he might just take things into his own ghostly hands to teach her a lesson.

Abe also knew that nobody in the room had considered the final wild card: Halasat. He knew about it through his interactions with Ychir. Until then, like everybody else he had thought Halasat was a pointless little village at the edge of the world. He was very surprised to learn that Iwizadi had grand plans for Halasat, even if Ychir's understanding of them were vague.

It was for that reason that Abe had then sought out Iwizadi's mind again. Iwizadi had felt a presence exploring his mind, and was unnerved when he could not discover its identity. There was no magic that was beyond him, he assumed. Whatever was visiting his mind was an unnatural power, and he had been deeply troubled to discover it.

Abe learned the truth about Halasat's origins from Iwizadi. He could hardly believe that within the nation he had ruled over there was a secret community of magic users. To think, the Department could have discovered Substance M years earlier without the problem of 'resettling' the Blue Island refugees.

It was interesting, but still too vague of a threat to bother with. Nevertheless, the knowledge would come in handy later, he thought. For now, he would continue with his plan to disrupt Alvilda's arrogance.

Ychir didn't feel Abe entering his mind. He was not aware of him until Abe started talking to him.

"Hello again, my friend."

Ychir heard the voice clearly in his mind and paused where he was. He was in the middle of going to a meeting at the tavern and ducked into a side street to avoid being seen acting strangely by anyone.

"What do you want? Do you have an army for me yet?" Ychir asked the voice in his head, whom he still believed to be Osbourne. By now he was used to it, after having been contacted a number of times before.

"Not yet. But, before you get angry, you should hear the information I've stumbled across."

"Okay, I am listening." Abe could see all the emotions Ychir felt. Though anger dominated his thoughts, he still had a good amount of curiosity. There was, however, little patience.

"I overheard some discussions going on at the Capital. It seems Abe's successor has great plans for your island home, and for the nations in the east."

"What? Haven't they learned from the last time we defeated them?"

"Apparently not."

"What are their plans? Sending more false magic soldiers?"

"No."

"Then what?"

"They have underestimated you in the past, and they have not learned their lesson."

"What do you mean?" Ychir's curiosity was growing all around Abe.

"They still see your people as primitive and incapable of political planning. But we know better. And your future will depend upon it."

"What are you talking about?"

"The Capital plans to play off Naha and Nyika against each other."

"So what?"

"They don't care if the war continues here or in the east."

"Then the Khun will again be caught in a war." Ychir was finally piecing together the problems. "Then hurry up and send your soldiers to help. The Capital can still help."

"That is a complication. With the Capital's new plan, I will not be able to send soldiers. We cannot be seen to support one group over another, else Naha and Nyika will team up against us and not kill each other."

"You bastard! You promised me soldiers!"

"And you will get them, but it will take longer."

"How long?"

"When Naha and Nyika have hurt each other so badly that the Capital is forced to step in and save the day."

"How long?"

"Several years."

"Years! I need to take the book and get rid of Iwizadi now! I cannot let our nation suffer for years of war, under his leadership. Do you think he will try to defend us against Naha and Nyika?" Ychir's mind was once again raging.

"Take it or leave it."

Ychir sighed heavily and gritted his teeth. His vision for the Khun was falling apart, but he was at the mercy of the voice in his head.

"There is more that I want to tell you."

"Go on then."

"The Capital thinks that neither Khun nor Arazi are important players in the world. They refuse to even consider any sort of alliance between you."

"Arazi? They are lunatics. An alliance is not possible. They are not even allied with themselves."

"So thinks the Capital too. But in case it were somehow achieved…"

"Then the Khun could defend themselves from Naha and Nyika."

"Exactly."

"And you are sure that the Capital thinks it is impossible?"

"Yes."

"What do you know about Arazi? How can I make this happen? If it will save my people from the war, I have to try it. Maybe I can use their soldiers to make up for the ones you promised."

"Let me do some research for you. I will visit their country and discover what they truly want. Then we can find out how to use them."

"But what about you?"

"What about me?"

"What is it that you want? Why are you helping me?"

"Like I told you before, I want that book. And I am willing to go to extraordinary lengths to get it."

"Even betraying your own Capital? You have no honour."

"Perhaps. Let's just say that I am not very fond of the

current leadership in my country. You and I have that in common."

"So, if the Khun and Arazi form an alliance and prevent the Nahans and Nyikans from destroying Gazar again, won't that ruin the Capital's plans? What are you hiding?"

"I would like to tell you, but I'm afraid it will not do either of us any good. Instead, I will help you ally with Arazi, and you will get me the book."

"I am starting not to trust you. What if I choose to keep the book?"

But no answer came. Abe had already abandoned Ychir's mind and gone off into the north, searching for another mind to take over. The Arazi had long since abandoned their places on Gazar, since there were no soldiers to torment and rob, so instead he went seeking them out in their own land.

Being impulsive as always without considering the consequences in any detail, Ychir went to the tavern with Arazi on his mind. He walked in and shook some hands. Some people clapped him on the shoulder as he went to his usual table, where someone handed him a beer. But he was distracted, and did not respond with his usual enthusiasm. People took this to mean that he was busy strategising, which he was, just not in a way that they expected.

"What do you think we should do next, Ychir?" someone asked him. Everyone wanted to know, after their last attempt to storm the mountain fizzled out and went nowhere.

"I am thinking," he replied. He went over his conversation with Abe a few times, and started to seriously consider the Arazi. That night in the tavern was more subdued than previous meetings. There were no grand speeches and no attempts to arouse the mob's violent tendencies. It was a more casual meeting between like-minded Khun, who wanted to brainstorm their movements.

"I think we should train our colleagues to fight," one of the men at the table said eagerly. "We only use magic for cooking and cleaning and farming. Why can't we use spells like *he* did to us? We could take over like that."

"It isn't so simple," Ychir replied. "Mostly because we don't know those spells ourselves, and it would be too risky to underestimate him." The other man leaned back and drank a few mouthfuls of beer.

"That makes sense," he admitted. "Do you have any ideas, then?"

"I do have one idea," Ychir began. "But it is crazy, and I'm not sure if it is worth saying."

"Well, say it now that you've started," said the man opposite Ychir, whose name was Teneg.

"Arazi."

"What about it?" Teneg asked aggressively. His massive meaty forearms rested on the table and he held tightly onto his mug of beer, his hairy knuckles bulging with arthritis.

"I believe we could use an ally." Ychir was careful not to say too much, because he was still formulating his idea.

"An ally? Arazi?" Teneg laughed. "Now it is official, everyone: Ychir has lost his mind." Everyone at the table laughed, except the first man who suggested fighting Iwizadi with magic.

"Maybe he has a point," he said. The laughter died down, but Teneg still looked bitterly at Ychir. "Let's hear it Ychir."

"Shut up Sonsokh," Teneg interrupted. "It's an idiotic idea. There's no point in talking about it."

"You shut up Teneg," Ychir said, and chugged the liquid in his mug. He hiccoughed. "Our enemy has magic that is stronger than ours. Our advantage is our number. But we lack destructive magic or weapons, and that is why I think we need an ally."

"Why Arazi though? Aren't they the ones who caused so much damage when they entered the war last time?"

"We cannot ever trust the Nahans, after what they have done to our home these years. Nor the Nyikans, who are essentially the same people but too stupid to realise." Ychir was finding his element again, as the idea made more sense to him. His voice grew more confident. "And we certainly cannot trust the Capital, after so recently trying to conquer us.

"So, who is left? There is that nation of Iwizadi's, Halasat, who we don't know anything about. They are the ones we want to prevent from coming here at all. Finally, there is Arazi. They are the only nation who is strong enough to help us defend our land, and not interested in digging the Noi out of the ground."

"And remember how we once fought alongside them ten years ago, Teneg? Remember the Battle of the Endless Night?" Sonsokh was coming to like the idea. Some Khun nodded at the terrible memory, but Teneg looked stubbornly at those around him.

"So what?" Teneg said. "What makes you think they would help us fight? What can we offer them in return?"

"That is the part I am trying to work out," Ychir answered. "But when I do, we will be able to gain their weapons and numbers, and throw Iwizadi and Aisling out of our land."

"The idea makes sense," Sonsokh admitted. "Though practically, I can't imagine how you will make it happen."

"You see? The whole idea is pointless. Not worth discussing." Teneg and Ychir often butted heads when discussing strategy. It was their default response to say the other had stupid ideas. Ychir was not offended because he was used to Teneg's brash behaviour.

"Shut up, Teneg, I will make it work." Ychir ignored his opponent and spoke to the others at the table, who thoughtfully nodded. "Leave the alliance to me. I can leave tomorrow to seek them out in their homeland."

"And what if war breaks out again before you can return?" Sonsokh asked.

"I will hurry. We will have to hope that there is enough time," Ychir said. "If not, then I will arrive late with an army and save the day."

"You coward, Ychir," Teneg taunted, trying to get under Ychir's skin. "You fled our country with Chuluun the traitor, sixteen years ago, and now you are fleeing again as we are once again on the verge of war. You should stay and fight. We don't need Arazi mercenaries to win this war. We only need Khun to fight together." A growing crowd was listening to their discussion, standing around the table. Many of them agreed with Teneg, but many others agreed with Ychir that they needed extra help – even foreign help. "You are weak. You want to rely on foreigners to help you in your fight against foreigners? You are just like Iwizadi. You are just like Chuluun."

The Khun in the tavern listened intently, waiting to see how Ychir would respond. He and Teneg had previously broken into fist fights over lesser disagreements. But Ychir knew he had the assurances of Osbourne in the Capital, and restrained himself from engaging with Teneg. It was a tense environment in the tavern, and the bartender called out, telling them to go outside if they wanted to fight:

"Too many broken glasses in here last time."

"Maybe you're both right," suggested Sonsokh. "I think we do need more people on our side, foreign or Khun it doesn't matter to me. But I also think we have to be firm in our motives. We cannot make any concessions to our nation or to our integrity. We are not cowards. I agree that Ychir should seek an alliance with the Arazi." What Sonsokh did not explain, was that he wanted Ychir out of the picture and for Teneg to take control of their little faction. He shared a look with Teneg, who understood that he should not say anything more.

"Then I will leave tomorrow, and return with an army," Ychir concluded to applause from the room. "Now, let us drink!" The applause exploded and there was cheering and toasting. Teneg shook hands with Ychir and gave him a difficult stare.

"Good luck, Ychir." He did no let go of his hand. "I do hope nothing happens in your absence that will make life difficult. For any of us."

Though Ychir could hear a veiled threat, he chose to ignore it, knowing that he had the power of the magical spirit Osbourne to help him. He would leave in the morning. He would form an alliance to drive out Iwizadi and save Gazar from his grips. He would keep the book for himself and betray Osbourne. After all, if Osbourne refused to help, why should he get anything? He would come home a hero.

But before leaving on his diplomatic mission, Ychir would get roaringly drunk with his supporters in the tavern, and stagger home to fall into bed. He had learned that when he was drunk, there were no voices in his head, and sometimes he preferred it that way.

Chapter 7

Nearly two months. That was how long it took Chuluun to reach Halasat. Most of it was uneventful, and it eerily reminded him of the time when Iwizadi had calmed the sea as the Khun returned to Gazar from abroad. Was Iwizadi responsible again for Chuluun's easy journey?

Every day was the same, and it wasn't long before the boredom got to him. The perpetually good weather and monotonous views made him wish that something interesting would happen. A storm, a pirate ship. Anything.

At night he would find a beach or some other land where he could safely tie up the boat, come ashore and set up a tent. He tried to find concealed bays when possible, as he was traveling illegally through the Capital. It would have been a disaster if he was caught and questioned by the immigration officials. At night he would set up a fire and cook fish that he caught during the day and eat whatever fruits were nearby. But over time he was getting a bit tired of this repetition, and everything permanently smelt like saltwater.

Even worse than the boredom however was the thought of his task. Iwizadi had sent him to Halasat to bring its people back to Gazar to supplant the Khun. He didn't want to do it, but Iwizadi had made clear the consequences if he refused, leaving him with no choice. So, reluctantly he had set sail again, barely a month after arriving back home. He knew that they were magic people too, but knew nothing else about them except that they were unable to talk with Kraka; they had no Bird magic. What did Iwizadi want with them?

Chuluun had little idea that there was any discontent in his beloved city. Throughout his journey, he had received some birds from Khuch, but these were few and far between, and only in the first week. Chuluun wondered if Iwizadi was somehow preventing them from finding him.

When he left, he had made sure that Aisling was prepared for her new role. She had the support of her mother and Khuch, and they should be alright until he returned, he thought. If he returned at all. She had Iwizadi to help her if she needed.

Chuluun had waited too long to simply give up Gazar at the first sign of trouble. Being realistic though, he thought that anything could happen on his trip. Nobody knew what the people of Halasat were like. If they were like Iwizadi, he and all the Khun might all be in trouble. But if they *were* like Iwizadi, why had they stayed hidden in the farthest corner of the world? They didn't make sense to him.

Finally, when Chuluun was approaching the distant shape on the horizon that was Halasat, he felt his boredom replace itself with anxiety. He was not normally an anxious person. During sixteen years of exile, he had led his group of refugees through one crisis after another, and finally returned them home safely. But this felt different. It was too unpredictable. He wished there could have been some way to prepare for his meeting with the new people.

The shapeless blob on the peninsula ahead of him slowly morphed into distinct buildings, and he could make out a pier of some kind. As he got closer, more and more birds filled the sky with pirouettes and squawking. Sea birds. Reliable, trustworthy birds. He desperately wanted to send messages home, but the distance was too far for these types of gulls. He needed an eagle.

His boat drifted closer to the pier, carried forward on the waves as if by magic, and he saw human shapes. He stood up and waved to them. They waved back and continued their activities. That was a good sign at least.

It was late afternoon, and the sky was full of clouds. The moon had risen early, and for a few hours both sun and moon were visible when the clouds were generous enough to get out of the way. There was a strong wind on the way, and water lashed the sides of the pier. It was a good time to make landing. Finally, something interesting was happening.

As he moored his boat and tied it up, the two men who waved at him came closer to greet him. They were very tall, and wore clothes of a style he did not recognise. They were stained with fish and the sea, but underneath the grime, they had ornate and colourful geometric patterns. The two men had faces unlike others that Chuluun had come across in the Capital. There was more of a resemblance to Iwizadi in their angular bones.

They looked at him with intrigue. They pointed to his boat and one of the men said something in his local language. The other man laughed, and said something to Chuluun that he didn't understand.

He thought their language sounded vaguely like an antiquated form of his own, like the text in the Book of Boloi. They saw that he didn't understand, and looked at each other, as if unsure how to speak to a foreigner. Almost as if they had never even seen a foreigner before. Chuluun wiped his brow with a sleeve, removing a layer of salt and sweat, and tried to greet them in Khun.

They gave a hint of confused recognition, but he guessed it was the same feeling he had upon hearing their language.

Then Chuluun tried using the language of the Capital, and the two men lit up with understanding. When they spoke back, they had a peculiar accent, as if their tongues were too far back in their mouths and too stiff.

"What are you doing here?" The man with darker hair spoke first. He had a very large Adam's apple, and Chuluun saw he was missing a tooth. "We don't see many outsiders. Are you from the Capital?" Chuluun decided that these people had no concept of the world outside their village.

"No, I come from further than that. My name is Chuluun. I am from Gaz… Blue Island. I have been at sea for nearly two months." He wondered how much he should tell them. Should he even bother trying to convince them to follow Iwizadi? If he returned home alone and said he had tried, would Iwizadi know it was a lie?

The men spoke to each other in their own language, and shrugged. They were not familiar with Blue Island.

"I am Ikenna. This is Faruq. How did you come so far in that little boat?" The man was simply curious, and asked without suspicion. He extended a hand to Chuluun, and they shook. The lighter-haired man Faruq did the same. "We know boats well. Yours is not built for open sea travel. You were lucky not to capsize."

"Very lucky, I know." Chuluun agreed, still not sure what he was doing.

"You should have used a bigger boat." Faruq had a much higher voice. Chuluun saw a little scar on his neck and saw that he had trouble speaking.

"Yes, you're right."

"Is that why you're here? To buy a boat?" Ikenna asked.

He started pointing at various boats moored around the pier. "Some of these ones we can sell. Then you can continue your trip right away. We don't want to hold you up for long in our little town."

"Actually, sir," Chuluun realised the men were not so receptive to foreigners as they first appeared. They were trying to get rid of him already. But he was still unsure if he wanted to go through with Iwizadi's plan. "I would like to rest here for a night, have a hot meal and some dry clothes. Look at the sky: the wind is picking up and a storm is coming."

Without hesitating, the men began to welcome Chuluun. They were like actors reading a script.

"Well, welcome to our village," Ikenna said, turning to gesture to the buildings with his whole arm, his palm face down. "We don't have an inn because nobody ever comes here. You can stay at my house tonight. Then in the morning, you will buy a bigger boat and go." He shook Chuluun's hand again and smiled, showing off his blackened gums.

"No inn?" Chuluun was more surprised than he should have been. Even though Halasat was ignored by the rest of the world, and preferred to stay isolated, he thought at least they would have an inn. He noticed that a few more people on the shore were looking at him and the men on the pier. They were all exceptionally tall and thin. They were carrying various daily items: bags, clothes, children, food. And they had the same style of clothing as the men with him, though theirs were more vibrant and undamaged.

"My home is not far," Ikenna said as he led Chuluun towards a cottage on the eastern edge of the village and away from the people who had stopped to look. Faruq walked behind Chuluun, as if marching a prisoner. "You will be dry and fed."

"Very kind of you, sir." He looked at the buildings and saw a faint trace of the kind of architecture used in Gazar before the war. Some buildings had a similar decoration to the kind used in the mountain palace.

"I only want to help you on your way," Ikenna answered. Chuluun knew he was being arrested in a way, but it was so expertly done, and so polite that he was compelled to agree with Ikenna. The whole town was creepy enough to be vaguely threatening, even though there had been no overt threats made. Chuluun did want to leave, but he had to at least try what he came to do.

Or all the Khun would be killed.

Some Khun like Ychir believed that it was better to die with honour than to seek out their next coloniser. They protested Chuluun's acceptance of Iwizadi's plan, and urged him to side with them against him. Sometimes he felt selfish, like he was putting his own desire to live above his peoples' honour.

Just like he did during the war.

Ikenna opened the door to his home and called out something, while pausing at the threshold. A pleasant voice came back, and a moment later a woman was standing at the doorway. She began a hurried, whispered discussion with Ikenna, even though Chuluun couldn't understand it at all. They made a lot of rapid gesticulations and a flurry of facial expressions.

Chuluun peered inside past the woman. A Noi generator sat in the middle of the room, with various appliances around the room connected with wires and lit up with blue. The more modern Noi batteries had made use of a new wireless technology, transforming homes from jumbles of wires. When Chuluun had lived in the forest near Nelasive in the north-east of the Capital, he could only afford a used generator and salvaged wires. Luckily it was only used when outsiders visited and so cost him almost nothing during the whole time he lived there.

It was strange though, he realised. The people of Halasat were supposed to be magical. Why was there a Noi generator in use? He remembered seeing another older one at the pier, too.

Everything about Halasat was telling Chuluun to get out and go home. It was unsettling to be there.

Ikenna and the woman stopped arguing, and she reluctantly stepped aside to let the men in. She glared at Ikenna, but gave Chuluun a fake warm welcome, as her culture demanded she show hospitality to guests.

"Welcome to our home," she said in the same heavily accented Capital language as Ikenna. "We hope you will be well-rested here to continue your travel tomorrow."

"Thank you, ma'am."

She smiled frostily and returned to a small office to the left of the entry where she had a desk stacked high with electronics and books.

"My wife, Ediye." Ikenna showed Chuluun to a living room, ducking under a wire connecting the lights to the Noi generator. "I am sorry we have no bed for guests, but you can sleep in here tonight. I will get some blankets and then start to prepare food."

The room was stuffed full with rugs on every surface and huge cushions. They were expertly made with the same sorts of designs on the Halasetters' clothing. Ikenna dragged a low table into the middle and arranged the cushions so they could all sit and talk.

"Thank you very much."

"Do you like manya?" Ikenna found himself enjoying the

stranger's company more than he should. At the mention of manya, Faruq's ears pricked up and he looked expectantly at his friend. Not knowing what it was, Chuluun hesitated. They saw his hesitation and tried to put him at ease.

"Sit," said Faruq in his raspy voice, guiding Chuluun across the room with a hand on his shoulder. Chuluun did as he was told and eased himself onto the floor, where he occupied twice as many cushions as Faruq. "We drink manya."

It must be a local spirit, Chuluun realised. As much as he liked spirits, he thought maybe he should refuse. But before he could object, Ikenna had produced three tall, skinny glasses from nowhere and Faruq was already pouring a thick, golden liquid into them. The glasses themselves were beautiful works of art, and Chuluun was afraid to touch them. They were inlaid with elaborate designs, but even more impressive was how they changed colours when filled with the manya. When he picked it up in his giant hand it looked tiny, but in the hands of Ikenna and Faruq it looked elegant.

"Munsha." The two Halasetters upended their glasses and watched the insides eagerly as the manya dripped into their mouths. Chuluun repeated the word and did the same as the men and was amazed at the way the designs appeared to change before his eyes as the manya slid past them. The glasses were crafted specifically to give a light show to someone drinking manya from them.

The manya tasted like honey and berries, and despite its thick, syrupy texture, it melted in the mouth and slid down the throat easily. Initially, Chuluun thought it might not be alcoholic, but after two more glasses he knew he was very mistaken.

Ikenna and Faruq were only superficially affected, but

Chuluun felt that he needed to slow down. His head felt heavy and his eyes drooped. Unfortunately for him, Faruq kept pouring more and more until the small bottle was empty. The local men became quite chatty in their own language, and Chuluun strained his attention, trying to understand their words. It was a very weird feeling for him to hear a language so like his own in rhythm, yet completely incomprehensible.

Ediye emerged from her office looking defeated, and surveyed the scene. She started berating Ikenna, who got up and apologised to Chuluun.

"She is mad because I promised to cook, but now we are drunk instead." Faruq laughed loudly with his strained voice, and Ediye glared at him. Chuluun examined Ediye's face and decided that if someone were to take Aisling's face and stick it on Iwizadi's head, she would be the result, and he laughed at his own imagination. The others looked at him in confusion. Ikenna stood up from the cushion he had been sitting on, and went towards the next room to cook. Before leaving, he told Ediye to take his place and then produced more manya. Faruq immediately poured her a glass before she could refuse. His gangly legs were drawn up to his chest yet he looked perfectly comfortable sitting on the floor.

"Where are you going tomorrow?" she asked Chuluun after draining her glass. He hadn't thought yet how he would answer any interrogation. He didn't even know if he wanted to invite these people back to Gazar.

"I don't know yet."

"Where you come from?"

"Blue Island. Gazar" He said this, and she scratched her chin for a moment, as if trying to remember the world outside Halasat. Faruq poured her more manya but she ignored him.

"You are Khun?" Her demeanour had changed. She was more astonished than cold now.

"Yes." He was surprised that she knew that.

She slapped Faruq on the back of the head, then got up to find Ikenna. Chuluun heard them arguing in the kitchen and tried to name the various spices he could smell. It was hard to tell with the sweet taste of manya coating his mouth. Faruq stared at Chuluun, grinning and swaying. He was about to pour another glass but stopped and asked him:

"You are really Khun?"

Chuluun felt that the evening had suddenly taken a new direction, and instead of their desperation to be rid of him, they were curious about him, even eager to know more. The arguing in the kitchen ceased and Ediye came back to take her position on the cushion. The sounds of cooking got louder as Ikenna drunkenly clanged pots and pans around and banged ingredients and utensils clumsily.

"My idiot husband did not know you came from Gazar." Chuluun remembered that he said he was from Blue Island, deliberately using the Capital name for his home, unsure of whether it was still a danger to be Khun in that country.

"We thought you were just another man from Capital, or some other powerful country, come to do damage."

"Damage?" Chuluun was unaware of the history between Halasat and the Capital. He didn't know that Halasat was regarded as strange and not worth conquering by the old leader, the one before Abe Brown. He still thought Abe was in charge. Nor did he know that their local version of the Iwizadi story was a story about a returning messiah and a prophet. He did understand however that a history of poor relations with foreigners can lead to a general feeling of suspicion and distrust, and he didn't blame them for trying to get rid of him.

"Never mind about that." Ediye slammed back another glass of manya, which Faruq wasted no time in replenishing. Chuluun had long lost count. "Khun man, Chuluun, why are you really here?"

"I came…" Chuluun gulped down another glass of manya and was by this time sufficiently drunk and reckless, that he thought he should just tell them. "I came to deliver a message from Gazar. The message is-"

"No! Don't tell us three in here." Ediye interrupted him and her eyes bulged wide with interest. Her colourful fabric head scarf had come loose and now threatened to fall off. "It is far too important. You will tell all of us tomorrow. The whole town."

"I thought I had to go tomorrow."

"No. You can stay. Khun are welcome here. We wanted you to go before, because we thought you were from the Capital."

"Why can't I just tell you now?"

"Because in our small country, we have an ancient story that when a Khun man comes from Gazar, he will bring good news of our leader."

"Your leader?"

"We believe Iwizadi will come back for us."

Chuluun shifted on the cushions, rearranging his tailbone where his weight was balanced uncomfortably. Tomorrow, he had to tell the town what he came for. He had to tell them Iwizadi had sent him. The news that they had been waiting for him was unsettling, and it would be harder now to betray Iwizadi, if that was what he decided to do.

"How do you know that the first man from Gazar will bring good news? What if it's the second? Or hundredth?" He was searching for any way to relieve the pressure.

"Because we believe he would not do us wrong like that."

Ediye was unflappable. Chuluun was drunk and anxious. "Tell us about Gazar. What is it like now?" He would have preferred to learn more about Halasat first. It would have been nice to know about these people and why Iwizadi wanted them and why they worshipped him.

"Gazar is still at war."

"What war?" Ediye asked bluntly. Chuluun stared at Ediye, just coming to terms with how remote and isolated Halasat really was. They had no idea about any of the Khun's struggles. He relaxed into a familiar storytelling mood, and began to talk about his experiences with the war.

"Over two decades ago, soldiers from the east started arriving in Gazar. At first, they didn't do much, but then they discovered Noi and began fighting over it. It was not long before their violence spilled into the lives of the Khun and we were forced to flee."

"It is always a problem of Noi," Ediye shook her head. "Here they leave us alone because we have none."

"You are lucky people."

"In that respect yes. In others, not so much. But what soldiers came? Which countries?"

"Naha came first. Then Nyika and Arazi joined them." Chuluun saw the blank expression on Ediye's face and realised she had no knowledge of geography. "From the east."

"Ikenna," she called to her husband, ignoring Faruq who was still sitting with them in a stupor and with a glazed look on his face. Ikenna poked his head through the doorway, and they rapidly discussed something in their own language. Ediye turned back to Chuluun. "We don't know those countries. Was Capital involved?"

"Eventually yes, but not until much later."

"Dinner is nearly ready," Ikenna called out.

"Through the fighting, I and many others fled Gazar. The war grew fiercer until it was not safe for us. A few Khun stayed behind and joined the invaders. They were traitors. But I left the island with my son, who was a baby then. Sixteen years ago. We sailed to the nearest shore of the Capital continent, away from the homelands of the soldiers, and we waited there until it was safe to go home.

"Then only three months ago, I learned that our time had come. The soldiers were going home, leaving Gazar free for Khun again. We returned, and started to rebuild our lives."

"I have questions," she asked directly. There were some cultural similarities between the Khun and the Halasetters, Chuluun noted.

"What questions?"

"How did you learn that your time had come?"

"Iwizadi," Chuluun said, and watched as a knowing satisfaction dripped smugly over Ediye's face. Faruq registered the name, but made no comment. "He visited me in a dream. He said he had made it so."

"Then you are really the prophet from Gazar." Ediye kneeled up high and leaned forwards to touch Chuluun's hand. He pulled away, not wanting to be revered in such a way, and she awkwardly grabbed for his feet instead.

"No, I am no prophet."

"But you are. Our leader has spoken to his people through you." Her eyes shone with admiration and hope.

Chuluun remembered the hopes of his own people. How he had kept them optimistic during sixteen years of exile. His own fervent hope that he could return home one day. He knew how powerful that feeling could be, but he wished it was happening to someone else.

"What other questions do you have about Gazar?" Chuluun was careful not to let her ask about his dreams.

"When was the Capital involved? What did they do?"

"Just after we returned home, the Capital sent its own soldiers to conquer Gazar and steal its Noi." He was careful not to mention the true details of that day. How the Capital had tried to steal the Book of Boloi and how they had found an artificial source of magic. "We fought them in a battle and defeated them."

"They are greedy people. They have unimaginable riches of Noi here in this land and they still want yours too." Ediye shook her head sadly, and Ikenna came into the room with some plates and placed a huge pot of some kind of stew in front of them all. "You Khun must be strong fighters to defeat Capital soldiers." It was dangerously close to being forced to reveal about their magic. But then again, Chuluun reasoned, he was talking to a supposedly magical people, who seemed to worship a physical, God-like Iwizadi.

"We fought bravely to defend our home." He decided not to reveal all his secrets just yet. Ikenna gave him a large serving and urged him to take some bread. It was thick and brown, and Ikenna encouraged him to eat. Chuluun noticed that nobody else had been served yet, and they were waiting for him. Not wanting to be rude, he broke off a chunk of bread and used it to scoop out some stew, as there was no cutlery. It tasted like beans and was very salty, but not bad. He made some token sign of approval, and Ikenna started serving everyone else, pleased with himself.

"There is still a lot I want to know about Gazar, and about its prophet Chuluun."

"I told you, I'm not a prophet."

"You are."

"For me to be a prophet, you must believe Iwizadi is a god or something like that?" Faruq mindlessly gnawed on some bread, and seemed to just enjoy being in company and hearing noises around him. Ediye ate a few mouthfuls before answering.

"He is like our god, yes." Chuluun wished it wasn't true, thinking about the cruelty he had witnessed. He remembered how effortlessly Iwizadi had manipulated them, had threatened them, had nearly killed dozens of Khun just because Chuluun didn't agree with him. He might not be a god, but he acted as if he were. Who would worship a god like that?

"Tell me more about your country." Chuluun needed to find out more. He needed as much information as possible before deciding whether or not to fulfil his mission. He frequently imagined the look on Iwizadi's face if he returned alone. But how could he risk it, seeing the way Iwizadi treated the Khun? His pride was not worth their lives.

"We have an ancient claim to this land. According to legend, we were founded by the survivors of the great fall of Libalele, which you call Khot."

"What fall?" Across from Chuluun, Ikenna was gulping down vast quantities of stew. Faruq had begun to eat properly and his vision was more focused. Chuluun and Ediye only ate a little as they talked.

"Our story begins and ends with Iwizadi. In the ancient times, he led the true believers from Libalele, where they were persecuted."

"For what?"

"For magic. The city collapsed from the weight of its own corruption, and Iwizadi freed the believers. They survived due to their magic. And he led them across the world to wait until a new city was rebuilt for them. And we have waited here for over one thousand years."

Every country had its origin story, Chuluun knew. Even the Khun had theirs, the *Buteelin Domog*. They said they came from nothing, and fell from the sky. There was a time when he was young and naïve, and had believed it literally, and he could see the same blind, uncritical belief in Ediye. Why did he have to be the one to destroy her faith? He wished Iwizadi had never come into his life. Life in exile was hard, but he had hope then, and a purpose. Back then he could work for the good of all Khun. But Iwizadi ruined it all. He had no purpose of his own now and no hope for his people.

"Do you believe in magic?"

"All people here believe. Some of us have seen it. Our town has also had prophets in the past, those people fortunate enough to be visited in dreams by Iwizadi."

No wonder she believed everything he was saying.

"Have you seen magic yourself?"

"Yes. I am one of the lucky ones. There is magic in my blood. I have the gift of Light." Ikenna shuffled on his cushion a little.

"Can I see?" Chuluun asked politely, feigning wonderment.

"Yes. But you must know that I am only choosing to show you because you are the Khun prophet from Gazar. No people from the Capital know our secret."

"They don't believe it." Ikenna butted in.

"Yes. The truth is that in the past, some of us have revealed our beliefs to the Capital, but we were laughed at. Tonight, I will show you."

"Before you do, can you tell me if your stories say anything about the Khun?"

"Only a little. We know you believe, and you live on Gazar but that is all."

"That is a great shame. Your history is founded on Gazar, but you have lost track of the island's story since you left it."

"We moved forward with our new home, but we have

always waited for a sign that it was time to return. Now you have come."

Chuluun disliked her explanation. He was a man of action. When he was in exile, he did everything possible to learn about his war-torn home, and make a way to return. His lost home was everything to him, but it seemed like the Halasetters had accepted defeat. Maybe he wouldn't tell them to return. Maybe they didn't deserve it, and they were happy enough where they were. Or maybe it was him who lived in the past.

"Will you show me your magic now?" He changed the topic.

Ediye concentrated on the lights in the room, and though they were still connected to the Noi generator, they intensified. The room lit up brighter than daylight for a few seconds. Chuluun was disappointed though. He knew the spell she had used was one of the most basic, one that all Khun children knew, and despite looking flashy, it required very little magic concentration.

"You said you were one of the lucky ones. What did you mean by that?" The lights returned to normal.

"There are many of us who cannot perform magic at all. Even though we are all receptive to it, and we believe in it, there are only a few who can do like I do."

Chuluun had to think hard about this. What did Iwizadi want with a group of fanatics who could not even use magic? Did he know their limitations or did he expect them to be fully magical? What would he say if Chuluun returned home with them? Would he be disappointed?

"You don't look impressed," Ediye said. She took another bite of her meal. Ikenna and Faruq were already finished. "Maybe I am wrong to assume this, but perhaps you can also perform magic?"

"I can," he answered, but with the hope that she didn't ask him to perform anything.

"Please show me. Show us all. So that we can believe you are truly the prophet."

Chuluun felt like he had been backed into a corner. If he showed them magic, it would mean that he would need a very good excuse for not inviting them back to Gazar. But if he refused to demonstrate a spell, they would throw him out as a liar, and Iwizadi would take his revenge on all the Khun back home.

He thought back through the years to when Aisling and Peter had first joined the Khun. They were amazed and scared when he had first shown them magic. Peter took some time to adjust his worldview, but Aisling absorbed magic faster than anyone he'd ever known. Maybe all the Halasetters needed was someone to spark their imagination. Maybe Iwizadi knew that.

The meal had grown cold as it sat half-eaten in front of him through the conversation. He felt the pressure of Ediye's gaze upon him, and reluctantly, he performed the same spell he had shown Aisling and her father. He straightened his spine, feeling that he was getting older and stiffer, and half closed his eyes. A second later, light began spewing from his fingertips, and he could point at various objects to light them up. He traced some circles on the ceiling.

"Is it true for all Khun?" Ediye asked, admiring the ease with which he cast the spell. In some ways, she reminded him of Aisling as a young girl, even though she was at least forty. She watched the circles, mesmerised, then studied Chuluun's hands and tried to imagine how it worked.

When Aisling had seen the spell, she stayed up all night trying it herself. She was like that. Stubborn. Patient.

Determined.

What should he tell her? If he said that all Khun were magical, he could upset her, and set off a chain of events that ended with them coming back to Gazar with him. If he said it was just him, there would be too many questions to answer: Why was it just him? Why was he so effortless? They would be convinced he was a prophet. He didn't have enough lies left in him to pretend.

"Most Khun use magic." The answer he decided upon was decidedly non-committal. He didn't describe how often, or how easily, or how powerfully. And he left out the important fact that magic was an integral part of their cultural identity.

"It is amazing." Ikenna stood up unsteadily and cleared away the plates and remnants of dinner. He looked upset and muttered something to Ediye in his own language. "My husband thinks our leader Iwizadi favours the Khun over his own people."

This was an accusation Chuluun never thought he would face. Maybe if he told them more about him, they would reconsider their worship of him.

"That is not true. Tomorrow, when I tell you my reasons for coming, I will explain all that I know about him too." He made up his mind to tell them he was violent, and did not care for Khun at all. He would tell them that he had come only to save the lives of his people. They could not possibly think that Iwizadi favoured them. With any luck, they might rethink their devotion to him. He would leave them free to decide their own fate. The power to control their own destiny was a gift he had not been granted.

"I want to believe you." Nodding sagely, Ediye was processing all that had happened that night. She changed the topic back to life on Gazar. "You have a son, you said."

"Yes. Khuch Chaddhal."

"And when you fled from the war, he was a baby." Chuluun had a suspicion where Ediye was leading the conversation, and really wished she wouldn't. Faruq was sober enough to begin pouring more manya for everyone. He and Ikenna eagerly swallowed another mouthful, again admiring the light show that played out inside their glasses.

"Yes." *Please don't ask.* There were parts of Chuluun's memory that had been kept locked up for decades, and he really did not want to look inside.

"What happened to his mother?" There it was. Chuluun felt his face heating up. Perhaps it was from the manya, or the hot meal, or the room was getting stuffier. The windows had fogged up, and it was a hot night outside. He felt cornered. He had not talked about her since the war. Since her ceremony was ungraciously rushed, under threat of the soldiers discovering them.

"She died. If you don't mind, I would like to go to bed now. It has been a long day, and I should rest before tomorrow."

"Yes of course." Ediye could tell that Chuluun was not prepared to speak on the subject. And even though in her culture it was not rude to press someone on an issue, she chose not to insult her guest. She did not want the prophet to be upset and vanish back into the far reaches of the world, especially on the eve of an important announcement.

In a flurry of activity, Ediye made Ikenna and Faruq get up and find some pillows and blankets for their guest. They cleared a space and filled it with cushions and pushed the table away to the side of the room. They laughed a lot while doing it, and found great humour in their uncoordinated movements. Faruq tripped over his own feet and Ikenna howled with laughter until Ediye smacked him on the back of the head. She scolded him, presumably telling him not to embarrass her in front of their guest, the prophet. Ikenna and Faruq resumed tidying up in a demure and solemn mood.

As the night deepened, and Chuluun lay awake, his mind whirled with memories of the war and the thought of addressing the town the next day. He wondered what was happening in Gazar at that moment. Was Khuch safe? Was Aisling alright? The lack of birds over the last month had been very hard and lonely.

Around the time he fled Gazar, he saw her face often in his mind. But as time went on, and he and the others adjusted to their new life in the far reaches of the Capital, he saw it less and less. His duty was to the Khun surrounding him. He wanted to give Khuch a good life. Even in their storytelling, he could not bring her up by name. While the other Khun reminisced about their dead and missing family and friends, Chuluun felt his throat close up every time he thought of her. He could not get on with life when her ghost was with him, hurting him with their good memories together.

There were sounds of murmuring and movement through the house, as Ediye and Ikenna moved about the other rooms, trying not to disturb him. Faruq had gone home, or rather Ediye had practically guided him out the door.

The month before Chuluun left Gazar, the fighting between the different armies was getting worse. They had already been present for four years at that point, and engaging in short skirmishes over their Noi mine. But it got much worse when the two main armies formed an alliance and teamed up against a third. The Khun were caught in the middle of it all.

In the beginning, the Khun tolerated the Nahan soldiers who were first to arrive. They kept to themselves and didn't bother the Khun too much. There was no sign that they wanted to stay on the island permanently, so the Khun decided to let them come and go. Some Khun made friendly relationships with them and learned their language. It was a generally peaceful time. Chuluun joined in too. It was seen as a very progressive thing amongst the Khun to welcome the newcomers and learn about their country. It was the cool thing to do, and Chuluun being a young man at the time, did not want to find himself part of the crowd of old, fearful Khun who avoided the Nahans.

Soon after the arrival of the Nahans, another army arrived further south. The Khun learned that these were the Nyikans, and they were at war with the Nahans. The Khun decided that their friendship with Naha had to end, because with two opposing forces gathering on the island, they could not be seen to be favourable to either. It would be too dangerous for them. They thought by doing this they could avoid being dragged into the war, but they didn't realise they were already part of it.

For a few years, not much happened. There were tensions between the two armies, and the Khun kept to themselves. Chuluun remembered sometimes hearing news of a small skirmish taking place between them. Most other Khun ignored the armies. For them, their forces were only temporary and their fighting mild.

But that all changed when the Nahans discovered the huge amounts of Noi buried under the earth on Gazar. Chuluun had tried to block his involvement in it from his memory, because it was so shameful to think about. He had kept it secret ever since, but sometimes he wished he could tell someone and hear them say 'it's alright. It's not your fault'.

Her name was Athena, and she was part of the early Nahan expeditions, while it was still considered cool and trendy amongst the Khun to befriend them. Chuluun remembered the way she showered him with affectionate interest and curiosity, and he remembered loving the attention. It was so foreign for him to witness overt displays of emotion, and he found himself visiting her very often.

At first, they could only communicate very rudimentary ideas. But as time went by and he learned her language, they were able to discuss broader concepts and get into details about how their cultures worked.

She wanted to know about how the Khun lived without Noi. It was the first time Chuluun had ever heard of Noi, and when she explained it to him, he was shocked. He found it bizarre the idea that the blue substance that was commonly found all over the island could be used to generate a type of magic.

Of course, he could not reveal anything about the Khun's magic. That was agreed by all to be the most important thing, and that no matter what, the soldiers must not know. So, he told Athena lies about their life without a source of power like Noi or magic. He made up things about how they used regular old fire for cooking and washing. She lapped it up, believing every word, because in her mind, why would a curious young native man lie about his culture? There was nothing to suspect.

The greatest mistake of Chuluun's life came when he revealed to Athena how common Noi was on Gazar. She thought he must be mistaken when he told her it could be found close to the surface, and you could trip over it if you walked near the mountains in the north. She thought he must have misinterpreted her meaning, because there was no way Noi could be so plentiful, especially amongst a people who had no need for it.

When she made it clear that she didn't believe him, he got all cocky in the way that arrogant young men do when they feel their integrity being challenged. 'I'll show you', he told her, and they set off from the Nahan camp on the east coast.

The Nahan soldiers were given a lot more freedom on the island than other units back on the continent. They were pioneering, the army said, so discipline was more relaxed. It was easy for Athena to get away from the camp.

He led her north-west, through an area of scrub that skirted around the edge of the great crater. The Nahans were aware of Khot in the centre of the crater, and had little interest in it. On their trek, when they reached the northernmost point of the mountains that ringed the crater, Chuluun carved a path northward, towards a distant cluster of mountains. Those mountains were higher and more jagged, but he told Athena to look at the ground as they approached. Just an hour later, she was surprised to see the first scar in the earth where a vein of Noi had erupted.

Bending down to examine it, she then jumped with excitement and flung herself at Chuluun, kissing him on the mouth. 'You don't know the good you've done!' she exclaimed. He was proud, and had a great feeling of being proven right. He kissed her back, then with a great rush of passion she took off his shirt. He took off hers too and she stroked his hairy firm chest as he caressed her neck and breasts.

They made love there, bathed in the blue light of raw Noi, unaware that together they had changed history.

Twenty years later, as memories of that time came to Chuluun lying awake on the sofa, he tossed his head around, wishing he could turn back time and wring her neck instead.

He wished he'd never met her. But if it wasn't him, then another Khun would have done just the same. They had no control over the direction of their lives, and all paths led to war.

He tried to justify his choices by saying that the war was going to happen no matter what he did. It was always just a matter of time. He tried to feel better about his choices, but in his heart, he knew the mistake he had made.

And there he was, in a house in Halasat, with the power to hurt his people again. He saw no way out of his situation that did not result in suffering. There was to be no happy ending.

Athena returned to the camp with the good news. She showed her superiors where to find the Noi, and then for a while, not much happened. Then after a couple of months, a lot more Nahan boats started appearing, and soldiers began moving huge serious-looking equipment north to the mountains. The Khun had never seen such huge machinery and watched in awe as the soldiers moved in a great convoy, carelessly smashing a path through the wilderness.

Then the mining began, and the Khun saw the damage being done, and they were unable to stop it. They watched as the Nahans drilled and blasted their land to pieces, and scooped out huge barrels full of oozing, dripping Noi. The barrels were sealed and put on boats going back to the continent.

A feeling of betrayal came over the Khun. And shame at having believed the Nahans were harmless. They yelled and made noise at them to stop, but their protests were met with brutality. Chuluun protested along with the most fervent Khun, feeling as though it could somehow absolve him of the guilt that he felt for revealing the Noi. He was there when the Nahans first got violent towards them, and words became pushing and shoving. He was there when the first shots were fired, and the first Khun was killed defending his land. That was the moment the war began for the Khun in earnest. That was when they realised they were already deeply involved.

Athena was at that time back on the continent, unaware of the escalating violence. The soldiers only toured for up to a year at a time before being sent home for other duties She would have been unsurprised to know, however. When she returned to the island after several months back home, it was not the place she remembered.

The main Nahan base had been moved inland and further north, closer to the mine, and a secure corridor had been built to transport Noi between the mine and the port. A secondary port was established further south to distract the Nyikan army from their new focus on Noi extraction, and for a long time, it worked.

When Athena returned to the island, she wanted to see Chuluun. She wanted to praise him for helping her people progress, and tell him all the good things that Noi was doing on the continent. But when she found him, he refused to speak to her, saying she had betrayed him and his people.

The Nahan army had started putting its roots down in the city of Khot now, pushing some of the Khun from their homes and driving up prices of basic items. Ostensibly, they were there to prevent any further protests or uprisings. Many Khun who were most strongly against the occupation found themselves harassed and intimidated by the soldiers, and taunted them back, saying 'Why do you need our houses? For such a great and powerful army, can't you even house yourselves?'

Of course, with the soldiers now living in the city amongst the Khun, it was impossible to use magic without being seen. Crops failed where they had once depended on it for growth. People went hungry. Illnesses spread, where in the past they were easily cured by a healer. The soldiers became convinced that the Khun were primitive savages with no knowledge of farming or hygiene.

Despite the tougher conditions, the Khun still protested the mining of Noi when possible. Though their protests were ineffective, they were satisfied that they were doing good, and refused to give up. Some did give up however, and either fled to more remote areas, or joined the Nahans in order to receive reliable food and healthcare.

Athena found Chuluun again one day and asked him if he would talk to his people on Naha's behalf, to convince them that nothing was wrong. He refused vehemently, and was disgusted by the suggestion. Athena assumed that would happen and then insisted that Chuluun take up her offer. 'If you don't help them to see the benefits of our operation, I might have to tell them how exactly I discovered all the Noi', she had threatened. Years later, her soft and harmless voice still tormented Chuluun's mind with its words. Sometimes when he heard her echo in his brain, he wanted to slam his head against a wall until there was nothing left to hear.

Faced with the eternal shame, one way or another, he chose to speak to the Khun on Naha's behalf. But he didn't have to do anything as spokesperson because thankfully, Nyika attacked the mining operation, setting off the next phase of the war.

He was lucky that time.

And he was lucky that some aspects of life continued as normal, even throughout the occupation. During that year, Chuluun's family organised his marriage to Emelt Yavdal. The families had known each other for generations, and it was decided that the wedding would go ahead sooner rather than later.

It was neither a surprise, nor unwelcome news. Emelt was not been beautiful like the goddesses were often described in stories. Instead of the divine standard of beauty, she had dark hair like all Khun, and was a lot smaller than Chuluun in width and height. The goddesses were tall and fair-haired, with pronounced cheek bones, but Emelt had a soft and round face with dimples. The goddesses were always described as very stern and dignified, whereas Emelt was a woman who got her hands dirty working hard and cheered and supported others, and Chuluun thought those were the best qualities to have.

As the occupation dragged on, life for the Khun seemed to have been stalled in a timeless vacuum. Every day felt like the same struggle to survive. But as they got used to it, the days started whizzing by, and without warning, they came to realise that it was a year since the Nyikans had attacked the mine.

Then things changed again and the war became more complicated.

When Arazi joined in, the whole dynamic of power changed, and for a while it was unclear how the three warring armies would affect the Khun. They were used to life under the Nahans with Nyika fighting for supremacy. They knew the Nahans only attacked them when provoked with protests at the mine, and after a year of living such a way they had been able to reach an uncomfortable stalemate. The Nyikans left them alone because the Nahans lived in Khot.

But when Arazi joined in, and the Nahan and Nyikan armies joined together in an uneasy alliance, the Khun were left wondering what their future would hold. Not even the soldiers seemed to know what the Arazi wanted: were they after the Noi? Or did they simply seek to create chaos?

They learned quickly that the Arazi were brutal. They were far more violent than either of the other two armies. Attacks on the mine were common, and the violence often spilled into the territory nearby. Protests stopped when it became obvious that the Nahans were just trying to keep alive. There were attacks on the city too, aimed at the soldiers residing there. Unfortunately, there was a lot of collateral damage, and many Khun were caught in the middle of it, losing homes and lives.

"I'm pregnant," Emelt had told Chuluun, as explosions rocked the city just a few blocks from their home. It used to be a quiet city, but now the front gardens that most Khun once cherished lay barren and dusty.

"We have to go." He held her close through the rumbling, wishing that this happiest moment was not tarnished by the blue and red fires erupting from his neighbours' homes. "We have to leave Gazar."

Stupid. He thought while lying there awake in Ikenna and Ediye's home, looking at the stars through the window. *I should not have abandoned them.* It was a familiar pattern of thoughts.

"I don't want to go." Shouts in the streets pierced the tenderness of the moment. A part of him wished they would blow up his house right then so they wouldn't have to think anymore. If only someone could make the choice for him. He felt his clothes dampen where her face was buried.

"Then we will stay."

But the argument returned often as the danger persisted. It was not the Gazar he wanted to raise a child in. Maybe that Gazar would never come back.

"I will not leave my home and my family." She was firm every time. He admired her for it, but he also wished she would reconsider. Not for him, but for their child.

She was stronger than me. He found the star he was searching for, and traced out her favourite constellation: the Raven.

They continued arguing during the first year of Khuch's life – the last year of Emelt's. By that stage, attacks on the city were less common due to Naha and Nyika organising their alliance better. They had managed to drive the Arazi back from the mines and into the remote north.

But that meant that mining resumed. In turn, that led to protests resuming.

And Athena returned for another tour of duty. After nearly two years, she missed the excitement of the island and volunteered. She went to look for Chuluun again, and was surprised to see he was married and had a son. A family man; not the impulsive and spontaneous young man she once knew.

She wanted to know if he had grown to see her point of view. If he could see mining as a good thing yet.

He told her to get lost.

She asked to come inside his home while walking in, not waiting for an answer. From Emelt's perspective, she was just another soldier throwing her weight around.

"We have nothing to talk about." He held the door open for her, waiting for her to go. Instead, Athena introduced herself to Emelt.

"We have a long history, from before the fighting started." A look from Emelt pushed an explanation from Chuluun.

"Yes. In the early days, when Khun were friendly with Naha. Before the fighting." He still kept the door open. It was uncomfortable with Athena near his wife. Relationships with foreigners were not unheard of, but they were taboo.

"Chuluun, why won't you speak to your old friend?"

Emelt asked him.

"Khun are not friends with soldiers now."

"Did something happen? Did you have a fight?"

"We had a war."

"I believe friendship is stronger than that." Emelt's way of standing firm by her beliefs was one of the reasons Chuluun loved her. Uncomfortably, it dawned on him that Athena was the same. He wished he agreed with her, but he didn't. The war was bigger than Athena. The mine was tearing apart more than the earth.

"You make me sad, Chuluun." Athena made as if to leave, but stopped. Spitefully, but dressed up in innocence, she turned to him on the way out and flippantly said: "What we had was stronger than the war we started."

And she left, her perfume lingering behind her. Chuluun locked her out and could feel his wife's confused anger boring a hole into him.

He wished for a bomb to wipe their home out of existence right then. He wished to disappear in a violent bang, so he would not have to answer the questions that were coming.

But no bomb came, only the barrage of accusations. He denied everything, like he had denied himself the truth ever since it happened. His truth would never be *the* truth, if it was never told. Anything else suited him better.

There were no answers and no satisfaction. Emelt joined the next protest as they had planned. Their marriage was not going well since Athena had planted images in her mind. What had she meant about starting the war? What had she had with her husband?

And where was Chuluun? He was supposed to be with her, after taking Khuch Chaddhal to stay with her parents. He must have been held up on the way.

Then the protest began in earnest. It was the roughest one yet, and it did not take long for fierce violence to erupt. Emelt was near the front of the crowd at the flimsy fences set up to mark the boundary of the Nahan operation. On the other side of the fences were around one hundred armed soldiers, tired of waiting anxiously for something to happen. The Khun pushed forwards into the barrier and almost without any resistance, the fence toppled forwards in seconds. Those at the front felt the hideous crushing of bodies behind them and were relieved when the fence gave way. It crashed to the ground but its sound was not heard over the war cry of the crowd and the shouting of the soldiers.

The Khun had numbers on their side, but the soldiers had weapons.

The crowd surged forward as if to trample the soldiers and overwhelm the mine. But they were disorganised and aimless in their quest. There was no pattern to their movements. They clambered over the fallen fence, and ran towards the Nahan soldiers who were taking some hesitant steps backwards while keeping their weapons trained forward.

A signal came from the Nahan side and the soldiers fired into the crowd. Some of them aimed high, but more than a few fired directly into the crowd. Khun at the front leading the charge saw their neighbours collapse with bloodstained clothing and mangled body parts. The crowd was momentarily stunned, but they regrouped and knew who the enemy was. There was another signal and the soldiers fired again, this time with more deadly accuracy. Bodies fell in the front line, but they were swallowed by the surging crowd.

Chuluun had arrived late and was near the back of the

crowd. He heard the shots, and saw that some of the crowd was running back to him, away from the mine. It was pandemonium. They were running everywhere, screaming, shouting, shooting. Someone near him threw a Nahan grenade forward over the heads of all the Khun, and by some miracle it landed just in front of them, killing three soldiers. Someone whose face was stained red with blood pushed past Chuluun, stumbling away from the carnage in a concussed stupor.

In the battle, he lost sight of the purpose of the riot, and all he could think to do was find Emelt in the crowd and escape with her alive. He shoved past people, trying to get deeper into the swarming hoard, trying to find his wife while all around him there was panic and anger. He pushed forward and somehow burst through to the front line where he suddenly came face to face with a Nahan soldier he recognised.

"Go, Chuluun! Get out of here!" he yelled, and tilted his rifle upward, firing into the air above Chuluun's head. Chuluun felt the heat of the air as the bullet rushed overhead, just millimetres from killing him. The sound was deafening and the crack of the rifle left him momentarily stunned. His ears rang and he could not hear anything happening around him for several seconds.

As if in slow motion, he saw the soldier's panicked expression as he tried to fend off the disorganised and murderous Khun nationalists. He saw that the soldier was just a man who was ordered to kill, but had no reason to obey, and he pitied him.

Chuluun turned back, and still watching the battle occur slowly around him, felt like he was in a story, that he was only a character in a story told by his old grandfather around a fireglobe, and no matter what he did at that moment, his fate was already decided. But it wasn't the way the story was supposed to go. He wanted a different story. It was all his fault.

His ears were still ringing painfully from the rifle exploding in front of his face, and there was so much noise from the crowd that he could not hear Emelt calling his name. But he saw her, stuck in a swell of Khun trying to overwhelm a Nahan truck full of soldiers, not far from him, close enough that he could see her desperation as she tried to wriggle free. She was trying to fight her way out of the crowd but there were too many of them and she was swept up in their movement. Blood dotted her face.

He fought his way toward her, not thinking about how he would manage to drag her from the crowd. His only motivation was to be with her, and she saw his determination as he struggled to approach her, and in that moment nothing about his past mattered to her. She needed to be free, to escape the riot with him and raise their son together. It was all that mattered.

But it wasn't the way the story was going.

Chuluun was still not close enough. He had reached the edge of the crowd, and could not penetrate it to reach her. He felt a rough pair of hands grab him by the neck and drag him away. The pain was horrible and he struggled to breathe, and found he could not shout anymore. Emelt saw the soldier drag him away and raise a rifle to him, but she lost sight of him before she heard the bang, and felt her whole world collapse and her body went limp, and she would have let the crowd squash her, if they hadn't suddenly stopped pushing forward.

There was a huge cheer, and the truck full of soldiers tipped over, catching fire. Gun shots were still ringing through the air, but the Nahans were realising they were vastly outnumbered, and had underestimated their opponents.

The scene was full of the sights and sounds of violence and the tastes and smells of blood and sweat and Noi, and the feeling of a thousand bodies pressing against each other forcefully, preventing individual movement in any way. Emelt was overwhelmed by the power of all the stimuli assaulting her every sense and by the shock of Chuluun's murder. She managed to squeeze out of the mosh pit and gain a second to herself, to rest against the side of the upturned truck, and could not control the stream of tears gushing from her face. Even without the crushing pressure on her chest, she could hardly breathe, and the wailing that came from her mouth sounded like someone else to her, like a faraway voice.

Chuluun had managed to wrest the rifle from the soldier just as he squeezed the trigger. The bullet was so close that it tore his sleeve and grazed his arm, leaving a hairless burn. But he was alive. And even though he still felt like he was not in control of his body throughout the battle scene, he was lucid enough to grapple with the soldier and steal his weapon. The soldier ran back, and Chuluun once again turned to the crowd, but he had lost sight of Emelt. A thousand angry Khun continued their violent assault on the Nahans all around him, and he saw their collective effort succeed in turning a truck upside down.

Then he saw Emelt emerge from near the front of the crowd, gasping for breath. She moved around the truck and stood there still, and he realised she must have heard the gunshot when he was taken.

He tried yelling her name, but his throat was badly hurt and no sound came out. He felt painful fire when he tried to speak and knew he could not possibly get her attention.

There was no hope.

Then the Nahan reinforcements arrived and the Khun were driven back. But Emelt stayed where she was in her grief. And while soldiers continued firing at Khun all around him, he stayed there transfixed, watching as one of them approached her, as she lifted her head sombrely and made no effort to run, as he lifted his rifle as if with pleasure, as she stared down the barrel, as she gave up, and he saw the blue flame erupt from the barrel of the rifle, and the splash of blood from her chest, and he saw her fall forwards to the soldier's feet then slump to the side, and he saw that the soldier had already moved on.

Other Khun all around him were dragging him backwards, away from the mine and back to the city. The Nahan forces had increased, and continued firing even as the Khun retreated.

I did all this.

He let them drag him back, thinking that he had caused all of this carnage, and that everything would have been better if he had just kept his mouth shut.

His feet moved on their own as he went further from the danger. Did they get what they wanted? Did the Khun achieve anything?

One final glance back at the Nahan army, and he recognised Athena, standing proudly in her uniform. *Would she have killed me?* They made eye contact across the battlefield and she smiled coquettishly at him.

Many Khun had already left Gazar by that stage. The riot was the final straw for Chuluun, and he left that day with his son and Emelt's parents, and as many others as would fit in their boats. They went west, away from the land that had given birth to their oppressors and into the unknown. They promised to come back, if they ever survived the journey.

Eventually, lying on the sofa in Halasat, Chuluun fell asleep, haunted by the memories he had tried to erase. What was the point of his mission? Everything he did seemed to cause pain and destruction. That was his story that he could not escape. If the Halasetters came with him, would he be starting off another war like last time? If they didn't, would Iwizadi start the war instead?

The next morning, as he looked at the faces of all the people assembled in front of him. He saw their hope and their faith in him. He knew what he was supposed to say, but he remained silent for a moment, the heat of the bright sun already making his head sweat. He was sent there on a mission, but one that he had never understood or seen the benefit of. He could only envision what could go wrong. Is this what it would have been like had he accepted Athena's offer to address the Khun?

The crowd was full of people looking at him expectantly to fulfil one of their oldest prophesies. There was a great weight of responsibility on his shoulders, and the sun shone blindingly in his eyes. The people looked at their long-awaited prophet with all the hope he recognised from his own time abroad, exiled from the home he loved.

He knew they loved it too. But whose home was it?

Would he tell them the words they wanted to hear? Would he give them a reason to return, and be the prophet they had already written into history?

Or would he deny them their hope? Would he tell them a lie and that their collective identity was based on fairy tales? That their life was a lie.

He saw that they were just like he was, waiting and hoping for the day that they could go home, and he was filled with pity for them. The words clumped together in his throat as he prepared to announce their future.

There could be no happy ending

Acknowledgements

I've never been good at these things. How can I think of everyone who deserves to be acknowledged? There are so many, and all their contributions to my stories are different in quality and quantity.

To the authors of all the books I've read in my life: thanks for writing them. I've read a lot of them, and I will continue reading until my eyes won't allow it anymore. I didn't necessarily enjoy reading them all, but I certainly enjoy having read them. Those I did enjoy, which is the vast majority (I can only think of maybe three or four that I thought were painful… and by the way, I don't believe in giving up. I will read it through to the end even if I'm not enjoying it), have given me lots of joy and broadened my imagination. Those I did not, I still learned something from you. While on the topic of books I did not enjoy, I might use this opportunity to give a great big 'no thanks' to my high school English curriculum (not my teachers, who were all fantastic, I want to make clear), which sucked all the pleasure out of reading for years by insisting on close critical readings of texts and attributing meanings to the author's words through tenuous and dubious pseudo-intellectual whisps of threads, until I rediscovered English literature for literature's sake, ironically in a classroom in Spain. If anyone wants to subject my work to the same high school treatment, go ahead, but know that my words are just words. Anything else is your own imagination.

To the people who gifted or recommended me books: thanks for your choices. In recent years, Bridget has been a big contributor in this sense, and I am always grateful to receive a book for my birthday or Christmas. It has become something of a joke between us for her to give me biographies of people who I either despise or know nothing about. Some of the best ones include Ant Middleton (possibly the least likeable personality I can imagine) and Sinéad O'Connor, whose paradoxical life of equal parts tragedy and success could quite easily inspire me to write future stories. I am really a very easy person to buy gifts for.

Finally, and it might be completely unrelated, but I want to acknowledge my friends who got married last year in Colombia and gave me a great reason to go traveling there.

About the Author

A. C. Smith is a nerd with a background in linguistics, political science and psychology. He is fascinated by the interplay between these fields, and the roles that language and personal choice play in regards to power. Originally from Sydney, Australia, he has also lived in Spain and The Netherlands.

In the Iwizadi Trilogy, Smith explores how words can be used and abused, and examines the spaces where different truths overlap.

www.ingramcontent.com/pod-product-compliance
Lightning Source LLC
Chambersburg PA
CBHW070113120726
47909CB00002B/581